A SONG FOR JESSICA

RUBY MONTALVO

MONPENDO PRESS

Copyright © 2018 by Ruby Montalvo

All rights reserved.

This book is a work of fiction. The characters, incidents, and dialogue are drawn from the author's imagination and are not to be construed as real. Any resemblance to actual events or persons, living or dead, is fictionalized and coincidental. For any inquiries regarding this book, please email: ruby@rubymontalvo.com

No part of this book may be reproduced in any form or by any electronic or mechanical means, including information storage and retrieval systems, without written permission from the author, except for the use of brief quotations in a book review.

Created with Vellum

For Mark

CHAPTER 1

It was a year ago, almost to the day, that I was on my way to work and Jessica called with her news. She was still on summer vacation and calling before eight so I knew it had to be important.

"Allie, I'm engaged!" She gushed with excitement and kind of screamed it out.

I was stunned. It was one of those crazy moments that happen in slow motion. It took a second for the message to get from my ears to my brain. I pictured her beaming face. *David proposed. She's engaged. She's getting married.* Tears rose up from somewhere catching me totally by surprise. "Oh my God. Jessica! Congratulations!"

I wasn't surprised exactly. I knew it would happen, but I wasn't ready. I thought I'd have more time to prepare myself.

She'd be marrying this awesome, super brilliant guy who was making plans for a permanent move to the west coast. They'd be leaving San Antonio in a year or so. Their engagement was the start of what feels something like skidding down a steep hill dreading the inevitable hard landing.

She and David were in love. He was good to her. It made me happy to see her happy, but part of me wanted to cry like a baby. *Jessica's getting married. She'll be leaving me.*

My mind still seemed to be going in slow motion when she surprised me again. She got all choked up and said she loved me like a sister and asked me to be her Maid of Honor, said I didn't have to answer right then, that she didn't mean to put me on the spot. I could think about it and let her know.

Was she kidding? She had been my best friend my whole life. In my twenty-eight years, I had never had another friend like Jessica. Of *course* I'd be her Maid of Honor.

Now, my dog, Chewy, and I head out for our walk on a hot and steamy late-summer morning before the neighborhood's fully awake. It's calm and quiet and I can let my thoughts pinball off the insides of my brain in peace. Today things are kind of a jumble.

We're one day away from Jessica's Bachelorette Party weekend and I need to snap out of this pity-party-funk I'm in. Time to be happy for crying out loud. "I'm happy for her," I try to remind myself. But it's complicated.

After a year of bridal showers, bridesmaid dress shopping and fittings, and other wedding stuff, the date's coming up fast. It's hard to believe what seemed somewhere in the distant future is now just a few weeks away. And, in my mind, our weekend getaway kicks off the "it's about to get real" stretch, the point of no return.

I'm feeling the pressure of Maid of Honor duties and I want everything to be amazing and memorable. The party's at a resort in Louisiana—Sables Blanc Resort, one of those all-inclusive deals. It's perfect because it's within driving distance from San Antonio and Jessica loves road trips.

I hope everything falls into place. Being Maid of Honor truly is an honor and I don't want to screw anything up but something's gnawing at me, something I can't quite put my finger on.

It's weird. I'm excited. It should be an amazing weekend, but for some reason I can't seem to shake a sinking feeling of gloom. And sadness maybe?

Maybe that's it. Part of me's sad that Jessica's getting married. How pathetic is that?

I would have hoped I'd be nothing but excited for her, thrilled that she's found her soul mate, someone she loves so completely that she's ready to jump at the chance to build a life with that person, without the slightest reservation, that she's ready to stand before God and anyone who cares to listen and say those two little words that will change everything for her. But everything will change for me, too.

My life will never be the same. Never.

The thought leaves me with a sense of dread and I don't want to be a downer when it's a time for celebration.

It's not that I want her to stay with me forever, but I know our relationship will be different. Things will change. But how? Will Jessica and I stay close? People drift apart all the time.

I realize it sounds ridiculous. I think, "What's wrong with me? What am I saying? I *am* happy for her. Of course." For months I've tried to ignore these annoying thoughts running through my head. I hate feeling sorry for myself. I tell myself, "Things are supposed to change. It's time for us to grow up."

But I can't help it. Jessica's getting married. She and David will be moving away. I'll never see her. And I can't imagine my life without her.

That's huge, but it's more than that. Something even bigger than possibly losing my best friend. It's pitiful, I know, but I feel like life is passing me by, that everyone is doing something with their lives except me. What am I going to do with my life? The same thing I've always done? Go to work, go home, hang out, except now without my best friend? Nothing changes for me.

Heck, I'll be thirty in a couple of years. Thirty. My parents had two kids and a mortgage by the time they were thirty. That's weird to think about.

I don't know what's wrong with me. Why can't I stop feeling sorry for myself? Sometimes I feel stuck.

If things were different with my family, they'd be different for me. If I didn't have to worry about my mom so much it would be easier. She's got no one. No one but me. I'm it. My dad's not around. No telling if or when he'll re-surface. She doesn't have any friends.

I feel bad for my mom. She's still heartbroken. I get that. It was horrible for me to lose my brother. I can't imagine how much worse it would be to lose a son. But it's been a long time. Fourteen years. I wonder if she'll ever be able to move on. I keep hoping. Maybe one day. Until then, I have to deal with how she is now, which is an almost daily challenge. And really, the wedding has been a nice distraction.

I check the time on my phone. "Oh crap! Chewy, we gotta go." Here I am taking my time and now I'm running late.

When we get home, sun rays shoot out from the horizon through white, puffy clouds that cast a bubble gum pink glow across the brightening sky. "Look at that, Chewy," I say. She looks at me as if to say, "Are we going in?"

On my way inside, the pink rose bush by the front door catches my eye. My grandmother's roses. Crap. I keep forgetting to water them. I'll do it when I get home tonight for sure. I can almost hear her calling down from heaven, "My roses, Mija!"

I live in my grandmother's house. Well, it's mine now, but to me, it'll always be hers. It's old and small, but perfect for Chewy and me. What I love best is the back yard. It's quiet and shaded by a huge pecan tree that's been there as long as I can remember. I thank my grandmother every day, not just for the house, but for everything.

She was a strong woman. Lucky for me because if it weren't for her, I would have been on my own when my brother, Oscar, died. I was just fourteen and she was the only adult in my life who seemed to care that *I* was still alive. Even though she was as heartbroken as anyone, she understood the way life twists and turns and sometimes knocks you down, but you have to find a way to move forward.

I was an emotional wreck about my brother, too. I felt guilty for ever being mean to him, angry at my parents for their constant silence, and just plain miserable most of the time. My family was falling apart and there was nothing I could do about it.

One day I lost it. I broke down and unloaded all my anger and frustration on my grandmother. But she didn't get mad. She just held me close without saying anything for a long time. Finally she said, "It's terrible to lose someone you love. It feels like you can't go on, but you're stronger than you think. You'll find your way." It wasn't until much later that I realized how lucky I was to have her. She helped me find my way through that terrible time. I wish my mom had gotten through it.

What makes one person able to go on living after such a loss and not another? Not just breathing and taking up space but truly living life. I wish I knew. All I can do is hope my mom some day finds her way, that it's not too late for her.

I get my car keys and lunch bag. "Okay, Chewy. Be a good girl," I say to my dog before I head out the door. "One more day of work," I say to myself. "I can do this."

After work today, it's back home, pack for the weekend, and then we'll officially be in the homestretch to Jessica's wedding.

CHAPTER 2

I get to work a few minutes early and there's already a stack of folders on my desk. First things first. I pour myself a cup of coffee.

I'm glad to be busy. I work on my reports, read and send emails, and answer phone calls.

Ding. A meeting reminder pops up on my desktop. I'm scheduled to meet with my boss today for my six-month review. *Oh God. I hope this goes okay.*

Mr. Hernandez, my boss, is an older guy, probably about fifty, and he's been with the company a long time. Very professional. He always wears a neatly pressed dress shirt and slacks to work, unlike most managers who push the limits of business casual. He's always pleasant and courteous even when he's telling me I screwed up.

Everyone says he's a "hands off" type of manager, that as long as you're doing your job he leaves you alone. Too bad I've met with him pretty regularly in the six months I've been at my job.

These past few weeks I've tried hard to double check my work, but still don't expect a rave review today.

My job title is Account Specialist. I write reports and price bids for computer hardware, network support, and other systems-related stuff.

I'm the link between sales and accounting. Part of my job is to piece together what a customer wants with what we can provide and get prices for all of it and send it to the Sales Rep to submit to the customer. Exciting stuff.

For the first ninety days on the job I had to send bids through an extra Quality Check before I could send them to Sales. All new Account Specialists go through this probationary period and the extra step made sense to me. During that time, I didn't have any major problems. I thought I was doing a good job. No one said otherwise.

I worked on small bids at first and did fine on those, except for a few minor errors. At least I thought they were minor. Then I started getting requests for bids that were a lot more involved. I should have asked for help, I guess, but I didn't.

One bid, in particular, nearly got me fired. It was for a Sales Rep who submitted this complex and detailed quote to his client without even reading it. And, wouldn't you know it, I had made a couple of key errors that threw everything off. That dude screamed like a spoiled brat to my boss and made a huge scene demanding I be fired on the spot. *Jerk.*

I thought for sure I was done, but instead, my boss, Mr. Hernandez called me in and lectured me on the importance of accuracy and asking for help when I need it. I honestly didn't know I needed help and had no idea I had screwed up. Of course that didn't matter.

After that I had to send Mr. Hernandez all my bids so he could make sure they were correct before they went to the Sales Reps. I felt like a kid in time-out, like I was taking a giant step backward. Instead of getting better, I was getting worse.

I know I screwed up, but I think I've gotten better since then.

I'm nervous to see if Mr. Hernandez agrees.

When it's time for my meeting, I head to the conference room. The door is open when I get there.

Mr. Hernandez sits at the head of the table surrounded by small stacks of paper. He's straightening his stacks and making notes when I knock on the door.

He looks up from his paperwork. "Hi Allison. I'll be just a minute.

Come on in. Go ahead and close the door and have a seat." He motions to a chair on his left.

He makes a final mark on a form with a ballpoint pen then stuffs the paper in a pocket folder. I sit with my legs crossed at the ankles and clasp my hands in my lap.

"How are you, Allison?" He smiles at me and rests his elbows on the arms of the office chair.

I'm a little nervous, Mr. Hernandez. I guess I'm not getting a raise, huh? "Fine. I'm good," I say.

"Great. It's hard to believe you've been here six months."

"I know. It's gone by fast," I say.

"Yes, it has. How do you feel you're settling in? Are you happy here, Allison?"

Isn't that always the big question? And I've thought about this a lot these past several months. I started here when my other company, where I'd been for three years, got bought out, went through a massive restructure and let me go. I was unemployed for a few months and when I got the call that I'd gotten the Account Specialist position I was grateful to have a job even though I wasn't thrilled about the work. That pretty much sums it up. I'm happy to have a job. The pay is good enough, the benefits are good enough, but the work is repetitive and dull. Honestly, I'm a terrible employee. It's true. I don't care about technology solutions for businesses. I don't. So given all that, how do I answer Mr. Hernandez's question? I can't tell him all those things. I need this freaking job.

"Am I happy here?" I say, surprised that he'd ask me that. *Is anyone happy here?* "Yes. I am. I ..." I stammer, " I mean…yeah. It's fine."

"Good. Having been here six months means your probationary period is over." He opens the folder and turns to me. "I'm going to be real honest here, Allison. I'm concerned about your job performance," he says in the nicest way a person could say something like that.

Dammit! "Okay?" I say. Maybe I'm not improving as much as I thought I was.

Mr. Hernandez says, "We like you, Allison. You're dependable. You're a hard worker. We don't want to let you go, but we need to see some improvement in your performance." He gives me a stern look.

He said they don't want to "let me go." I get a flashback of the day they "let me go" at my other job. That was awful. I don't want to have to look for another job. Again.

"I understand, Mr. Hernandez. I don't *want* to go. I think I can do a good job here." My throat starts to tense like it does when I'm fighting back tears.

"I think you can, too." He nods his head. "Since I've been reviewing your bids, I've discovered some inconsistencies in your work. I've covered most of those with you."

"And I've corrected those mistakes. Is there still a problem?"

"Well, we'd like to see error-free bids from you. We're not set up to double and triple check every bid. I believe you can do this, I think you need a little more coaching." He leans back in his chair. "I'd like to have you work with a Coach for a few weeks."

"A Coach? Like a Nesting Coach?" All new hires work with a Coach right after initial training. They call it the "nesting period" in which the new Associate sits with an experienced Associate to see what they do, how they organize their work, the processes they follow, etc. Nesting usually lasts a few weeks. It's like using training wheels to learn how to ride a bike. I went through my "nesting period" six months ago, now he wants me to do it again?

"Yes," he says. "It so happens a new group is completing initial training and their nesting period starts Monday, so you'll be able to get some extra coaching and participate in a daily debrief."

"Okay. If you think that'll help." I think about this for a second. What he's saying is I'm going to be in a remedial class with new hires even though I've been doing the job (though, not perfectly, I admit) for months. *This sucks.* I feel like a reject.

As if he could hear what I'm thinking, he leans forward and makes a note in my folder. "Now, Allison, this is a good thing. Please don't think of it as a negative or that you're in trouble or anything like that."

Of course not. Why would I think it's a negative? Except you just said this is what happens instead of getting fired. This is my last chance. I get it. I can't help my sarcastic mental rant.

"I'll do better," I say and my voice cracks. I fight back tears.

"Allison, I don't want to put any unnecessary pressure on you. We just want to close any gaps that might exist, for whatever reason." He smiles as if to reassure me. "There's a place for you here and after nesting, we'll check-in again. I'm confident this will help."

"Thank you," I say because I don't know what else to say.

"Alright then. Your coach is busy with some new trainees today. I'll reach out to her tomorrow so you can meet her."

"Oh, I won't be here tomorrow. I'm going out of town."

He stops and thinks. "Oh, that's right. Your friend's wedding."

"Bachelorette party," I say. His daughter got married a couple of months ago and we had a conversation about all the stuff they do for weddings these days and how much everything costs. "The wedding is in October," I say, to clarify. *He doesn't care.*

"I see. Well then, Monday. I'll schedule a meeting Monday morning so we can go over the details. Will that work?"

"Yes, sure. Thank you."

I eat lunch at my desk, then put on my headphones and listen to music while I work. At five o'clock, I leave the office without speaking to anyone.

CHAPTER 3

When I get home, Chewy waits by her leash that hangs on a hook by the door.

"It's too hot, Chewy. Your paws will burn," I tell her and we go out to the back yard instead.

A warm breeze blows and, even though it's hot and I start sweating after a few minutes, the fresh air is calming.

I think about my job and how close I came to getting fired today. What do I want to do with my life? What would be the perfect job for me? I can't even imagine.

I read somewhere that we all know what we're meant to do in life by the time we're seven years old. That perfect thing we were born to do that will give our lives meaning and purpose is seeded deep inside us, and by the time we're seven, if we're paying attention, we know what we're meant to be when we grow up. I was ten, not seven, when I thought I knew what I wanted to do with my life. A few years late of course.

My grandmother took me to a show at a local high school. *West Side Story*. Everything about it amazed me. The story, the dancing, the actors, the music. The whole experience was like peeking into a different world. I had no idea the actors were kids just a few years older than I was. To my ten-year old eyes, they were flawless and perfect. I had never seen anything more beautiful. When I saw them up there, I thought, I want that. I already knew I loved to sing, but it wasn't until that moment that I dared to imagine what might be possible for me.

If things hadn't happened the way they did with my family, it might have been possible. It's no one's fault. That's life. Sometimes life buries dreams. I accept that.

But now I need to face another reality. I suck at my job. I've tried to be better at it, to like it more, but it's not happening. Now I have to get extra coaching and my secret will be out. The whole office is going to know I suck. I almost don't want to show my face. I guess I should be grateful for another chance.

Maybe extra coaching will help. What am I going to do if it doesn't? It's true, I don't love my job, but it pays well and it's not hard. There's no reason I can't do this. I have to get my shit together or get ready to look for another job.

Yes, I'll have to give that some serious consideration, but there'll be time for that later. I can't stress over that right now. This weekend is all about Jessica.

"C'mon Chewy. We have to finish packing." She's lying on the grass in a small patch of sunshine and when I open the door, she prances toward me, panting. "I know. It's hot."

This bachelorette party won't be the typical wild and crazy drunken last hoorah of single life, for various reasons.

Jessica's not a big partier. Neither am I.

I mean, I like to go out and enjoy a nice meal, listen to music, go to shows and that type of thing, but I don't go out and get drunk and wild because alcohol makes me sick. I think I'm allergic, although I've never gotten an official diagnosis.

My first experience with alcohol caught me totally off-guard. Thankfully, Jessica was with me that day.

We were Seniors in high school and Jessica's brother, Chris, had invited us to his fraternity's back-to-school bash. It was great for a while. There were lots of cute college guys and Jess and I were like, "Yeah, this is cool."

We drank this sweet, red punch that we found out later was called

"Trash Can Punch." With a name like that it couldn't have been good, but what did we know? I drank a whole cup of the stuff on an empty stomach. Within thirty minutes a rush of nausea came over me and I was hugging a pillar on the front porch of Chris's friend's beautiful house hurling pink vomit on the shrubs. Disgusting.

Jessica held my hair and helped me to the car.

She called her brother. "We're leaving. Allie's sick. Your punch is poison."

"Allie's sick? Is she okay? Are you okay to drive?"

Jessica frowned and looked at me as if to say, *Can you believe this guy?* "Yes, I'm fine. We're going to grab a bite then I'm going home. Thanks for the invite to your fancy frat party," she said.

"Yeah, you're lightweights."

Chris was right. We were lightweights. I was in bed by midnight.

For a long time after that, I couldn't look at a bottle of alcohol without feeling like I needed to lie down. Even the smell of wine made me gag, so communion at Sunday mass was a little unpleasant.

It took me a while to realize I might be allergic. I didn't know there was such a thing. It turns out certain types of alcohol are okay in very small amounts. Usually. "The good stuff" Jess calls it.

The only sure way to prevent a reaction is to not drink at all, but occasionally, I take a chance. A small chance.

We were lightweights then and we're lightweights now. Some might consider us the "boring bunch," but I don't think so. We have a good time without drinking and as long as Jessica's happy, that's the most important thing this weekend.

Even though it'll be pretty tame, we plan on eating, dancing, swimming, and relaxing.

I double-check my luggage to make sure I got everything. Easy enough. I've heard Louisiana is even more humid than San Antonio, so I'm packing extra hair product to keep my mane under control. I couldn't have gotten my mom's straight, tame hair. I had to get my dad's thick, wavy, frizzy hair.

I pack Chewy's bed, food, and leash. "You're going to stay at the kennel for a few days, okay?" This is the first time I've boarded her and I'm a little nervous about it.

I wish I could leave her home and have my mom check on her a few times a day, but my mom's not the most dependable person in the world. Asking her to do anything out of her normal routine of work and home seems to be asking too much. Leaving Chewy at the kennel is easier. More expensive but less hassle.

I'll drop Chewy off in the morning on my way to Jessica's house. Hopefully, every one will be on time and we can hit the road and be at the resort by dinnertime.

CHAPTER 4

In the morning, I load my car, drop Chewy off at the kennel, and head over to Jessica's parents' house for an estimated departure time of 10:00 AM.

I park and get my overnight tote, garment bag, and small suitcase from the trunk.

Audrey, Jessica's cousin, is just getting out of her car.

I set my bags on the driveway and give Audrey a hug. She's a year younger than Jessica and her only female cousin. She hung out with us a lot when we were younger.

"How are you?" I ask.

"I'm good. Hangin' in there." Audrey looks the same as she did in high school, fit and athletic. "I guess you heard. Steve and I broke up," she says as she drops her bags next to mine.

"Yeah, I know. I heard. I'm sorry."

"Thanks, Allie. Yeah, I'm fine," she says smiling. "I'm getting used to being single."

Audrey's breakup was rough. She and her boyfriend, Steve, met when they were students at The University of Houston and they'd been together for a while. After graduation they got jobs in San Antonio and moved into a cute little townhouse near downtown.

We all thought they'd be engaged before the end of the year. Steve seemed like a great guy, funny and sweet. Then one day, Audrey got home from work and he was sitting at the kitchen table waiting for her. His car was packed. He was leaving, moving back to Houston, had already gotten another job. Said he was sorry, it wasn't her it was him. Left her money to cover his part of the rent and left.

The breakup hit her hard, mostly because she didn't know there was a problem and that he'd been unhappy for months.

I felt terrible for her and the way it all went down, but at least he manned up and let her go if he didn't love her, or didn't love her enough. That's way more kind than dragging it on for years, letting her think he was with her when he wasn't. I wondered if there had been any clues that he was planning to leave. I didn't think so. You would have never been able to tell by seeing them together that he wanted to be someplace else.

It's been rough for her, but Audrey's smart, pretty, kind, fun. She deserves a guy who'll love and appreciate her, not some jerk who settles for her.

She says, "Maybe it's a good thing. I've decided I want to travel and see the world before I settle down."

"Wow, that's great, Audrey. Well, you look great. I love your new hairstyle. So chic." Audrey's always worn her hair long. Now her light brown hair is cut to shoulder length with wispy bangs.

"Thanks. Something different," she says with a shrug. "How's everything going with you?" Audrey asks.

I don't want to explain everything, so I just say, "Everything's good. I'm excited about our road trip." That last part is true.

I look at the small pile of luggage stacked on a flat dolly in the driveway. I tried to keep my packing to a minimum but still have three bags. Six women, four days. Of course there's going to be a lot of luggage.

"Can we leave the bags out here for a while?" I ask.

"Yeah, they'll be fine."

"Let's see who's here." I grab my purse and Jessica's gift out of my car and Audrey and I head inside.

When we walk in, Jessica greets us with a smile. "Hey! You're here!" She hugs me, then holds me at arms length. "You okay?"

"Great!" I say, forcing a smile. "How 'bout you?"

"Excited!" she says. "Thanks for everything, Allie." She looks vacation-ready in her white, flowy sundress and sandals and her hair tied back in a pony tail.

"Of course! Yeah, it's gonna be fun." I see Jessica's mom, Mrs. Reyes. "Let me go say hi to your mom."

"Yeah. Mom, Allie's here," she calls.

"Hi Mrs. Reyes," I say. I hug her.

"Oh, Allison, you look so pretty."

Jessica's mom is always so nice to me. "Aww, thank you. How are you?"

She seems to think about the question and then says, "I'm good. Just getting ready for this wedding. It keeps getting bigger and bigger and bigger." Her shocked expression makes me smile. "But it's getting close now. Thank God. And having Jessica here has made it a lot easier. In some ways." She laughs.

Jessica and her mom are close. Not quite like the type of mother-daughter that are more like sisters and tell each other everything, but close. It's funny to see them get on each other's nerves because even though they get frustrated, they get over it right away. They don't stay mad at each other.

"How's your mom?" Mrs. Reyes asks.

"She's fine, thanks." My mom *is* fine. She has a job, a home, a car. She's well enough to do what she needs to do and not much else.

I notice the clock on the wall. Nearly ten. Time to get going.

Everyone's here: Vivian, Jessica's teacher friend; Susan, Jessica's sister-in-law who's married to Jessica's oldest brother, Jonathan; Candace, her other sister-in-law who's four months pregnant and married to Chris; Audrey

I say, "Okay, everyone."

Conversations continue.

Jessica whoops, "Hey! Allie's talking."

In a few seconds the room is quiet.

"Wow. Thank you, Jessica." I grin.

"You're welcome," she says as she bows her head.

"Jess, before we start this amazing party in your honor, we have a gift for you." I hold out the black, quilted tote bag with her name embroidered on the side. "From all of us."

"Oh wow! Thank you guys!" She touches the pale pink embroidery. "This is beautiful."

"There's stuff inside, too, Jess," Audrey says.

"Oh yeah!" She laughs.

"Here." I take the bag from her and she pulls out each item: personalized stationery and post it notes, "Bride" tank top, satin floral robe, hand lotion, and a mini-veil.

"Oh my goodness! This is gorgeous!" She holds it up: layers of ivory tulle attached to a pearl-studded headband.

Audrey says, "Vivian made it."

Jessica looks at Vivian. "You made this? It's perfect. Thank you," she says as she admires it.

"You have to wear the veil all weekend," Candace says. "Even at the pool."

"It's too nice to wear to the pool!" Jessica says.

Vivian says, "It's waterproof. It'll be fine."

"Okay, but ya'll have to help me keep track of it so I don't lose it."

"That's Maid-of-Honor duty," Susan says. "Allison, that's you!"

"Okay, fine. Keep it on your head, Jess," I say. There's no way I can be in charge of her veil all weekend.

She puts it on. "Does it look okay?"

"Wow, it's looks great, Jess," I say. She looks like a bride. This is really happening.

"And we got you a spa day at the resort. Massage and facial," Susan says.

"Wow! That sounds fantastic. Thank you all so much," Jessica says. "For the beautiful gifts and for being here. It means so much to me that you've taken time out of your busy schedules and time off work to celebrate with me. Thank you." She turns to a box on the sofa, "And, I have these for you all. Just a few snacks and things for the trip." She hands each of us a canvas tote bag, each with a different design.

My bag is navy blue with a silver, heart-shaped, word cloud. The dominant words are "love" and "friend". Inside the bag are: a "Bride's Crew" t-shirt, satin sleep mask, a CD music mix, a framed picture of me singing karaoke onstage, a nutty snack, a beach towel, flip flops, hair ties, hair wrap, and a journal.

"Jess! I love this. All of it. Thank you."

"Of course. Thank you. For helping me plan the wedding and for being at all my showers and for this amazing party. And for just being so good to me."

Jessica's my best friend, I feel like I get much more from her than I give. I know her whole family, all her stories, and she knows mine. If I had a sister, I can't imagine we'd be any closer than Jessica and I are now. *She's getting married.* That familiar mixture of happiness and sadness tries to surface.

"Aww, Jess." I hug her. "Of course."

Susan says, "Okay everyone! Candace and Vivian are driving. Leave your keys in case Mr. and Mrs. Reyes have to move your car for some reason."

"Let's get this show on the road!" Audrey says.

Jessica and I will ride with Vivian. Susan and Audrey will ride with Candace.

We load our luggage and finally set out for Louisiana.

CHAPTER 5

We make it to Lake Charles, stopping twice along the way. The first time, two hours into the drive, at a bustling rest stop right off the highway, and the second time at the Louisiana Visitor's Center at the Texas-Louisiana border.

None of us have been to the Sables Blanc resort, but Susan has friends who rave about it. I researched it online, and the reviews were good. We liked that it was driving distance from San Antonio. I hope it's nice.

We get off the highway and follow the signs to the property but can't see the hotel at all. The driveway seems a mile long. Palm trees and Bougainvillia dot the rich, deep green lawn. We drive through a canopy of palm trees and emerge at a circular driveway. Resort attendants dressed in tan smocks and black pants open our car doors when we stop. The resort entrance oozes luxury and I get the feeling this is going to be perfect. Seeing it online is nothing like seeing it in person.

The attendants collect our luggage and place the bags on wheeled carts. Even though it's breezy, the air is thick and muggy and I can feel my hair frizz almost immediately.

"Welcome to Sables Blanc," they say.

The lobby is open and airy, the front desk positioned directly opposite the front door. The ceiling must be thirty feet high. There are large marble pillars throughout the lobby, white tiled floors, leather lounge chairs and sofas positioned around dark wood coffee tables. Through the back window, I catch a glimpse of the famous Sables Blanc pool and beach.

We check in and get our room assignments. I'll be rooming with Audrey. Jessica with Vivian and Candace with Susan. Our rooms are side by side on the third floor and each have a balcony overlooking the pool with its white sandy, man-made beach. It's clean and white and I don't care if it's fake. Not one bit because it's gorgeous and it's going to be awesome.

Our room is dark when we enter. I open the curtains to let the light in.

"Brrr!" says Audrey. "Mind if I turn this down?" She adjusts the thermostat.

"Not at all," I say as I check out the room amenities. Two queen beds with white duvet covers and lots of tan pillows, dark wood furnishings, a flat screen television, a desk, a bathroom with a granite double-sink, toilet, and a large, granite-tiled shower, plush white towels, and two thick, white cotton bathrobes in the closet.

"How was ya'll's trip? Everyone getting along?" I ask Audrey.

Audrey thinks Susan can be snooty and superficial, insisting on expensive designer shoes and bags, shopping every weekend for even more clothes to add to her already overstocked closet. Maybe I haven't spent enough time with her. I haven't seen her snooty side. She's always been nice to me.

"Oh yeah," she says. "Candace and Susan talked about being pregnant and pretty much giving every detail you never want to know about having a baby."

"Too much?"

"Yes! Susan was showing off her stretch marks and telling us about a 'procedure' she's looking into to take care of them since her baby factory's closed." She clarifies, "Her words, not mine."

"That doesn't sound too bad," I say. "Which bed do you want?"

Audrey touches up her makeup in the full-length mirror by the bathroom. "By the window is fine. I guess it wasn't too bad except for the graphic details about blood and placenta and dilation levels and… trust me. If I were pregnant with my first baby, I woulda told her to shut up, but not Candace. She wanted more."

"Yeah, I don't think I'd want to know either," I say, hanging some things up in the closet.

"Right?" Audrey says looking at my reflection. "I finally changed the subject and asked Susan about her job."

"Where does she work?"

"She's works for this company that sells medical supplies or something. She's a sales rep. Man, she is bankin' some cash right now."

"She told you how much money she makes?"

"Not exactly, but her bonuses are more than my salary. Let's put it that way."

"Oh wow. Well, that means she has cash for her 'procedure' I guess."

"True. She makes a lot and she spends a lot." Audrey smirks at me in the mirror.

"Good for her," I say. At least *someone's* doing well at work.

Audrey shrugs her shoulders, "I guess."

We step out to the balcony and Jess and Vivian are on their balcony too. "Hey," I say to them. Jess's veil floats up around her head.

We lean on the railing and take in the view. The pool's impressive. It's as big as a football field with a curvy shape. There's a white sandy beach on one end and a high, rocky waterfall on the other. White lounge chairs, two deep, line one side of the pool. Only a few chairs are occupied.

"Are ya'll hungry?" Jessica asks.

We decide to go to dinner, then maybe come back and change into our swimsuits and head down to the pool.

The dining room's on the first floor, near the lobby. The tableware sparkles and cut crystal centerpieces with floating flames set the room aglow. We're seated at a round table covered with a white linen tablecloth.

"Hello Ladies. My name is Ray and I'll be your server," says our extremely good-looking waiter. He's about six feet tall, has light brown, curly hair, dimples, and pale-blue eyes. He smiles and adds, "And here's the bride to be!" he says and goes over to shake Jessica's hand. "Congratulations! When's the big day?" We look over our menus at Ray and then at each other.

"Hi Ray. Thank you!" Jessica smiles and shakes Ray's hand. "October twelfth."

"Well, we're honored to have you here to celebrate."

"Thank you, Ray." Jessica smiles. "We're happy to be here. This place is beautiful. It's amazing." She looks up at the crystal chandelier that hangs from the ceiling.

"Perfect. Ladies," he says to all of us, "food is a very important part of the Sables Blanc experience. It's our goal to treat you to fantastic food and impeccable service, and for you to relax and enjoy this happy occasion worry-free." Ray explains resort dinner schedules and restaurant options. "If you have any questions at all, please do not hesitate to ask."

When he takes our drink orders, he asks each of us our name and smiles when he repeats the order.

When he leaves Jessica says, "Wow, he's so sweet!"

"And so cute!" Audrey says.

I nod my head in agreement as I read the menu and try to decide what to order. Everything sounds delicious. Finally, Jessica, Audrey, and I each choose a different entree that we'll share.

I'm relieved our food arrives quickly because now I'm pretty hungry.

It's probably terrible manners to share off each other's plates like we're doing, but we've found this is the best way to sample as much as we can.

"Just take it," Jessica tells me and motions to the shrimp scampi on her plate. "Oh my gosh, David gets so upset when I get food from his plate. The first time I did that we hadn't been dating very long and I guess it's a bad habit, so I reach over and pick a piece of shrimp off his plate and he's looking at me like I'd just, I don't know, goosed him or something." Jessica frowns and sits up straight, impersonating David.

"And I'm totally clueless...I know, big surprise...and I'm just yappin' and talkin' about I don't know what, and I bite into that shrimp and it was so good and I look at David and he's got this look on his face, like …" Jessica's jaw drops slightly and she looks from her plate to Vivian's with a confused look on her face.

"And I see him and have no idea what the heck's wrong with him. And I'm like 'Are you okay?'" My mental image of Jessica just being her spazzy-self and totally catching David off-guard like that makes me laugh. He had no idea what he was getting into.

"And he's like, 'Did you just take food off my plate? And eat it?' and I'm like, 'Oh wow! I guess I did. I'm sorry.' I didn't even realize I had done that, but inside my head, I was thinking 'Is that a problem?'"

"Oh poor David. He had to learn the hard way," Audrey laughs.

Jessica and I share food all the time, although we usually offer or ask before grabbing. That just shows she's been completely comfortable with him from the very beginning.

The food is delicious. My favorite was the baked Fettuccine Alfredo. The shrimp scampi was a close second. We order two desserts, crème brulee and chocolate molten lava cake, for the table and enough spoons for a taste of each. Delectable.

Jessica says to Ray, "Oh, my goodness. Dinner was amazing!"

"So glad you enjoyed it. I hope you all have a wonderful evening," he says.

"You too," Jessica says.

"Thank you, I will. I get to tuck my daughter in tonight."

"Oh, how old is your daughter?" Jessica, the teacher, asks.

"She's five. She starts school this year so we're trying to get her to bed early, but she won't go to sleep until I'm home to tuck her in."

"Oh my goodness! You look way too young to have a five year old!" Susan says.

"Well, I started young, but, hey, she's my everything. I can't imagine where I'd be without her," Ray says.

I would have never guessed this handsome, charismatic, young guy is a dad. And a devoted one at that.

"How beautiful! Well, enjoy your daughter. Thank you, Ray," Jessica says as we stand to leave.

When we're out of the dining room, Jessica says, "Who wants to go to the pool?"

"I do," Audrey says.

Vivian, Candace and I nod our heads.

"Sure, let's go. But don't forget we have a table at the dance club reserved tonight at ten o'clock," I say.

"Oh right. Well, it's almost seven. I think we'll be okay if we don't stay long," Susan says. "I probably won't swim, but I'll go check it out."

"So, let's get changed and we'll meet at the pool," Jessica says.

CHAPTER 6

When I get back to the room, I pull my phone from my purse to put it in the room safe, but I see that I have two missed calls from my mom. She hasn't left a message. *Why the heck doesn't she ever leave a message?* I wonder what she needs. I know I told her I'd be gone. Maybe she forgot. *Oh no, what if something's happened?*

I put on my swimsuit and tell Audrey I have to call home, to go ahead without me. I'll be down in a minute.

My mom's phone rings and rings and finally goes to voicemail. Okay, she just called. I'll give her a few minutes to answer. I go to the bathroom and brush my teeth. I read the room service menu, then try my mom again. Voicemail. I shake my head. "Dammit!" I say. I check my phone again. She just called thirty minutes ago. *What the hell?*

I lie on the bed and look up at the ceiling. I'm sure she's fine. I sit up and try again. It goes to voicemail: *"Hello. I'm sorry I missed your call…"*

I think about putting my phone away and calling her tomorrow, but I feel like I need to try again. What if something's happened? What if she needs me? She rarely calls me. And twice in a row? I sit on the bed in my swimsuit and cover-up and look at myself in the mirror. My jaw is clenched.

I walk out to the balcony. It's nearly sunset and the pool is in the shade. I spot Jessica's veil and then see everyone on the far side of the pool by the waterfall.

I want to go to the pool. I come back inside and try my mom one more time.

It rings and she answers. Rustle, rustle, rustle. Silence.

"Mom!" I say.

No answer.

"Mom!"

"Hello?" she says.

"Hello?" I say. "Mom, are you okay?" I ask before I say anything else, trying not to sound aggravated.

"Yes, I'm fine. Are *you* okay?" she asks.

Oh here we go. Give me a freaking break. I take a deep breath. "Yes, mom, I'm fine. I'm in Louisiana with Jessica. Remember? For her bachelorette party?"

"Oh I thought you were going for the weekend. Today's just Thursday."

"It's a long weekend. I'll be home Sunday."

"Oh, okay," she says. "I'll just talk to you when you get back."

"Are you sure? It's fine. I can talk now. What's the matter?" She hasn't said why she called. She doesn't sound sick. She would have gotten home from work hours ago. "Did you go to work today?"

"Yes, I went to work today. I'm fine." She sounds annoyed.

So she's not sick but something's up. "Well then what's wrong, Mom?"

"No, I don't want to spoil your weekend."

I think about this and wonder if I even want to know what she's talking about.

"Mom, please tell me what's going on." I don't really want to hear it. I want to throw my phone across the room and let her figure it out for herself, whatever it is. She's not sick. She went to work. What is so urgent that she has to call to tell me about it but makes me guess why she called because she won't tell me what's so urgent that she had to call?

I try to calm down because anger has a way of coming back to bite me in the butt. I always end up hurting myself, somehow.

Finally, she says, "Your dad came back today."

My dad came back today? "What do you mean 'came back'? Came back where?"

"Back home. Here."

Are you freaking kidding me? He just decides to show up? What could he possibly want?

"He came to get a few of his things he still had here," she says and pauses. "He said he wants a divorce," she says. Her voice cracks. She sniffs.

"Really?" *Oh, thank God. It's about damn time.* My dad left years ago and he's only been back for days at a time. My parents' marriage died a long time ago, they just haven't buried it. Never made it final. But my mom's in denial, which seems as crazy to me as one of those bizarre stories you hear about people who keep their spouse's corpse in their bed for years.

"Well, Mom, maybe it's for the best. I mean, he has been gone a long time. And now maybe you can get on with your life. Maybe this will be a good thing." My dad. I just thought of him the other day and I tried to remember the last time I saw him. He pops into my head sometimes, like one of those idea bubbles. He's smiling and handsome like he used to be a long time ago.

"How could you think breaking up a family could *ever* be a good thing? You don't even know what you're saying!"

She's dreaming. Do I just tell her what she wants to hear or do I tell her the truth? She's living in LaLa land if she truly believes what she's saying. I'm twenty-eight years old. My dad's been mostly absent since I was fifteen. My mom has hung on to the hope that he'll someday return, her knight in shining armor, in love with her once more. I can't imagine it.

"No, Mom. Breaking up a family's not a good thing." It's easier to agree with her for now.

"Then how can you say that? You don't know how I feel! He's still my husband! Of course you don't know anything about that!" She's crying openly now and raising her voice.

Silence. That stings. Especially now, but I refuse to be pulled in.

"Mom, let's talk about this Sunday. I'll be back early and we can go out to dinner. We can talk about it then."

"No, I don't want to go out to dinner. I'm fine. I'll just deal with it myself," she says. "I have to go. Bye."

And she hangs up.

Well, shit! I wish I could let her deal with it herself, but she can't do it. She doesn't get it. Not even a little bit.

I sit on the bed and take a deep breath. My stomach is unsettled and my face is hot. I know I'm scowling, the crease between my eyebrows accentuated by my frown. I start to turn my phone off and put it in the safe, but I imagine my mom at home all alone crying about my dad yet again. He's the one who keeps hurting her, but she's mad at me? Well, too bad. I won't lie to her any more.

Should I call her back? What do I want to say? I don't want to do this. Not at all.

I play out different conversations in my mind and how she'll react if I say this or that.

I decide to call her. Maybe she'll answer. She does.

"Mom, I'm sorry I upset you. I only want the best for you. I apologize for what I said."

"Is that all?"

"Yes, that's all," I say.

"Okay then. Have fun on your little trip with your friend."

It's hard for me to ignore her sarcasm. "Thank you. I'll call you Sunday."

I think I hear her say, "Hmpf" and hang up.

I decide to keep my phone on me in case she needs me. She doesn't sound good. I go to the bathroom and run the cold water. My cheeks are bright red and warm to the touch. The water jolts me but feels cool and calming. "Can't get away from it," I say to my reflection. All those years of wondering where he is and if he thinks about us and if he's okay and if he ever wonders how I turned out. He didn't care enough to find out. Why should I give him a second thought? *He made his choice. We're better off without him.*

I get my room key and head down to the pool.

CHAPTER 7

I get in the elevator with a guy wearing jeans and a gray, plaid shirt with sleeves rolled to just below his elbows. His face is stubbly and his hair's wavy and mostly dark brown with some gray.

He nods as I get in the elevator.

"Hi." I nod and smile.

"How you doin'?" he asks.

Terrible. I'm so frustrated with my mom I just want to shake her.

"Fine, thanks," I say.

"It's a nice night for a swim," he says.

"Yeah, looking forward to it. The pool's beautiful."

"It is," he says.

I look at my feet and notice the contrast between my sparkly wedge flip-flops and his well-worn boots.

The elevator door opens and he holds it, waiting for me to exit.

"Thank you," I say.

In the lobby, a few people lounge around on the oversized chairs. Their voices echo off the glass and granite.

I notice Susan sitting at the far end of the room with her cell phone in one hand and a glass of wine in the other. She doesn't look up.

The automatic doors shwoosh open and a blast of air hits me as I walk through and the doors close behind me. It's dusk.

The pool and patio lights click on. I make my way around the right side of the pool and toward the back waterfall where I spotted Jessica earlier.

Audrey's climbing the rocky cliff, and calling out to Jessica. "Come on, Jess!" She and Vivian hang on blue hotel floating boards.

"Be careful, you nutcase! Please don't split your head open!"

"Jessica. You're cursing me. Now, watch me fall on my ass!" Audrey says.

Candace sits on the side of the pool with her feet in the water, watching Audrey climb the rocks.

Audrey steadies herself as she stands on the small cliff, holding her arms out to her sides. She shouts, "On your mark! Get set! Go!" and leaps into the air, arms stretched wide, her wet hair momentarily lifts off her head and she grabs her legs in a cannonball. Jessica and Vivian brace themselves. Audrey smacks the water and sends a wave of water over them.

"Audrey!" Jessica says.

Audrey comes up and takes a breath, swimming to Jessica.

"It's fun, Jess! Try it once."

"It looks like fun when *you* do it. It'd be a trip to the ER if I do it," Jessica says.

Audrey sees me and says, "Allie, you're just in time."

Jessica says, "Allison Deleon! There you are. Everything okay?"

"Oh yeah. Fine. I was on the phone with my mom."

Jessica knows my mom and even met my dad years ago. I don't complain about my mom to anyone except Jessica and that's only when I feel like I'm going to explode unless I get it off my chest. I don't want to be the annoying friend with all the issues and drama and it's so exhausting being in it. Sometimes I don't even feel like talking about it because nothing makes it better. Jessica knows and understands as much as anyone can. She reads my face for a moment and then says, "Well come and join us. The water's perfect."

I thought about just sitting on the side with Candace, but the water looks too good to pass up. I take off my shoes and cover-up.

"You're not getting in?" I ask Candace.

"Not tonight. I'm good right here," she says as she rubs her belly.

I dip my toe in the water. It's warm. I get a float and lower myself down at the ladder.

I stretch my arms across the float and lean my chin into it. I try to relax but can't stop thinking about my mom. I imagine her in front of the TV watching the news or one of those sappy movies where the girl always gets the guy at the end and they live happily ever after.

"Allie, we were just talking about all the activities they have. They have like three different auditoriums all with a different show. "

"Oh yeah? Cool."

"Right? I think they have a Beatles review at one. And another one has a talent show."

"Oh yeah? Hmm. Sounds like fun," I say. I stand up and re-do my hair in a high bun on top of my head so it doesn't get soaked.

"Watch out. I'll try not to fall on you, but if I do, I apologize in advance," Audrey says. She's trying to balance herself on the float that's just slightly too small. She wiggles around and it shoots out from under her making a loud farting sound as she splashes in the water.

Jessica won't look at her and I can't *stop* looking at her. It's like watching a baby attempting her first steps. She's got it, she's got it....she falls! Oh, so close. Audrey tries again and she kicks one leg hard in the water as she leans her torso on the board and rests there to catch her breath.

"She wants me to look at her, but I'm not going to look at her," Jessica says.

"I need to get up on this float. Why don't they make them bigger?" Audrey says.

She grabs both sides of it as she lifts herself again and the float wiggles under her grasp as if it's trying to get away from her and she brings her knee up and catches the float on the edge. It shoots high up in the air.

"Whoa!" I say as Audrey falls back slapping her arms on the water.

Jessica wipes water from her face. "Nice job. You almost had it!"

Audrey swims to Jessica's float and Jessica moves over to make room for her. Almost immediately the float is under water. They have to keep kicking their legs to keep from sinking themselves.

"Audrey!" Jessica says.

Jessica gives up the float and swims to the side.

"Finally! She's gone!" Audrey says laughing.

Jessica dries off and a little while later, we all kick to the ladder and climb out.

I get a hotel towel and dry my face first. The thick towel feels like a pillow and the night breeze chills me as I stand there dripping wet. I wrap the towel around my body, tucking the end tight to keep it in place.

Candace and Susan have been sitting at a table by the pool talking.

"Okay, it's time to get this party started," Susan says. "Time to get dressed and get ready to go dancing, ladies."

"Woohoo," Vivian says.

"Let's go!" Jessica says.

I look up at the night sky. Only one star visible so far. I think about my mom. God, she makes me crazy. Sometimes I feel like she drags me down, like I'm trying to stand on a float in the water and she keeps kicking up waves so there's no way I can stand on my own. I don't think it's intentional, but that doesn't make it any easier. And my dad filing for divorce is bound to make it worse. Who knew it could possibly get any worse?

I try to forget about it for now. Nothing to be done now. This weekend's about Jessica. Everything else will be waiting for me when I get home.

CHAPTER 8

We decide we'll go back to our rooms, get dressed, and meet in Jessica's room by nine-fifteen.

"Do you want to shower first?" Audrey asks.

"No, you go ahead." I can get dressed in a snap since I don't have to do my hair.

I unpack the rest of my clothes and pick out a black wrap dress and my black wedge sandals for tonight.

Generally, I don't dress up much, but I wanted to make sure I have at least a few stylish outfits for the trip. It's taken a lot of effort for me to get to this point. I'm not a total misfit, it's just that fashion has never been a priority for me.

My parents sent my brother and me to Catholic school and we didn't have a lot of money when I was growing up, so I rarely went shopping. When I could shop for some special occasion, my mom kept me on a strict budget so my choices were limited. Maybe that's why I didn't know what I liked, never found my own style. I'm sure that's part of it.

The other thing is I always felt guilty about asking for anything. It's just the way I was raised. My mom didn't see a need for extra stuff. We got gifts at Christmas and for our birthdays, but that was it. We used what we had. If we didn't have it, we didn't need it. That's what my mom used to say. But when I was in fifth-grade, I wanted a new dress for our class end-of-year dance.

The dance was a big deal. Most of us would be going to different schools the following year, so we were very dramatic, "We'll never see each other again," teary-eyed. My mom said I could go and gave me money for my dance ticket, but I had nothing to wear except my school uniform and a blue hand-me-down dress I had worn for Easter the previous year. My mom had gotten the dress from one of her work friends whose daughter had worn it probably ten years before.

I didn't want to wear my school uniform (plaid skirt, white blouse and black shoes) to the dance. Everyone was going in regular clothes. I didn't want to be the only one in my uniform.

One afternoon I stared at my open closet again, as if bluebirds and mice had magically spun my perfect dress while I did my chores. But no, all I saw were the usual stuffed animals and toys, board games I didn't play with anymore, shoe boxes, some of my mom's old clothes, my brother's and my baby clothes, special dresses from my younger years, like a pink eyelet dress my mom made me for Easter one year, and a red velvet jumper I wore for Christmas when I was in kindergarten.

My mom came into my room with laundered clothes. "What are you doing?" she asked.

"I'm looking to see what I can wear to the dance." It was a week away and all my friends were talking about their new outfits and I had nothing but that stupid blue dress and my uniform.

She looked in my closet. "Why don't you wear your blue dress?"

"The one from last Easter?"

"Yes," she said. "It's still good."

The dress was ruffly and made of some kind of scratchy material and it was hot and I never liked that dress.

"I guess," I said. The thought of wearing that dress made me sad and discouraged. I wanted to go to the dance because all my friends were going, but I didn't want to feel like a total dork wearing some hot, scratchy dress I never even liked. I thought about asking my grandmother for help, but my mom wouldn't like that. I turned away from my closet and started putting my folded clothes in my dresser, and in my frustration I closed one of the dresser drawers a little too enthusiastically.

"If you don't want to wear that dress, just say it," my mom said.

"No, it's okay." I couldn't look at her or I would start crying and I didn't want to cry.

"That dress is beautiful and expensive. It looks good on you."

"I said okay!" I faced her and then turned away.

The one thing that would set my mom off was talking back. She saw it as disrespectful and intolerable. She looked at me for a long second.

"Don't talk to me like that," she finally said in an even tone. "I'm your mother and you don't talk to me like that," she said as she left my room.

Two days before the dance, she said, "Let's go. We're going shopping."

"What for?" I asked. I hoped it was for a dress, but what if it wasn't?

"For a dress. For you. For the dance," she whined to mimic me.

That made me mad. I didn't even want to go anymore, but I couldn't wear that blue dress and showing up in my uniform would have been the worst, so I went.

My mom picked out a few things for me and I picked out a few things to try on. I had such little experience shopping and picking out my own clothes, I had no idea what I liked or what would look good on me.

When I picked something out my mom would say, "*That* won't fit you." I didn't even know what size I wore.

With an armful of dresses, we went into the dressing room and I started trying everything on. Every dress my mom approved of, I didn't like and every one I liked she found something she disliked about it.

I finally accepted one of her recommendations as being ten times better than the scratchy blue dress and was satisfied.

"I hope you're happy," my mom said on the way home.

The way she said it made me wish I'd never mentioned the dance, but I said, "I am. Thank you, Mom."

That's my standout nightmare shopping experience. Online, in person, whatever. It doesn't matter. Shopping is a dreaded chore, so once I find a style that works for me, I stick with it.

I even keep my work-style super simple. It's almost like I still wear a uniform. Slacks and a blouse. That's it. Colors vary slightly. I generally stay away from patterns. Texture's very important to me. I still don't like itchy stuff. Ease of use, also important.

When I *do* have to shop, I prefer to shop alone. I find it very stressful to shop with friends. After 15 minutes or so, I'm ready for breakfast/lunch/dinner/coffee, anything to get me out of there. Getting myself together and ready for this weekend required discipline and effort, but I like my new clothes so it was all worth it.

After my shower, I bend upside down to spray my hair with hairspray. I think this is the longest my hair's every been. I kept putting off getting it cut and then all of a sudden, it was long, falling almost to the middle of my back.

"That dress looks great on you, Allie," Audrey says. "Very flattering."

"Thanks."

Audrey's still in her robe and doing her makeup. "I haven't even asked you how you like your new job. Do you like it?"

I shrug. "It's okay. I can't say I love it, but it's a job. Can't complain."

"Yeah, I hear ya," she says.

I sit on the bed and watch what Audrey's watching.

"You can change it. It's just on. I'll be ready in five." She takes her clothes and goes into the bathroom.

I hit the up arrow on the remote and stop at a channel showing *Coal Miner's Daughter*. Loretta Lynn. There's a woman who found her style. And her voice. She started off with nothing and music changed her life. What if her husband hadn't pushed her into singing? What if they would have settled for being poor, barely getting by? What if leaving her kids and her home to be on the road would have been too much for her? That couldn't have been easy.

She was talented, sure, but that's not enough. She had support, smarts, and focus. She didn't quit. She got knocked down, but she always got up again. Where does that come from?

I used to love to sing. When I was little I used to want to be a singer on stage, Broadway shows. Oh those crazy dreams. It's funny how when you're a kid, people say, "You can be anything you want to be." And you think, "Yeah, I can be anything I want to be."

But when you try to do it, they want you to do it their way and if you can't do it their way, you feel like an idiot because you're doing it wrong. It's enough to make you want to forget the whole thing.

I wonder if people tried to make Loretta Lynn feel stupid. Did it make her want to quit? I guess the only thing that matters is that she didn't.

Audrey comes out of the bathroom dressed, hair and makeup done. "Sorry. That was a little more than five minutes. Ready?"

"Yep," I say. I get my small clutch with the wrist strap and make sure I have a room key. "Let's go."

CHAPTER 9

*A*udrey knocks on Jessica and Vivian's door with the first part of a familiar door knocking rhythm.

We listen for the response from inside, but instead we hear loud voices and laughter.

"They must not've heard me," she says. She knocks again and looks at me as we listen again for the response.

Loud laughter. "Hell-o. People. Let us in!" Audrey says. She's about to knock again when Vivian swings the door open. "I thought I heard something," she says.

Audrey walks into the room, "What's so funny?"

Jessica says, "I was telling them about my first week in the classroom when that kid threw up all over my brand new two-hundred dollar alphabet rug."

"Oh, poor little boy," Audrey says.

"I know. And my rug," Jessica says, and then continues, "So poor Trevor's standing there, puke all down the front of his shirt and all over my brand new, perfect, beautiful rug. And he's kind of waving his hands like 'What's happening?' and, I'm standing there in shock." Her eyes widen. "And then he throws up again!" Jessica grins. "And oh my God. It smelled so bad. I start gagging. I'm like…" Jessica covers her mouth as if fighting her gag reflex. "I seriously thought I was gonna lose it too."

"Oh, nice!" Susan says.

"I know. I had no idea where to start to clean it up. I mean the stuff was everywhere. Yep. My first week. I didn't think I'd make it," she says shaking her head.

"And now, here you are. An old pro," Vivian says.

"Well, I don't know about that," Jessica says.

Susan's at a makeshift bar she's set up on the desk. "And on that note, Audrey, Allie, would you care for a drink?" she asks. "We have rum, vodka, scotch, cranberry juice, orange juice, and ginger ale. Pick your poison."

"Hmm. I'll take a Cape Cod, please and thank you," Audrey says as she finds a spot on the edge of the bed.

"Allie?" Susan asks me.

"No thanks. I'm good." I can sometimes stomach vodka in small doses pretty well, but what can I say? It's not worth the risk. I'd hate to get sick and start vomiting all over myself like that kid who ruined Jessica's rug.

Jessica says, "This is the good stuff, Allie, if you want to give it a try."

Susan says, "Oh, excuse *me*! You only drink the good stuff?"

"You know she's allergic," Jessica says to Susan.

"What? No way!" Susan says.

Jessica nods. "Yes! Can you believe that? We learned the hard way, right Allie?"

"That's right," I say.

Vivian says, "I knew you didn't drink much. I thought it was by preference."

"I guess it is. I prefer not to be puking my guts out when I'm out trying to have a good time. It tends to be a buzz kill," I say.

Jessica tells the story of our first adult experience together at Chris's fraternity party when we were Seniors in high school.

Candace says, "Well, Jess, I have to ask, do you have any more vomit stories? You told two just now."

"Oh wow! I did, didn't I? I'm sure I could come up with a couple more if I put my mind to it."

"How about cranberry juice, ginger ale, and a splash of vodka?" Susan asks me.

"Sure, I'll try it," I say. "Hold the vodka." I smile at her. "Please and thank you."

"Oh, fine," she says.

"Well, I was watching the channel with the resort activities and there's a talent show tomorrow night that I really want to go to," Jessica says.

"Oh right, you mentioned it at the pool," Audrey says.

"Yeah. I was thinking one of us could be in it. Doesn't that sound great?" Jessica says.

I watch Susan mix my drink like a pro.

"Jessica. You're going to be in the talent show?" Audrey asks.

"That's awesome," Candace says. "You could tell vomit stories."

Susan says, "That would be hilarious. Do it as a stand-up routine."

"Not me. Allie!" Jessica says motioning to me.

"Uh-oh, Allie. Jessica's ready to sign you up for a talent show. Run!" Candace says.

"What's your talent?" Vivian asks me.

"Nothing. I have no idea what she's talking about."

"Not true, Allie. Audrey knows, but you guys may not know that Allie can sing. She's got an amazing voice," Jessica says.

"She does. Allie, you do," Audrey says. "Amazing. Blew me away."

"What?" Candace says.

"Really?" says Vivian.

"I had no idea," Susan says as she hands me my drink.

"When did you hear me sing?" I ask Audrey.

"In high school. One of your concerts, maybe?"

"That was a long time ago." I sip my drink. It's sweet and refreshing.

"You should do it, Allie. That'd be awesome." Candace says.

"No thanks," I say, shaking my head.

Jessica says, "Yes, Allie. Do it! For fun. No pressure."

Audrey chants, "Do-it! Do-it! Do-it!" Everyone joins in.

"Jessica. You need to stop," I say.

"No, this would be perfect, Allie. Seriously ya'll. She's really good."

Audrey starts again as she walks over to make herself another drink, "Do-it! Do-it! Do-it!"

Susan says, "I mean, if you got it, why not flaunt it, Allie? That would be freaking cool. Representin'!"

"Alright, alright. Jess, I'll do it if you do it," I say.

"Oh no you don't! This has got your name all over it, Allie," she says. "Come on now!"

"Are we going dancing or what?" I say. "It's getting late and it's past Candace's and my bedtime. Right Candace? Plus, we have reservations. They're gonna give away our table."

"Way to change the subject, Allie," Susan says. "But I don't think you're going to get off *that* easy."

Candace says, "I hate to be your excuse to stop this unfair peer pressure, but yes, I won't last much longer. Junior and I have had a long day." She pats her belly.

"Oh yikes! It *is* late," Jessica says checking the time on her phone. "Alright. You're off the hook for now but not forever." She looks in the mirror and touches up her lipstick. "Everyone ready?"

At this point, I just want to call it a night and go back to the room, get under the covers, and finish watching *Coal Miner's Daughter*. Why would she put me on the spot like that? I swear. Jessica.

Jessica wraps her arm in mine as we walk down the hall. "Well, will you do it?" she asks.

At first I can't even look at her. She blindsided me and I don't appreciate it. I finally turn to her. Her mini-veil floats around her head. "How could you put me on the spot like that, Jess?"

"I know. I'm sorry. But come on, Allie! This is the perfect opportunity. You don't know anyone here but us. And we love you. You can just go up there and leave it all on stage, like, give it all you got."

She's always been so encouraging. President and only member of my fan club. Totally biased. I think she'd always tell me I'm great even if I suck.

But she's right. That was my dream once upon a time. I remember Loretta Lynn. It wasn't easy for her. Being a musician is a hard life. And competitive. There are so many people way more gifted than I could ever hope to be. Hugely talented people.

Jessica doesn't stop believing in me, even way past when every one else has. Even when I have. I've thought about getting back out there, but something always stops me. I end up shaking my head, shrugging my shoulders and saying, "I just don't know. Maybe I don't want it bad enough."

She has a point about no one knowing me here. Would that make it easier? Even though I'm kind of pissed that she set me up, I wonder how I'd do. It's been a long time, but I'm sure I could make a respectable appearance. I wouldn't be horrible, I don't think.

"Oh, Jessica. You know what? Because this weekend is all about you, I'll think about it."

She smiles. "Excellent!"

CHAPTER 10

I'm not much in the mood to dance and it's late. If it were just me, I'd be down for the night. But I put on my happy face and give myself a pep talk. *You're the Maid of Honor for crying out loud. Get over your crap and be happy.*

"The reservation is for Reyes party," I say when I hear music in the distance.

The club's heavy bass thump greets us at the door. *Club Danse.*

"Boots and pants and boots and pants," says Audrey, moving to the beat as we walk in.

The dance floor's crowded and the club shimmers with strobe lights and a huge mirror ball that hangs from the ceiling.

Susan stops a waitress dressed in the tiniest black skirt and tuxedo shirt unbuttoned down to the middle of her chest so her breasts spill out. They shout something back and forth to each other, then Susan shouts something at Audrey. She nods and they start walking, so we all follow and snake through the crowd, up the stairs to the second level. We arrive at a table marked "Reserved" that glows with purple, red, and blue lights which pulsate with the music.

"This is perfect!" Jessica shouts. "Good call to reserve a table, Allie."

The waitress comes around for our order. Candace and I order club soda with lime, everyone else gets the house specialty—Hurricane.

I haven't been out to a dance club in a while and there's so much going on. Loud music, packed dance floor, blinding strobe lights, a mural of dancing silhouettes on a bright and detailed graffiti-style background that covers an entire wall. My chest thumps with the beat of the bass and we resort to hand signals and lip reading to communicate.

The waitress returns with our drinks and Susan raises her glass. "To Jessica," she says.

We tap glasses and drink just as the DJ plays a techno mix of old disco dance music.

Jessica dances in her seat and motions to drink up so we can go downstairs to dance. She drains her Hurricane then moves to the railing where I join her. We look out at the dance floor and she dances in place. Within a few minutes everyone's ready and we head down to join the throng of hot and sweaty bodies.

We dance song after song and I take pictures of us, mostly Jessica. She's laughing and the songs run together from one to the next, and we sing out to the songs we know, smashed together in a small circle in a corner of the dance floor.

Suddenly, there's a rush of movement right beside us and by the time I realize what's happening, I hear shouting and one guy, who must have a very loud voice, "Motherfucker!"

Right beside us, two guys go after each other, fists, arms, legs, flailing around, strong, all out punching. Two other guys try to pull them apart, but neither one to them backs down. A girl cries and I can tell she's saying, "Stop! Stop!" I duck and grab Candace, who's right beside me, and we, along with everyone around us, try to move away from the fight as the music continues to blare.

The guys wrestle on the ground and as I watch them I'm shocked to see Jessica crouched down and huddled on the ground right near them. *What's she doing? Oh my God, Jess! Stay down!* I tug Candace's arm and shout, "Jess!" I point toward where she is and Candace scans the crowd and I can tell by her shocked expression that she's spotted her. I start to go toward her, but Candace tightens her grip on my arm and pulls me back.

Finally, bouncers, neither of them much bigger than the guys fighting, show up and they each grab a guy from behind. One of the guys stops, but the other one who's closest to Jessica, a small, very drunk, young-looking guy, keeps swinging and kicking and the bouncer throws him to the ground and holds him there with his knee on the guy's back. He grabs the guys arms and pulls them behind his back, but he still tries to wiggle free, shouting and spitting.

The bouncer and another security guard lift the kid off the ground and walk him toward the exit.

The DJ says, "How 'bout that dancin'," and plays "Everybody was Kung Fu Fighting." My hands tremble and I walk toward Jessica just as she stands from her crouched position. She's talking to a girl, (maybe a friend of one of the guys?), helping her off the ground. The girl's friends gather around her now.

They put their arms around the girl and seem to be thanking Jessica.

"Jess, are you okay?" I ask as I look at her face. She looks pale and shaken up, but otherwise okay.

She nods. "I'm fine, I'm fine." She points toward the exit and starts walking toward it. We follow her out to the lobby and she stops at a bench. "I need to sit for a minute."

Audrey asks, "What the hell happened?"

I sit beside her. "Are you sure you're okay?" I ask.

She fans her face with her hands. Susan hands her a glass of ice water.

"Yes, I'm fine. Umm…The girl, the one I was talking to, I think her boyfriend got pissed because he thought the other guy was dancing up on her even though he wasn't or …I don't know. Anyway, they got stupid and started swinging. They hit her."

"They hit her?" I say.

"Was she okay?" Audrey says.

"Yeah, I don't think they meant to. She got between 'em." She shrugs. "I don't know, but it had to hurt. I saw the whole thing as it was happening otherwise I wouldn't have known what was going on. I should have gotten out of the way, I guess, but I wanted to make sure she was okay," Jessica says.

"Well it's a good thing they didn't hit you, Jess!" Audrey says.

"Yeah, Jessica. Those guys were out of control. You could've been hurt," Vivian says.

I agree. They weren't big guys, but they weren't playing. That's some scary shit. There we were minding our own business, having a good time when some assholes have to go and start punching people. It sucks.

"I know. You're right. But I'm fine. Thank God." She takes a deep breath and smiles. "Thanks for looking out for me."

"Don't even think about pulling that shit again," Susan says.

We laugh but I believe we're all relieved it wasn't worse.

"Well, I'll take that as my cosmic sign to call it a night. Have we had enough?" Jessica says.

"I have. I'm fine with that," Candace says.

"Stupid guys!" Audrey says.

"I know. Incredible. Grown men being idiots," Jessica says.

Susan says, "Grown, immature, *drunk* men being idiots."

On our way out of the club, the girl who was hit and who Jessica helped off the floor is on a bench in the lobby, talking on the telephone.

Her shrill, high-pitched crying voice echoes, "I know but he needs me." Pause. "I love him."

Wow. Could she be talking about one of those losers? Maybe even the guy who punched her?

We keep walking.

CHAPTER 11

We're slow to get up the next morning. I'm not sure what time I finally went to sleep last night. It was 2:30 AM the last time I checked. Audrey and I stayed up talking about everything, including her breakup, until we were all talked out. The breakup was devastating for her.

"I just cried and cried. I didn't want to tell anyone or see anyone."

"I can't imagine you like that, Audrey. How long did that last?"

"A few weeks. I mean I still went to work. My parents knew. I stayed busy, but I was sad all the time. I'd beat myself up a hundred times a day, like 'I'm so stupid. I should have seen it coming. Maybe I wasn't paying attention. Maybe there were signs.' You know. Regret. Maybe I was a little depressed."

"That's incredible. I can't imagine you depressed." When you know a person one way, it's hard to see them in a different way. You have to shift your view of them. "Well you sound great now. What happened? How'd you get through it?"

"I forced myself to get out. I'd go for a run or go to a movie. And then one day I was just done. Done feeling terrible. And so grateful that we didn't get married because I really thought that was the next step for us," she said.

"This might sound lame," I said, "but I'm happy for you."

"You're happy that I was knocked on my ass when my boyfriend told me he wasn't that into me?" Audrey laughed.

"Well, not that part. But now, you sound really good. You're strong and, I don't know, like a grown up," I said. "And that's awesome. You're not feeling sorry for yourself and having a pity party. Look at you, girl. You're good as new!"

"Thanks, Allie. I feel good. I'm over it."

I think of my mom and how she has gotten stuck in a state of sadness and grief. Will she get worse now that my dad will officially be out of the picture? Could she get better? Would it be strange for me if she changed now? What if one day she was smiling and happy instead of gloomy and depressed? Would I feel the ground shift under me?

∽

The plan is to meet for breakfast at nine outside the main dining room. My growling stomach wakes me up. It's eight-thirty. My alarm didn't go off. I hear the shower running, so I roll out of bed, put on my bathrobe, and step out to the balcony.

The sun casts a hazy, blinding glare and it's hard for me to keep my eyes open.

"Good morning!" Vivian says. She's on the balcony next door, dressed in a pale blue linen dress and embellished flip-flops, makeup completely done, and a cup of coffee in her hand.

"Oh hey!" I say. "Wow. Look at you. Already dressed and ready for the day. What time did you get up?"

"I'm an early riser," Vivian says.

Even on vacation? "Really? I admire that. You must get so much done," I say. "And you don't even look sleepy," I squint and block the sun from my eyes.

Jessica describes Vivian as the most organized and business-like teacher she's ever seen. Says she just got her Masters and wants to be a school principal. They met in education classes in college, then were assigned to the same school to do their student teaching. Vivian seems better suited to be CEO of her own company than a teacher.

"Jessica mentioned you just got your Masters. Congratulations," I say to Vivian.

"Oh thanks! So relieved to be done."

"Yeah, that's really great. And you want to be a principal?"

"Eventually. We'll see. I may be able to move into an assistant principal position this year," she says.

Audrey knocks on the sliding glass door to let me know the shower's available.

"Alright, I'll see you in a bit," I say to Vivian.

I shower and dress quickly, settling on a pair of khaki shorts and a white embroidered top.

On our way downstairs, Audrey says Jessica and Vivian will meet us, to get seated and they'll look for us.

The hostess seats us at a large round table and I'm starving. I order coffee and dig into the basket of bread and muffins in the middle of the table.

"Dear Lord, why are we up so early?" Susan says.

"Aren't you hungry?" Candace says. "I'm starving. I woke up hours ago. My stomach was growling so loud it woke me up."

We study the menu.

"Good morning!" sings Jessica as she pulls out her chair. Vivian follows behind her. "So sorry to keep you waiting." She picks up the menu. "How is everyone this morning?" she asks with a smile.

"You're in a good mood," Candace says. "I'm so glad you're here. I'm starving!"

"Sorry, sorry, sorry. I had to stop by Guest Services." Jessica looks refreshed in her pale, pink blouse. Her light brown hair falls past her shoulders

The waitress comes around and we order.

We talk about the resort and all the activities: casino, movie theatre, lazy river, spa, golf, tennis, yoga, and live music, to name a few.

My eggs Benedict tastes creamy and rich.

After breakfast, we'll be on our own, but we'll meet at the pool at noon.

"Yeah, we can float on the lazy river. We didn't do that yesterday," Audrey says.

"Oh, hey, that sounds like fun," Candace says. "You think I'll fit in a tube?"

"I don't know. We'll have to see," Audrey jokes.

"Jessica, don't forget. Today's your spa appointment. At noon," I say.

"Right. Allie, will you walk down there with me after breakfast? Just to check it out?" Jessica asks.

"Sure."

∽

The spa smells like eucalyptus and sounds like gentle rain. Black tile gives the place a sleek look. The woman at the front desk is tall and thin and her jet-black hair is pulled back in a bun with not a single stray hair. Not that I can see, anyway. She's wearing a very fitted, white smock buttoned up to her neck.

"How may I help you?" the woman asks.

"I have an appointment at noon for a massage and facial and I just wanted to check out the spa area."

"I'll be happy to show you around."

She gives us a quick tour: wet sauna, dry sauna, hot tub, thermal suite, massage, hair salon, nail salon.

We explore the spa common areas and the workout area. Treadmills line a glass wall that looks out over the the pool and lazy river. There's a free-weight area with benches and dumbbells and a spacious studio with a yoga class in session, its participants in downward facing dog.

We walk past the wall fountain at the entrance. "Well, Allie? Have you thought about the show? Will you do it?" Jessica says.

"I have thought about the show. You know, Jess, I have to tell you…" I hate to be mad at her, but I have to get it off my chest. "…What's up with you setting me up last night? You totally put me on the spot." It's not very often that I'm angry at her, but I'm almost more annoyed than angry.

"Yeah, I know. I figured you'd need some encouragement." She hooks her arm in mine as we walk.

"Oh, really?" I raise my eyebrows and nod as if surprised at the idea. "Is that what you call it?"

"Come on Allie. I know you want to do this. The other night when we went to hear that band, you were in awe of that singer. And, yeah, she was good, but you're as good as she was, or better."

A few weeks ago we met up at a bar with live music. The band was amazing and their singer was great. Her voice was strong and spot on. I don't think I'm anywhere near as good as she was.

"Yeah, right! No way, Jess." I know it's pointless to argue with her when she gets her mind set on something.

We're in the lobby now and sit on a sofa in the far corner of the room.

"You are, Allie. I'm not just blowing smoke up your ass."

"What?" I almost can't believe she said that. "Blowing smoke up my ass? Is that what you said?" We both laugh.

"I'm not," she says. "I'm serious. And! This is the perfect place. You'll never see any of these people again, so this is just for us. Me and you."

I look at her and can't decide if I'm upset or angry or just scared speechless.

"I'm not ready. It's tonight! There's no way, Jess. I can't do it."

"Sure you can. Keep it simple. You must have a song you already know, that you sing all the time."

"Oh, you mean a song I sing in the shower or something?"

"Exactly!"

I shake my head at her. She makes it sound so simple. *Yeah, just go sing in front of hundreds of people, Allie! No biggie!*

I visualize myself on stage with the spotlight on me. What would I sing? I'm out of practice. I haven't sung in front of a real audience in years.

"Allie, you don't look convinced, so let's put it this way," she says in that annoying teacher voice she uses when she's going to drive home her final point. "This is actually a double gift."

Gift? "Oh, really?"

"Yes. This is my chosen gift for me. I mean, my wedding gift from you."

Already my stomach is flip-flopping. I know I have a decent voice. That's not the problem. I just don't really want to do this right now.

I roll my eyes. "Okay. And?"

"Allie, this is my gift to you. This is a chance to get out there and give it all you got. Just leave it all on stage. No expectations, no risk. Just you and a song."

"Jess," I say, shaking my head.

"Allie, you're my friend. I love you. It would make me happy to see you happy. You must not know how good you are. You could do it as is. And you'll be great." She takes my hand. "You will."

She's nudging me in the direction she thinks I want to go but can't go on my own. I can see that. She wants to see me happy, see me spread my wings so to speak.

Jessica knows she can't do it for me, but she can give me a boost. I want to be pissed at her for pushing me, and maybe I'm a little pissed, but I'm also touched that she believes in me. That even with everything she has going on she takes the time to think about me and my happiness. Some people would tell her to back off and mind her own business. I don't think I'd ever do that.

Maybe she's right. What if I just go out there and sing my heart out? Who cares if not everyone's into it? I know at least one person who'd love it no matter what. And it would be cool to get out there again. How could I say no?

"Well? Are you ready to sign up?" she asks.

I nod. "Sure."

"You'll do it?" she asks.

"Yeah, I'll do it. What the hell," I say.

Jessica hugs me, grinning. "Allie! You're gonna be great."

I don't know about that. I admit that it might feel good to get out there again. When I saw that girl singing a couple of weeks ago, I was blown away. I wondered if I could ever be that good. Right now, I'm scared to death. I used to love it, used to want to do nothing *but* sing. Now I'm not sure what I want. Sometimes I want to be settled in my job, paid vacation every year, nice insurance benefits, 401K. I could build a good life with that, but even *that's* not as secure as I thought.

In my first year of college, I had to write about one of the best moments of my life, where the memory of it is something that I'd never want to give up. For me, that moment would be my Senior year of high school singing my solo in the school auditorium and feeling like I was on fire that night. It was a moment of pure joy, sheer happiness, of letting the damn break and holding nothing back. Fearless. That's what it was. No shame, no fear. That was a long time ago.

CHAPTER 12

*J*essica and I stop by guest services to sign me up for the show when I remember she needs to get to her spa appointment.

"You better get going," I say.

"Oh, right. Yeah, I better go. You got this, right?"

"Yes, I got this," I say.

When it's my turn, I step up to the counter.

"Is it too late to sign up for the talent show?" I ask.

"No, no, not at all. You know it's tonight, right?" the guy behind the counter asks.

"I know. Last minute decision," I say.

He chuckles and raises his eyebrows. "You're good. No worries. I just wanted to make sure you know it's tonight." He hands me a form to complete with my info, occupation, room number, what brings me to the resort, and then the questions that almost make me say, Never mind…Talent to be performed? Will I be providing my own music/accompaniment? Will I require props? What will I sing?

I do a quick run-through of songs I'd feel comfortable singing in front of a few hundred people in a few hours. Something I could sing in my sleep. It's a short list.

"Okay. All done," I say.

His name's Jeff and he's from Lafayette, Louisiana. That's what his name tag says.

Jeff looks over the form and says, "Okay, Miss Allison. You're all set. There's a short rehearsal at four o'clock in Blanc Auditorium to decide the order of performance and make sure you have the music you need, you know, the track, and all that jazz."

"Okay."

"Yeah, and they'll tell you everything else you need to know then."

"Okay, Jeff. Thank you."

"You're welcome, Miss Allison. Break a leg!" he says, smiling.

Well, I have a lot of time until rehearsal. I'm trying not to panic at the thought of being onstage without having rehearsed at all. Going on cold.

I told Audrey I'd meet her at the pool and when I get back to the room, she's in her swimsuit.

"Hey! I was just leaving. You coming?" Audrey asks.

I scrunch my nose. "Well, maybe for a little while, but I have to be someplace at four and I have to get ready for that."

"Where do you have to be at four?" Audrey asks. Just then, she seems to remember the talent show. "You're doing the show?"

"Yes, I'm doing the show."

"Oh wow, Allie! Exciting," she says. "That's so cool."

"Thanks."

She swings her beach bag on her shoulder. "Okay, Candace, Susan, and Vivian and I are heading down now. You want us to wait for you?"

"No, go ahead. I'll be right down."

She leaves and I change into my swimsuit, put my flip-flops on, and pack my beach bag.

I open the closet and look for an outfit for tonight. One of my new dresses, a white wrap, will do. It's exactly like the black one I wore last night.

Floating down the lazy river probably isn't the best thing to do right now. I should probably rehearse and go over the song again. It's on my playlist, so I get my phone and earbuds, search for the song, and head downstairs to the pool.

They're just putting their bags down in a shady spot between the beach and the main entrance to the lazy river. This is near where we were last night and I don't even remember seeing this area. How different everything looks in the daylight.

"Ready to float?" Candace says.

"Definitely," I say.

I don't have a water-proof case, so I decide to leave my phone. I'll have time to listen to it when I get back. I turn to follow Candace and start to ask her how she's feeling, when I scrape my little toe on the metal leg of the chair. "Crap! Oww! That hurts," I say as I limp toward them.

"You okay? What happened?" Candace asks.

"I tripped on the chair and jammed the hell out of my toe. Oh my God!" I stop to examine my toe. It's red and tender, but it looks okay. "I'm fine."

"Oh, I hate when that happens," Audrey tells me. "But, this is perfect!" She lies her head back settling in to the lazy river flow. According to resort information, the lazy river is three-quarters of a mile long and winds through the extensive beach area to the edge of the golf course. Today, the sun shines hot and hazy. I close my eyes and sing the song over and over in my head, making sure I know the words. I'll listen to it a few times before the show and I'll be fine. Good to go.

We make our way along the river fairly quickly. I decide to go around again and when we make it to the starting point the second time, I lift my head and roll out of my tube.

"I'm done," I say.

"Okay," Audrey says. "See you in a few."

I dry off and settle in a lounge chair. I reach in my bag for my phone and earbuds. My phone's not there. I take everything out of the bag. "Are you freaking kidding me right now?" I can't find it. I start to panic. I look around to see if I laid it down somewhere around my bag, but I don't see it.

All I can think is, "Crap! I need my phone. Now I don't have the song, I can't practice, and someone's stolen my phone."

I check the bag again, then out of the corner of my eye, I see it on the ground under the chair face down in a puddle of water. *Oh shit!*

The sight of my dead, dripping wet phone makes me want to cry. I dry it and try to power it on. No luck. *Oh no. Freaking stupid!* I need to dry it out. How do you dry out a cell phone? Of course I can't look it up because my phone's dead. Put it in rice? I've heard that works, but I don't have rice. Where am I going to get rice?

I'll go upstairs and dry it with a hair dryer. Maybe that'll work.

I get my stuff together, put on my coverup and head toward the lobby. I'm still dripping wet. My shoes make an annoying squishing sound with every step. I don't want to deal with this right now. I need to get ready to sing. Maybe I should have said no. If I would have just said no none of this would have happened.

When I get back to the room, I turn the hair dryer on high and get that warm air into every nook and cranny I can.

It still won't power on.

My phone's dead. I can't listen to my song. All my contacts are gone. And my pictures. I feel sick.

I turn on the hair dryer again and target every angle of the phone, but it doesn't do any good. My phone is ruined.

I get in the shower and let the water run over my head and face. I hold my breath for as long as I can, then turn away from the shower stream and gasp for air. I stand there and cry. Why does stupid shit like this happen to me? This sucks!

This performance is going to be a disaster. Without my phone I can't even listen to the song a few more times before I have to go out and sing it. What if I forget the words? I sometimes forget them when I don't have them right in front of me even when I know the song inside out.

I go over the lyrics in my head and then start singing. That helps calm me down. I'll be okay. I know this song. If I forget the words, I can make them up, I'll be fine. Yeah right, I'll be able to make up words that make sense right off the top of my head? I laugh at the thought. But really, it's okay. I won't forget them. And the show? It's a competition. I probably won't win, but that's okay. I'm not in it to win it.

Yep, my phone is ruined. It won't power on, which totally sucks, but it's not the worst thing in the world, I guess.

By 3:30, I'm dressed, my hair and makeup are done. I have plenty of time to grab a snack before check-in and get to the auditorium by four o'clock.

CHAPTER 13

The auditorium is dimly lit and a group of people are gathered in front of the stage. Their voices echo. Loud laughter.

I breathe deeply, slow and steady.

One of the men in the group greets me with a big smile that shows his white teeth.

"Hi! I'm Dave!" he says. "I'm the emcee for tonight's show."

"Hi Dave, I'm Allison."

"Welcome, Allison. Let me just check you in here," he says as he makes a note on a sheet of paper on a clipboard. "It's nearly time and we're waiting for one more person."

The theatre door opens and a gray haired man with a jet-black mustache walks in. He looks like a famous actor whose name I can't recall and I expect he'll speak in a Texas drawl because he looks like a cowboy. Or is it because the actor he looks like is usually a cowboy character. I'm not sure.

"Hi! I'm Dave."

"Hallo," he says. "Yuri ----vich," he says.

I'm surprised. Definitely not a Texas drawl.

"Welcome Yuri," Dave says. He makes a note on his paper then looks up eagerly.

"Alright beautiful people! You all signed up for tonight's talent show and thank you so much for sharing your talent with us tonight."

I check out the competition. Yuri looks like the oldest. A girl with the blondest hair I've ever seen and probably a little younger than me. Another guy, tall and thin, about my age. A cowboy-looking guy about Yuri's age. A woman quite a bit older than me. And another kind of big guy.

You can't tell by looking, Allison, I think to myself and mentally kick myself for doing it again.

"Okay, this is a chance to make sure you have what you need for your performance. I plan on having you out of here in about thirty minutes so you can go relax before the show."

Dave gives us the details about where and when to meet. He's holding his clipboard and looks like he's going over a checklist.

He says, "Now, a couple of rules for you all. First, please don't throw things out into the audience."

The cowboy says in a southern drawl, "That's a weird rule."

Dave says, "Well, we had a guest get hit in the eye with a tennis ball. Her face puffed up and her eye swelled shut."

The young blonde girl says, "Someone was playing tennis as a talent?"

"No! He juggled tennis balls. And not very well, either. A few balls got away from him, and chaos ensued. So in everyone's best interest, it's a rule. Before that people used to throw candy and beads and all kinds of things. Oh yeah. The crowd goes crazy for that stuff." He continues, "Rule number two is you have to keep your clothes on."

"I bet that's a way better story than the tennis ball story," the tall guy says. We laugh.

"I'll leave that to your imagination," Dave says.

Yuri says, "You sure you want me to keep my clothes on? Because I can …" and he reaches for the buttons of his shirt as if he's going to take it off to reveal more of his hairy chest.

"Thank you, Yuri, but yes. I'm sure. Everyone must leave their clothes on." Dave says. "I don't make the rules, but I do agree with them. Now, let's figure out who'll go when. Well, I'll just ask, would any of you like to go first?"

The cowboy and the older woman both volunteer.

"Ladies first. I'll go second."

"Okay, then first is Ruth, right? Ruth?" Dave says.

She nods.

"Then Charles will be second. Third?" he says.

The tall guy claims third (Andy), I'm fourth, then Yuri, the blonde (Kayla), and the big dude (Jackson).

"Excellent. I'm going to call you in order right now and just kind of go over what you're doing and make sure you have what you need. Is everyone good? Any questions?"

No questions.

Dave conferences with Ruth while the rest of us sit in the front row.

I sit between Andy and Kayla. "What are you doing tonight?" Andy asks me.

"I'm singing," I say. "You?"

"Dancing," Andy says. "What about you?" he asks Kayla.

"I'm doing a dance tumble routine," she says.

Dave calls Charles to the stage.

"I've never done this before. I'm a little nervous," Kayla says. "Are ya'll nervous?"

Andy says, "Nah. Don't be nervous. Just have fun with it."

Dave calls Andy. "See ya'll tonight," he says.

Kayla's from Houston. She's a pre-med student and was a high school cheerleader. I can see that.

"I'm trying not to be nervous, too," I tell her.

"Yeah, he's right. Just have fun with it. I mean I've done this routine a thousand times and I don't expect to win or anything," she says.

"That's the spirit."

"Allison?" It's my turn with Dave.

He covers the basics. "Are you going to use a track or would you like a piano accompaniment?"

The house band's in the pit and they're available for accompaniment. I prefer using live accompaniment, so even though the track is safer, I ask for the piano.

Oh, crap, I can't believe I'm going through with this.

The piano player's name is Gus. He says, "Oh yeah, I know that song very well. Sure," and he plays the chords and we cover the first verse and he says, "I'll follow your movements if that's okay. And I'll play it in C about this tempo," and he plays a few bars.

"Okay, great. Will you play the range at that key?" Gus plays the high and low chord.

"That should be good," I say. The range seems do-able and ideally we'd do a run-through of the whole song, but every one else seems so relaxed about the whole thing, I'll try to be too.

When I get back upstairs, no one's in my room or the other two rooms.

From the balcony, I pick out Jessica's miniature veil and see they're all out by the pool. I touch up my makeup, and decide I may add a little more when I go on stage. I pack a bag with a few things I might need.

By the time I get down to the pool, everyone's packing up. Audrey says, "There she is."

Jessica pulls me aside, "Allie! Wow. You look beautiful. Do you have a date or something?"

"Ha! That's hilarious." I tell her about my phone and about the pre-show meeting. "How was your massage?"

"Perfect. Really awesome," she says. "Susan also got me an appointment for a facial scrub thing and that was crazy."

"Yeah?" I say.

"Yeah, it was weird seeing all my dead skin being peeled away. It was freaky, but now my face feels as soft as a baby's butt." She laughs. "I'm sorry about your phone. That's terrible," she says changing her tone. "I haven't told any one else about tonight so I figured we'll make it a surprise. What do you think?"

"That's fine," I say. "I told Audrey. Are ya'll going to dinner soon? I have to be there by six-forty-five."

"Yes! I'm starving. We're gonna go up, get dressed and go to dinner, then to the show. I want to get there a little early too so we can get good seats."

"Okay, I'll be up in a minute. I'm going to walk around a bit."

I find a quiet spot in the shade and sit, take off my shoes, and close my eyes. The breeze is warm and soothing and I try to think of nothing at all, but my mind chatters about all kinds of things: the show, the song, my phone, my mom, Jessica, the wedding, my dog, my job, my future. Each time something pops in my mind, it wants to run around in there and I don't even realize I'm thinking about it. Breathe in, breathe out. Chatter, breath, and breeze.

A drop of sweat rolls down my calf. I put my shoes back on, stand up and go to the lobby, looking for a remote spot, but instead of stopping, I keep walking out the front door, past the parking attendants, into the parking lot.

I sit on the curb in the shade. It's much hotter out here than by the pool.

It's a little early, but I sing scales to warm up my voice. Then I sing my song, low at first, and then louder.

It's strange. Music used to be my heart and soul. Not any more. I let it get smashed into some dark corner of myself instead of being my center.

It wasn't just my family or what happened in college with Dr. Dumbkirk (I can't even say his real name), although that was a big part of it. When all that happened, I felt bad in a dozen different ways, none of which I wanted to examine or even think about. He thought I wasn't good enough and I accepted what he said as truth instead of holding on to what I believed, what I know. I gave up. Abandoned it. Will music always be there for me if I ask? I feel unworthy.

The sky goes darker and the air cools. Sun rays shoot through a billowy cloud like arms reaching toward some distant place. A black and yellow butterfly flutters above me, elegant and focused.

A surge of emotion wells up from inside me as if I've received a magnificent gift. Is it gratitude? Love? Forgiveness? All those things.

After a moment, I find a tissue in my bag and dry my tears and blow my nose. The sun shines bright and fierce again. The clouds have passed. The butterfly has flitted away.

I stand up and dust myself off, ready to meet my friends for dinner.

CHAPTER 14

We meet in Jessica's room before dinner. Every one's there and she's talking about her spa day.

"I felt like a total dork because I…I mean I've had a massage before, but this was so different, like, how do I say this? It hurt like hell! My massage lady's name was Blanca," she says with a faraway look and Spanish accent, "and she might have been a man, I'm not sure."

"Wait, what about her made you think she was a man, like did she have big hands, hairy knuckles, what?" Audrey asks.

"I'm kidding. No, she was so strong!" Jessica says. "She was like digging her fingers into my back and I was like, 'Oh! Wow!' Does that feel good or is that pain?"

Susan says, "Jessica, that's when you tell them, 'That hurts' and they'll back off. She probably didn't think she was doing it hard enough because you didn't say anything."

"I don't know. All I know is, whoa, she was strong," Jessica says.

"Jess, get your veil. We're going to dinner, right? Are ya'll hungry?" Candace asks.

"Oh yeah," Jessica says. "Where'd I leave it?" and she looks around the room for it.

"Allie, keeping track of the veil is Maid of Honor duty. You're slacking," Susan says.

"Oh, great. Jess, where's your veil?" That's stupid. How can I keep track of her veil? It's not like I'm with her every minute.

"Got it!" Jessica calls from the bathroom. "Okay, are we ready? After dinner we're going to the talent show!"

Only Jessica and Audrey know I'll be in the show tonight. I'm surprised they don't say anything.

It's better that no one else knows because that means I don't have to talk about it, even though I'm thinking about it. A lot. Talking about other things puts it more in the background.

We get a table right away and Ray takes great care of us. We get our food quickly and it all looks amazing, but I can't eat.

"Feeling okay? You aren't hungry?" Susan asks me.

"I'm okay. A little bummed."

"Why?" Susan asks.

I tell her about my phone. She looks sympathetic.

"Yeah, I tried drying it out with a hair dryer, but it didn't help," I say.

"You dried it out with a hair dryer? You know, that's probably the worst thing you can do." Susan takes another bite of her chicken Alfredo.

"Are you kidding?"

"No. Seriously. It fries the insides." She sips her wine.

That figures. "Great." I smile and shrug even though somehow that makes me feel worse. "That sucks."

The dinner dishes have been cleared and dessert is on the way. I ask Audrey, "Should we do a toast?"

"When? Now?" she asks.

"Yes," I say.

"Sure, go for it," she says.

"Not me. You," I say.

"No, Allie. You. It was your idea. I'll call it and you say it." Audrey taps her glass with a spoon. *Clink clink clink.* "And now, raise your glasses. Allie's going to make a toast."

"To Jessica! Beautiful bride to be. Thank you for bringing us together for this amazing time. And thank you for being a true and faithful friend. We love you."

Jessica's radiant. "Thank you," she says.

"Salud! Cheers!"

Desserts arrive. "And here are more spoons if you like," Ray says.

I taste the chocolate brownie a la mode. It's rich, warm, sweet, and delicious. Normally, I'd keep tasting it. Not today. The nerves are kicking in.

It's six-thirty when we wrap up dinner and head to the auditorium, stopping along the way to browse the shops. I tell Jessica I'm going ahead.

"Okay, Allie! You're going to do great," she says. "Try to relax and just be your awesome self."

"Thanks, Jess. See you after," I say. I feel like I'm in a daze.

"And smile, Allie! You got this." She smiles.

I keep telling myself, "It'll be fun. It's not a big deal. It's a song for Jessica. One song. That's it. No big deal," but I'm not very convincing. I muster a weak grin.

"You do!" she says. "Now, go break a leg!"

I get to the mostly empty auditorium and head backstage. Even with the backstage lights on it feels dark and shadowy.

The cowboy, Charles, is the only one there besides me.

"Hey!" he says.

"Hi, how are you?" I say.

"Now, tell me your name again?" he says.

"Allie. Allison."

"I'm Charles," he says. "Ready Allison?"

"Ready or not."

"That's right," he says. "That is right."

Charles is wearing a cowboy hat, jeans, and a western style shirt. And cowboy boots. He wrings his hands and asks, "Wanna see a magic trick?"

"Sure," I say. He seems so relaxed, like no big deal.

He shows me a quarter in one hand, rubs his hands together and rolls them around, then holds his hands up to show me his hands are empty.

I nod my head. "Cool," I say. I have no idea where the quarter could have gone. He smiles, then reaches for me like he's going to grab me and I'm thinking *Watch it, Dude*, then he pulls the quarter from behind my ear.

"Ahhh," I say and applaud lightly.

Kayla, the blonde, and Ruth, the older lady, show up backstage.

"Thank you," he says to me.

"Are you doing magic for the show?" I ask.

"Oh no. I just like to mess around a little."

He flips the quarter between his fingers. "I like magic because it's a good reminder that there really is such a thing as hocus pocus."

"Okay?"

He shows me the quarter, then cups it in his hands. "You may not realize it, Allison, but I'm diverting your attention even as we speak. And ..." Charles holds his hands up again, showing his palms. No quarter.

I check my ears. He laughs.

"What are you doin' for the show, Allison?"

"I'm singing," I say and I realize I'm not nervous at all. I'm actually looking forward to the show. *Oh, I see what you did there, Charles.*

"Well, it's about that time," he says and I follow him to say hello to the two women and everyone else who's just arrived.

We review names.

Ruth is first up and she'll be singing. She's wearing a very shimmery top and tight black skirt. She looks about my mom's age and I try to picture my mom in that outfit. Strange.

Charles is singing.

The blonde, Kayla, is wearing black yoga pants and a tight fitting workout jacket. She's doing the cheer-dance routine.

The tall, young guy, Andy, wears gray jogging pants and a black sleeveless t-shirt. He'll be dancing.

Yuri, dressed in black slacks and purple dress shirt, will be playing his ukulele.

And the big, construction worker-looking guy, Jackson, will be playing the harmonica.

I hope we'll have a good view of the stage. I want to see the show too. I'm getting excited. When Dave gets there, we talk quietly backstage and go through the line-up once more.

"Any questions?" he asks.

No questions.

"Alright we'll be getting started in just a few minutes. Listen for your name and come on out, we'll be ready for you. Okay, gather 'round, huddle up." He puts his hand in the center of the circle like I used to do with my middle school volleyball team.

"We're out here to have fun and share our talents and gifts. So the number one rule, besides the other two we've covered, is have fun!"

We nod.

"Okay, 'Smile', on three, quietly, one, two, three…"

"Smile," we say in a low murmur.

~

The house band warms up the crowd.

I wonder if I should have picked a more upbeat song, but yeah, it was a short list.

Dave starts the show and introduces the band who is an amazing group of musicians.

We sit in order of appearance stage right. The curtains open and Dave calls Ruth to the stage.

There's a loud roar as she walks out. She waves at the audience with both hands. We find out she's from a small town near Baton Rouge and she's on vacation with her husband and her sorority sisters from college and their spouses. When Ruth starts to sing, I can't believe that voice is coming out of that body. She looks like a grandmother, kind of dowdy and old, but she sings Gloria Gaynor's "I Will Survive" like a champ. She works the crowd and gets the whole auditorium to clap with her and she's amazing. I'm impressed.

Charles is next and he sings a Willie Nelson song, "Whiskey River." He works the audience, dances around and gets the crowd going. He's having a blast, doesn't look the least bit nervous. I get the feeling he's done this before.

Andy's up next. He's so charismatic and the crowd loves him. The soundtrack of a hip-hop song comes on and Andy gets the crowd clapping to the beat and then he starts flipping and spinning and doing a kind of Russian-style dance step, some Michael Jackson moves, like the moon walk, and then some crazy stuff, like he's on a pommel horse. When he gets backstage he's fired up and out of breath and sweaty. "You were freaking awesome," I tell him.

I'm next, and now my knees are shaking and my heart races.

Dave says, "And now, from San Antonio, Texas, Allison Deleon!"

My friends shout, "Al-lee, Al-lee, Al-lee!"

Dave greets me onstage.

Applause. "Al-lee, Al-lee, Al-lee!" my friends say, and the rest of the audience joins in.

"You have your own cheering section! Nice. Who's your cheering section?"

"Those are my friends and we're here for my friend, Jessica's, bachelorette party."

"Uh-oh, girls on the loose." That gets a laugh and whooping from the audience. "What do you do back in San Antonio, Allison?"

"I'm an Account Specialist at a technology company."

"Awesome. And today you're going to sing for us. Are you ready, Allison?"

"Yes I am," I say.

"Show her some Sables Blanc love, folks," he says. "Allison Deleon!"

The house lights go down and the spotlight's on me. I can't see much of anything except the feet of the people in the front row. I smile at the third row shouting my name and they get even louder.

I adjust the microphone stand so the mic is right at my mouth and when I speak, my voice fills the auditorium and sounds big and rich, not like me at all.

"This is a song by the late, great Leonard Cohen." It's "The Hallelujah Song", one of my favorites. It's been done a million times, a thousand different ways, plus one more.

I nod at Gus in the pit and he begins to play and I sing the only song

I can imagine singing at this time, mostly because that's how I feel. I'm up there with a Hallelujah.

And when I get to that last rise in the final verse I close my eyes for just a moment, then open them again and I'm overcome with this sense of magic of the moment, a mix of beauty and grace and joy and spirituality and happiness and absolute love.

I feel a surge of power hit me. I finish strong and loud, looking toward the spotlight, as if it's just me and the Lord of Song and I'm singing Hallelujah.

The audience applauds. My friends shout and whistle. I smile. *Wow. I did it. That was incredible. Scary as hell and so amazing at the same time.* I wipe a tear and walk off stage feeling dizzy. *Holy cow. That was so much fun.*

A couple of people backstage pat me on the back.

We sit and peek at Kayla and she does a dance-cheer-tumble routine to the song, "Hey Mickey!" She flips and does a back handspring on stage and the crowd goes nuts.

Yuri plays Queen's "Bohemian Rhapsody" on his ukulele. Amazing.

And the big, construction-looking guy, Jackson, plays Billy Joel's "Piano Man" on the harmonica.

Dave brings all of us back to the stage to decide the winner of the show. The vote is very scientific. Dave will hold his hand over each of us and whoever gets the loudest audience response wins. When he comes to me, my friends yell and scream. But Andy, the dancer, wins. He's a student from Dallas with a beautiful smile and dimples they can probably see all the way from the balcony.

His prize is a bottle of champagne, a trip to the spa, and a trophy with a #1 at the top. He does a flip when he's named the winner and the crowd cheers. Andy's awesome. I would have voted for him too.

"You've been a great crowd!" Dave says and closes out the show.

Before walking off the stage, we hug and say good-bye to each other and it's strange that I feel connected to them somehow. They're regular people, just like me, but something about putting myself out there, just like they did, makes me feel proud. Like a brotherhood, almost like a type of love. I think that's it. It's weird, but it feels like love. I didn't expect that at all.

My friends wait for me at their seats.

"Allie, oh my God, girl, you can sing!" Candace says.

"You were so good, Allie," says Vivian.

"You rocked it, Allie! You're badass," Audrey says.

"You should be on *The Next Big Superstar*, Allie. You'd win, girl," says Susan.

Jessica doesn't say a thing to me. She just opens her arms wide and grabs me and holds on. "Your song was so beautiful. It made me cry," she says. "What an amazing gift, Allie. Thank you."

All I can say is, "Thank you."

CHAPTER 15

*A*fter the show, we go for a late snack and drinks. Suddenly I'm exhausted. I head to the bathroom to see if I can wake up a little, get myself in the mood to celebrate.

On my way back to the table, a guy at the bar stops me and says, "Hey! You're Allison."

He's old, maybe 40 or so, wearing a western-style shirt and dark jeans. He looks familiar. *Where have I seen him before?*

He stands up from his bar stool and extends his hand. "Randy Smith," he says. "I saw you at the show."

"Oh right," I say. "I was wondering how you knew my name." Wait, he's the guy I saw in the elevator. That's where I've seen him.

"Girl, you rocked it tonight. I tried to catch you after the show, but couldn't get near you so this is cool that I get to meet you now."

I smile and nod. "Thank you."

"Yeah, you have a great voice. And that song. You nailed it. Beautiful."

"Thank you," I say. "I appreciate that. Yeah, I love that song." I'm ready to go back to the table.

"Can I buy you a drink?"

Is he flirting with me? "Oh, I'm good. Thank you. " I start to walk away and he keeps talking to me.

"Actually, Allison, I can't tell you how glad I am to run into you."

He pauses, then asks, "Are you playing with anybody right now? They said you're a secretary, right?" He scratches his chin and looks off in the distance. "At least I think that's what they said. Anyway, besides your job, are you playing with anyone?"

"You mean playing, like in a band?"

"Yeah, in a band or on your own, even." He leans on the bar.

I shake my head. "Not right now," I say, as if I ever had.

"Awesome. Well, I have a band and we're looking for a singer." His eyes widen.

I must look confused because he says, "I'm serious. This past year we went through a total transformation. Almost entirely. And we're looking for a lead vocalist."

"Oh yeah?" I look over at the table. Everyone's on the dance floor.

He continues, "Yep. We've been looking for just the right girl, and, I don't know, you may be a good fit. How would you like to audition to be a lead singer? I know the band will love you."

"Really? Uh, I don't know. What kind of music do you play?"

"It's a blend of country and blues, mostly," he says.

"Where are you from? I mean, where's your home town base type of thing?"

"Great question. We're based in the Dallas area," he says, "and we've been playing all around the city. We're getting ready to expand some, go on tour, so to speak. Next year. Or as soon as we can, really."

"You're going on tour? Where?"

On tour sounds cool. How does that even work? How do you get into it and start touring. I'm intrigued.

"Mostly Southwest, Texas, Louisiana, Oklahoma. After that, we're planning on expanding and branching out even more. Coast to coast, maybe Europe. Who knows?" Randy says.

"Oh," I say. This feels very strange. "What's the name of your band?"

"River Rangers. Named after the Red River. So," he says, as he checks his pockets for something. "Here's my card." He gets a napkin and a pen from the bartender. "And can I get your number and talk to the guys and figure out a way we can get together. You're in San Antonio, right? Did I remember that right?"

"Yes, I'm in San Antonio." What would it hurt to give this guy my phone number? Especially since I don't have a phone this weekend. I'll probably never hear from him, anyway.

I look over at the dance floor and Jessica's looking for a signal to come rescue me. I give her a thumbs up and give Randy my number.

"Thank you, Allison. I know it must seem strange for some stranger out of the blue to be asking you for your number, but I promise, it's a little odd for me too."

"Oh, you don't do this every day?" I say.

He smiles. "No, no, not at all. In fact, I was looking for you earlier and then I lost you. But when I saw you passing by, I thought 'Oh wow! Is that her?'"

"Well, thank you. I appreciate the encouragement."

"Absolutely. And I'll be in touch."

He extends his hand again. "Allison, very nice meeting you. You have an amazing voice. That's what we need. Maybe we'll be a good fit for each other."

The group is back at the table. When I join them Jessica asks, "Who was that?"

Susan says, "Did you tell him 'No autographs.'?"

"Not quite, but he did see me at the show and thought I was good."

"You weren't just good," Jessica says, "you were freaking stupendous!"

I grin and shake my head. "Oh Jess."

"See, it's not just us who think so, either," she says.

I smile at her. "Amazingly."

"Oh, Allie, come on. Admit it. You're damn good," she says.

"Don't. Stop," I say, "No, it's nice to hear it from someone I don't know. But come on. Let's dance."

"Okay. Let's dance," Jessica says.

We file out to the dance floor which is a lot smaller than the one last night. We sing loud and dance like we're the only ones in the place.

I'm a bundle of mixed emotions. Being with friends, singing, dancing. Having what I want, wanting what I have for the moment, at least, because everything will be changing soon. I try to re-focus, forget everything else and force myself to live in this moment. My heart takes a picture of Jessica, in all her love and happiness, singing all out, even if she's making up the words.

I think about all we've been through together. It's time. Things are supposed to change. That's life, like my grandmother used to say.

Time to settle down and do what grown ups do. Work more, play less. That's what my mom says. I've been doing that for a while, even though I don't want to be like my mom. How can I count the ways? To only exist, not actually live. That sounds horrible to say about my own mother, I know. I wonder how my mom would be different if Oscar had lived. How would everything be different?

The rest of the night is toasts, shots, and more dancing. We close the bar down. 2 AM.

"Move the party to our dance club just down the way and dance 'til four, beautiful people," the DJ says. "Have a good night!"

I'm partied out.

"I'm good to call it a night," Jessica says. "Whoa!" she says, stumbling slightly.

Everyone agrees and we finally get back to our rooms. I shower and get in bed and as much as I want to re-play my performance in my head, I can only see the spotlight and microphone before dropping off to sleep and dreaming.

I'm at a house, a big, Victorian-style house, bright with tall ceilings and hard-wood floors. My shoes make a loud clunking sound as Chewy and I walk down a long, dark hallway. We turn toward the light of an open door that seems like another room, but it's not a room. It's a tropical island with palm trees and ocean breeze. Absolutely beautiful and perfect. We get on a golf cart and then we're at a park, sitting around a picnic table with some other people I don't know.

I realize Chewy's not with me and I think, Oh my God! I lost Chewy! I call her and she doesn't come. I panic and scream, "Chewy! Chewy!"

And she's nowhere. I start crying and it gets dark and windy. And then it starts raining. And I stand in the rain calling, "Chewy! Chewy!" The rain's in my face and my sobs make it hard for me to breath.

All of a sudden, a girl named Ann, who I haven't seen since elementary school, is there. She has freckles and hair so blonde it's white, the same as she did in third grade, and she walks up to me and says, "Hi Allie!" She's smiling at me and I say, "Ann! I lost my dog. Have you seen my dog?"

She points down to the ground and says, "You mean that dog?" And when I look down Chewy is sitting there looking at Ann and then at me, and I say, "Chewy! Where were you?" And I pick her up and hold her and I cry and cry.

I sit up in a panic. Chewy! The room is dark except for the light from the hallway coming in under the door. Where am I?

Right. At the resort. Jessica's party weekend. Audrey's here. I look over to the other bed where Audrey is sleeping, but can't see a thing. My heart races and I feel tears in my eyes. The clock reads 5:25. Chewy's at the kennel. They would have called me if something had happened. I lie awake for a while hoping my dog's okay, and finally fall back asleep.

CHAPTER 16

We spend the rest of the weekend relaxing by the pool, eating, swimming, eating some more, and whatever else we want to do.

We explore the resort and get full use of the amenities: lazy river, pool, beach that's not a beach, and an awesome museum that features a few originals, by artists I've never heard of, as well as several prints of classic paintings, like *Starry Night, Sunflowers, Girl with the Pearl Earring, Torn Hat*, and others I don't know by name. I love the museum. From the moment of entry, it feels like I'm somewhere else. Thick, cushiony carpet, dark-wood paneling, and special museum lighting for each piece. Plus an explanation of each work, including where the original is housed and its estimated value.

Very interesting, even though it felt kind of weird walking through in my flip flops and sundress.

At dinner Saturday night, we see Ray for the last time and he's sweet and cheerful as always. We toast to Jessica once more and she toasts to us.

"To the best friends anyone could ever hope for. They say a true friend is the greatest of all blessings. My cup overflows. To good friends and happiness!"

"Here, here!" Audrey says. And we drink.

After dinner, we sit out by the pool with our feet in the water. It's calm and relaxing and warm. A bright white crescent moon glows beautifully alone in the darkening sky. Water splashes from the pool's rocky cliff.

It's our last night at the resort and we're partied out. We talk about going to the late show of the Beatles review, but it doesn't happen. Instead, we order drinks by the pool and talk and laugh for hours.

～

Sunday morning. Back to reality.

On the way home, I tell Jessica about Randy, the guy who stopped me at the bar after the show, and that he didn't just tell me I was good. "He wants me to audition for his band."

"What? You're kidding. Allie! That's awesome!" Jessica says. She turns toward me from the front passenger seat and reads my expression. "No? Not awesome?"

"No, it is," I say, "but I don't know. It's a little far-fetched, don't you think? Just some guy happened to see me and says, 'You're great! Come be in my band?'" I hold my hands up mimicking a fangirl. "It's crazy. And I'm not sure I could travel around with a bunch of guys."

"Well it won't hurt to check it out, Allie. You never know," she says.

Vivian says, "What a great opportunity, Allison. Go for it!"

"Thanks. I mean, I may not even like their music. And I don't want to move to Dallas," I say.

"Patience, grasshoppah," Jessica says. "Check out the band and see what you think. What kind of music do they play?"

"He said country and blues? I don't know. Yeah, I guess you're right." I want to tell her about my job because when we get home we'll be busy and I may not have a chance to talk to her about it. But I don't really want to because I feel like a screw-up.

"What?" Jessica asks.

"Nothing."

"Come on, Allie. Let's talk it out," Jessica says. She must think I'm thinking about the band.

I finally say, "Well, it's about my job. Right before I left work Thursday, God, it seems like so long ago, anyway, before I left work on Thursday my boss called me in for my six-month review. It didn't go well. He said he's concerned with my work performance."

"What does that mean?" Jessica asks.

"Well, it means they came really close to firing me, I think."

Jessica looks shocked. "Oh no, Allie. What happened?"

"Long story short, I made some mistakes on my reports and they think I've been there long enough that I shouldn't be making mistakes. So now, I have to work with a 'Nesting Coach.'" I explain to Jessica what that means and that it's like taking a giant step backward.

"But don't look at it that way. Maybe they're really trying to help you."

I lean forward from the center of the backseat. "I guess."

Jessica says, "That happens to teachers all the time. Right Viv?"

She's going to try to make me feel better about this somehow. I'm done talking about it, but before I can change the subject, Vivian says, "Oh yeah. Especially teachers who can't control their students. Yep. All the time."

I say, "It'll be fine. I'm not worried about it." It's not worry as much as dread.

"Yeah, I think the coaching is a positive," Jessica says. She starts talking about a teacher who was ready to quit because her classes were so bad and the principal got her some coaching and it helped her turn her classes around. Now she's an awesome teacher.

Vivian agrees and looks at me in the rear-view mirror. "Yeah, it saved her career."

Oh please. They keep talking about this teacher and I wish they'd stop. "What time do you think we'll be home?" I say.

Jessica gives me her "teacher look." One eyebrow slightly raised, blank expression.

And I give her a similar look that means *Can we talk about this later?* No offense to Vivian, but really? Do we need to talk about what a screw up I am in front of her? She's probably never screwed anything up in her life.

Vivian answers my question. "We'll be home around four."

. . .

*A*fter a quick stop for lunch and a chat with Jessica to tell her I'm fine and not to worry about me, we're back on the road.

I sit in the back seat and try to think about something good. The talent show. Even though I wasn't ready and I was nervous, I was okay. Not the best performance of even that small group, but it got me out there and I had fun.

As if she was reading my mind, Jessica turns and says, "Hey Allie, maybe this whole weekend…you know, the talent show and the offer to audition, are a sign that you should be doing something else entirely."

"Ha! That's crazy. I was just thinking about the talent show too."

She smiles. "Yeah? Were you thinking that you might do something in music again? Like find out about that audition? Or you could give school another shot," Jessica says.

I'm sitting in the back-middle seat, with my seat belt very loose so I can scooch up and lean toward the front seat, like a little kid talking to her parents.

"I don't know about the audition. I have to check out the band first I guess. And I actually have thought about going back to school. Not because I really want to but because I don't know what else to do. But I was never a good student, you know that, Jess," I say. I did well in the subjects I liked. Music and English. Usually.

"You weren't a bad student. Besides, it would be different for you now. And I could help you, Allie," she says.

No. She can't help me. "I know you'd want to, but you have your own stuff going on." She's got the wedding and school. Then she's going to be working on being a mom. And leaving. She won't be able to tutor me.

"Oh, I could still help you," she says.

"Thanks but I can muddle through the academic stuff. I don't have to make A's. I just have to pass."

"That's true. Do you think you'd go back to study music?" Jessica asks.

"Maybe I could be on the business side, like be a band manager or something."

"Really? If you want to do that, you probably don't need to go to school, Allie. Maybe you could work with that guy, that Randy dude, so you could learn the business first-hand," Jessica says.

"I can't imagine traveling around with a band. I'm too old for that," I say.

"But isn't that what you've always wanted? Didn't you want to travel in theatre, like *West Side Story*."

Of course Jessica knows I wanted to be like Maria in *West Side Story*, but hearing her say it out loud like that makes me cringe. It's almost embarrassing. "Yeah. I thought that's what I wanted," I say. "But that didn't happen. So whatever."

"You'll figure it out, Allie."

"Oh yeah." I love that she's so sure, but I have my doubts. There's no right or wrong answer, I guess. For now, I have to get my shit together and hang on to my job. How 'bout I start there?

CHAPTER 17

We get back to San Antonio with plenty of time for me to pick up Chewy from Happy Paws Kennel before it closes. When I walk in the door, she's sitting on an office chair directly behind the front desk.

"Oh, my goodness, Chewy. What are you doing up here?" I say.

She lifts her head but doesn't get up.

The girl at the desk says, "Hi! Oh, you're here for Chewy?"

"I am. But she looks like she'd be okay to stay a while longer." Chewy doesn't look very excited to see me.

"Yeah, she's been keeping me company up here. She's a sweetie," she says.

On the way home, Chewy jumps to the back seat and lies on the floor board instead of sitting up front with me. *Oh I see. Giving me the cold shoulder. You couldn't come with me. Sorry.*

As much as I want to drive straight home, I decide I better get another phone before I go back to work tomorrow. Though, I admit, it's been nice being truly disconnected this weekend.

"I'll be right back, Chewy." I leave her in the car with the A/C on. Lucky for me, the store is empty and I'm in and out in twenty minutes. I call my mom to see how she's doing and let her know I'm back in town, but she doesn't answer. "Call me when you get a chance, Mom."

When I get home, I start my Sunday night routine of getting ready for the work week. There's something positive to be said for routine. It helps me clear my head. It's familiar and automatic. Maybe that's why I'm dreading going to work tomorrow. Having to report to a nesting coach is going to be a pain. It throws off my routine and makes me feel like I don't know what I'm doing, which makes me feel lost and disoriented, like when you're driving and you get turned around and you don't know where you are until you get your bearings. I hate that feeling.

I tell Chewy about my weekend, the food, dancing, talent show, and about the guy who wants me to audition for his band.

"What do you think about that? Crazy, right? I didn't see it comin', that's for sure."

I had a blast performing at the talent show, but I'm not sure about the audition and singing in a band. I used to want to make music my life.

Jessica's right. That high school theatre performance made a huge impression on me. I decided I wanted to sing like "Maria" from *West Side Story* and I wanted to learn to play the piano, but things don't always work out as we'd like, do they?

My dad was all for it. He signed me up for piano lessons. My mom was less enthusiastic, but she didn't stop him.

At first, piano was easy. I learned the basics, then the music got more complicated.

My piano teacher, Ms. Susie, intimidated me. Every time I made a mistake, she'd purse her lips and shake her head. I could play a song from start to finish, then she'd say, "Start here," pointing somewhere in the middle of the piece.

I was never sure I was playing the notes she pointed at. Once I asked her, "How does that section go?" because I could play it by ear, but that's not what she wanted. She expected me to know the music. She frowned at me and said, "Allison, you should know this, my dear." Then she scolded my mom. "Mom, she has to practice." My mom said, "She practices every day." And I did. Ms. Susie raised an eyebrow as if to say,

"Sure she does."

Yeah, I couldn't read the music, but I faked it for a long time until she finally started catching on that I was lost. I could only copy what she played. I had a great ear, but that wasn't enough. No matter how hard I tried, I couldn't seem to make my teacher happy. I started dreading my lessons. It got so bad, I used to leave Ms. Susie's house in tears. I wasn't strong enough to face that kind of criticism.

I finally quit piano. No more lessons, no more recitals.

I still loved singing more than ever. I stuck with that through high school and into college.

But that miserable feeling of dread came flooding back when Professor Dumbkirk (his real name doesn't matter) came along.

He was a bully. Plain and simple.

He came in as an Associate Professor my second year in the music program and vowed to take the music department to the next level. His goal was to put our tiny, little music program on the same level as Juilliard. He came in "kickin' ass and takin' names." That was exciting to me. I was like, "Yeah, let's do it!" It turned out part of his plan involved weeding out the field and having only the best, most talented, and academically excellent students in the program.

He demanded that everyone in the program be expert at sight-reading (being able to sing a piece of music by reading the notes on the page). "You're music majors, people. You should be able to read music. Fluently!" he'd say about a thousand times a day.

Sight-reading was my weakness. I knew I was in trouble. No matter how hard I studied or what strategies I used, it was like a foreign language I couldn't master. I had gotten by for years, but I wasn't fluent. And truly, sight-reading is an important skill. It is. But it's not everything. At least, I didn't think so.

Once he knew for sure that I couldn't read music like a pro, he seemed set on driving me out.

He'd call me out in class, asking me to sing a new piece, and when I didn't respond immediately, he'd rush me, "Well do you know it or not? And if not, why not?"

I would muddle through it, but I was usually off. Sometimes way off.

That spring semester, he announced a mandatory sight-singing competition. He promoted it as an opportunity for students to stand out, to show their years of training in a definitive and concrete way. Really, it was a way for him and everyone else to see who was fluent and who wasn't. I was terrified.

I studied every day, worked with a tutor, practiced, and prepared as much as I could. The closer the competition got, the less confident I was.

The day of the competition, I was sick with anxiety and by the time my name was called I felt weak and distracted.

He handed me the music and I drew a blank.

I stared at it. I didn't know where to start. My knees were shaking and I looked at him for help, thinking maybe he could give me the first note.

He frowned his disapproval.

I hesitated, then stammered.

He rolled his eyes with a look of disgust.

Instead of just singing and doing my best, I stood there paralyzed with fear. And then the most ridiculous thing happened. I started to cry.

He must have rolled his eyes again and mumbled something to himself before shouting, "Ms. Deleon, collect yourself!"

But I couldn't. I left the room humiliated and ashamed.

I don't know if I would have failed the class or if he would have removed me from the program, but I beat him to it.

I dropped the class the next day, finished out my other classes that semester, and never went back.

The memory still stings. I'm bitter toward the professor. Definitely.

But I wonder if things had been different if I hadn't quit.

Could I have done something differently? Why didn't I fight back? Why did I let him treat me like that? Would I have had a chance if he hadn't ever landed at my school? I ask myself these questions all the time.

I'm not sure why I can't shake off what happened, just forget about the past and embrace my love of music again. The whole idea's kind of a jumble in my brain and just when I begin to see it clearly and it takes shape with hard edges and color, something or someone snaps me back to reality and it disappears.

I've come to realize something, though. It doesn't matter whether I quit, was driven out in shame, or just wasn't good enough. I left something I loved, something that was once a huge part of my life and dreams.

I didn't want to tell anyone the real reason I quit. At first, all I said was school wasn't for me. It took a long time to get over that disaster, but it left a tender scar.

I think my mom was relieved. She hated me studying music and supported my decision to quit. "Now you can stop wasting time singing and get a real job with benefits."

That's what I did. I worked retail for a couple of years before I got my last job where I got laid off and then I got lucky and landed the job at Micro Solutions. It's not a dream job, or even very interesting, but it pays the bills and gets me what I need. If I stop screwing up maybe I'll get to stay there a while.

But lately, music has new meaning to me. Sudden emotional reactions to a song, playing guitar and keyboard again, listening to live music, and now, actually performing on stage. It's great. I admit I love the encouragement I've gotten.

Who knows? Maybe Randy will call. Maybe I'll take him up on his offer to audition.

It might be cool to be "on the road" singing. I don't know. It seems crazy to consider that as a possibility. I should have started singing again a long time ago.

I'm not sure I'm cut out for a musician's life though. Too hard. Staying up late, no money, working in sleazy clubs, and what would I do with Chewy?

Anyway, who's to say he'll even call. I love to sing, but would I want to do it for a living? Live a Bohemian life. I imagine myself in a peasant blouse with a big ruffled skirt and Birkenstock sandals. Oh wait, country western. Black cowboy boots with a black dress and big turquoise jewelry. I'd let my hair be big and wild. That could be my signature look. My brand. I imagine being on stage and singing a country song.

My new phone rings an unfamiliar tone and it takes me a few seconds to realize that's my phone. It's my mom.

"Oh, you're back. That's good."

"Yeah, I got back this afternoon and I'm just getting ready for my week," I say. "How was your weekend?" I decide not to tell my mom about me ruining my phone or the show or anything else.

"Good. Everything's good. Just here."

"Are you okay?" I want to ask her if she heard from my dad again and has he already filed for divorce. I want details, but maybe it's best not to ask.

"Yeah, just been here. Okay well I wanted to make sure you got home," she says.

"Yeah, we did. You're going to work tomorrow?"

"Why wouldn't I go to work?" She sounds defensive.

"Oh, I don't know, Mom. Just wondering. You sounded pretty upset the last time we talked and you told me about Dad."

"I'm fine. I gotta go. I'll talk to you later." She hangs up.

My mom's not a big talker, but that was fast even for her. We're going to need to talk about my dad sometime. It won't be easy for either one of us. For different reasons.

CHAPTER 18

When I get back to work on Monday, I have two emails from Mr. Hernandez. The first one's a meeting invite at ten to meet my new coach. The second is a message saying he won't be in the office until ten o'clock for the meeting and hold off on my work files until then.

Oh I see. He doesn't trust me on my own. *Okay. Whatever, Mr. Hernandez.* I accept the meeting invite then make my way to the office cafe for the Tex-Mex breakfast of champions: a bean and cheese taco and a cup of coffee. I find a seat at a corner table and take out my phone to look up Randy and his band, The River Rangers.

Their website looks outdated with no current bookings listed, although they have a few live videos. They sound kind of country, but more like a mixture of country, blues, and folk. I guess Randy said that.

I like the music, though. Their singer's great. I'm nowhere close to being that good. And the guitarist is sitting and playing with the guitar in his lap. That's different. I can't see the drummer very well and there's a guy playing bass.

Randy's not on stage at all, or I can't pick him out if he's there. I thought he was in the band, but maybe he's the manager. Did he say that? I don't remember.

I finish up my breakfast and head back to my desk. I daydream about the band. What if he calls? Could I really audition? But that's crazy talk. What are the odds?

I clear out my email until it's time to head over to the conference room near Mr. Hernandez's office. I'm the first one there, so I sit at the table and wait.

Mr. Hernandez comes in a few minutes later and right after that another woman, who must be my Nesting Coach, gets there.

"Hey Roger," she says as she walks in and puts her laptop on the table.

"Angie. You made it."

"Yeah, sorry I'm late. It's been a hectic morning." She's out of breath like she's been running.

"You're fine. I just got here myself. Thanks for taking the time."

"Hi, I'm Angie," she says as she extends her hand to me.

"Hi Angie. I'm Allison."

Mr. Hernandez starts to say something, but stops himself. He says to Angie, "I'll let you get settled."

She pulls out a chair and sits in front of her open laptop. "Whew!" She opens her eyes wide. "Okay, I'm ready."

"Great," Mr. Hernandez says. "I explained to Allison that you'd be providing her some extra coaching and she could attend briefing sessions with your group."

"Right," she says.

"It might be easier if you explain the particulars so we're all on the same page here," he says.

"Sure." She clicks at her laptop then puts her hands in her lap and leans back in her chair. She says to me, "My group is in their first week of nesting, so this works out perfectly." She nods to Mr. Hernandez.

"Terrific," he says.

Lucky me.

"They'll finish up next Friday then they'll go to their assigned teams."

"Will I be nesting for two weeks?" I ask Angie and then look at my boss.

"Yes," he says. "I think two weeks should be plenty."

"Perfect," Angie says. "So for these two weeks, you can meet us in Training Room B at eight o'clock. You'll spend the day with your Nesting Buddy. Then you'll come back to the room at four for debrief. That'll give us a chance to share best practices and answer any questions you might have."

Mr. Hernandez says, "Allison, I want you to work on your current work files."

I nod. "Okay."

Angie closes her laptop and looks at me. She's smiling and seems to be waiting for me to say something.

"Thank you." I don't know what to say. This feels like way more coaching than I need. I think they're going overboard. I'm going to have someone sitting by me for two weeks, looking over my shoulder while I do what I've been doing for six months? It's stupid. But what choice do I have?

"So," she says as she stands, "let's go meet your Nesting Buddy."

She's so chipper. I cringe every time she says the word "buddy." I mean, she seems nice, yeah, but come on.

My Nesting Buddy, is a guy I've seen around the office, but never met before today. His name's Michael and he's always struck me as nerdy-looking because of the khaki pants and plaid, short-sleeve shirts he wears. I'd never noticed his round, smooth face behind his oversized black-frame glasses.

When I start to work my files, he stops me before I've even done anything. "Okay, now why are you doing that?"

I didn't think I was that bad, but Michael is taking his Nesting Buddy role very seriously. I don't seem to be doing anything right. I want to say, "Am I breathing wrong, Michael?" but I keep my mouth shut and remind myself, "He's here to help me."

Michael doesn't come right out and tell me what to do, but he makes lots of "suggestions," from how I update my calendar to the verbiage I use on my notes to the Sales Reps I support.

"Instead of saying, 'Here are the bids you requested…'" say, 'Please find the enclosed bids for — and then name the client — due on — and then list the date.' It sounds more professional that way, don't you think?"

Sure, Michael. "Okay," I say. He's like the perfect employee. At first I thought, I have to try and think more like this guy, but there's no way.

When it's finally time to go to the training room for the afternoon debrief, I'm not sure I ever did anything right and I'm relieved to get away from his hawk eyes.

"There you are, Allison," Angie says when I walk in. The trainees are sitting at their desks, talking and laughing.

"Am I late?"

"No, you're good. Have a seat." She points to a chair at the end of the row beside a woman with a loud, raspy voice. "Okay guys." Angie stands to get their attention and waits for quiet, but they're slow to wind down their conversations.

Angie smiles. She looks as chipper as she did this morning. "Awesome, guys. This is Allison, and she'll be nesting with us."

A big guy across the table from me says, "Hi Allison."

"Actually, I'd like to go around the table so you can introduce yourselves and tell Allison a little bit about yourself?" Angie smiles and raises her eyebrows as if to say, *Yes, Sound good?* "Natalie, will you start?" She nods to a woman sitting to her left.

Natalie wears black slacks and a blue blouse and flats and has her straight, dark-brown hair pulled back in a bun, like a ballerina.

"I'm Natalie. I have two girls, seven and ten, and I'm a student."

Angie nods at the woman to Natalie's left, "Maya?"

"Hi Allison! My name's Maya and I love these guys and love this job. And..." she says, as if she's on stage. "I just got engaged!" Maya flashes her ring.

"We've seen it," the big guy says. "At least a hundred times."

Maya flops her brown, curly hair over to one side of her head, then to the other. "Make it a hundred and one," she says. Every time she flops her hair, I can feel the whoosh of air as she cranes her neck to one side and then the other. She wears a heavy layer of makeup, severe blush, and very dark lipstick. And she's loud.

"Excellent. Thank you, Maya," Angie says. "Allison?"

I introduce myself and tell them I was born and raised in San Antonio. And that's it.

"Thank you, Allison. Welcome," Angie says. "Gerald?"

Gerald sits across from me. He looks like he's about sixteen, or maybe it's just his Super Mario T-shirt making him look like a kid. "I'm Gerald and I like to play video games," he says.

"Okay, thank you, Gerald. And last but not least, Todd," Angie says.

Todd has a round face with pink cheeks, fair, smooth skin, and red hair. He's wearing cargo pants and a wrinkled safari shirt that's at least one size too small.

"I'm Todd and I'm very grateful for the job and for this new opportunity. I love to cook and I love to eat, as you can see," he says patting his belly, seeming to make it bigger and rounder than it actually is.

"Thank you guys," Angie says.

She takes questions and clarifies a few issues, but it's all pretty straightforward stuff. I wonder how this is supposed to make me better. This group seems kind of oddball, not dumb exactly but not too bright. I don't know. Maybe it's me. Michael wants me to do everything exactly the way he does it, but is that really necessary? I'm not doing *everything* wrong. No one's perfect.

I had a teacher once who used to say: "Connection" is the key to success no matter what you do. If you're a teacher, you have to connect with students and parents and other teachers. If you're an artist, you have to connect to your work, yourself, and the people with whom you share your work. Parents have to connect with their kids and let them know that they matter. (Why is that so difficult?) Businesses have to connect with customers and develop relationships so they keep coming back.

I buy into that philosophy. Make a connection. Simple enough in theory, but, the way I see it, the key to making connections is caring enough to make it happen. It's not going to happen if you don't give a damn. And I'm not sure I do. At the same time I don't want to get fired.

I want to ask Angie, "Are we going to talk about how to care more? Because I think that might be what I need."

I give myself a good talking-to: Come on, Allison. Get your head in the game. It's not freaking rocket science. If they can do it, you can do it.

Of course I can.

CHAPTER 19

When I get home from work, I change out of my work clothes, sit outside and watch Chewy inspect the yard, then come inside and heat a frozen Italian flatbread for dinner. I'm watching the news and about to take a bite, when my phone rings.

"Hello?"

"Hello. Is this Allison?" It's a guy's voice, a low drawl.

"Yes it is?"

"Hi Allison. It's Randy with River Rangers."

Long pause. *Oh my God. He's calling me.* My heart beats faster.

"You sang at the resort talent show this weekend and you gave me your number and said you might be interested in auditioning? We're looking for a singer?"

"Oh, hi Randy." I try to sound calm. No big deal.

"Did you enjoy the rest of your weekend at the resort?"

"We did. Had a great time. Back at work today."

"Oh yeah, it's hard getting back to the real world, huh? That's a beautiful place."

"It is. Great place."

He waits. "Well, Allison, the reason I'm calling is I had a chance to talk to the band. Mostly to our guitar player, really. He's the picky one."

My mind flashes back to another picky musician who turned out to be a nightmare. He couldn't be that bad. Could he? "I see."

"Naw, he's a good guy. Just a stickler for the music. He'd love to meet you. Are you interested?"

I'm amazed that he's calling me, but I don't know. "Actually, I was looking at the band website. I wasn't sure I was looking at the right band. I didn't see you on stage."

"I'm behind the scenes." He laughs. "Yeah, I'm the manager."

"Oh. Okay. That explains it. You might've told me that." I ask him where they've played recently. I'm trying to get an idea about what kind of shows they play, trying to get a feel for the band, and just looking to see if I think we'd be a good fit.

"Yep, all that stuff on the website is from about a year ago. In fact, I need to completely update that thing. We've been totally re-working everything. New songs, new sound, and now we're gonna have a new singer."

"Okay," I say. They sound legit.

"I guess I shoulda told you all that. But no, this whole year's been a re-group and now we just need vocals. Our old singer left 'bout a year ago and we've tried out a few singers and no one's quite hit it right. Not yet."

"Alright."

"Now the video on the website, except for the singer, that's the band. Did you see the video 'Catch a Rocket'?"

"I don't remember exactly." That title doesn't sound familiar.

"Well, check that song out. That's a good sample of what we're playin' now. Mostly," he says.

"Okay, I'll definitely take a look," I say.

"So, what's your availability?" He stops himself. "Well, let me ask you this, Allison, before we go any further."

"Sure."

"Is this something you think you might want to do?"

Is it something I want to do? I can honestly say maybe. "Honestly, Randy, I haven't been singing much lately. But, yeah, if we could figure out how to make it happen, I'd love to audition and see where it leads."

"Alright. Good enough. Well, how's it looking for you this weekend? Do you think you might be able to come up this weekend?"

"Come up? To Dallas?" *How far is Dallas?* "I'm not sure. I'll have to check."

"If you want to bring your parents, bring your friends, whoever. We want you to feel comfortable, so that's fine. This is a legitimate audition for a legitimate band. All are welcome. And you know what?" His voice trails off and then returns. "I just thought o' this. You're in San Antonio?"

"Yes."

"I got a friend in Waco and maybe we can meet there. Not as far for you and we can do a little road trip ourselves," he says.

"Oh, okay," I say. *How far is Waco?* I don't even know. "That might work. This weekend? Saturday might work. I'll have to check. Can I let you know tomorrow?"

"You sure can, and that'll give me a chance to clear everything with my buddy there. He's a little ways off the main highway."

"Okay, umm, what can I expect from the audition? I mean, do you have specific songs you want me to sing or should I pick my own? How many?" I'm totally making this up. I have no idea what to do, but I'll have to sing something.

"I'd say be ready to sing about four to five songs. I guess sing what you want us to see. How 'bout that? We'll keep it simple and very low-key. We're not formal."

"Sounds good. I'd like to be ready in case we can meet this weekend."

"I understand. Alright, well, Allison, I hope I get to see you this weekend. You can call or text me back to let me know. Will that work?"

"Sure," I say.

I haven't even disconnected the call and I'm talking myself out of it. *That's crazy. You can't be in a band. You can't leave your job.*

At the same time I can hear Jessica's voice telling me to do it. *Just go for it.*

What's the worst that can happen? It's a public place. It's not like they're going to kidnap me or something. Right? That's why he said I could bring my family. I get it. Besides, they may not even like me and I may not even like them.

Even if they like me, would I leave my job to join a band? I know I'm not a model employee like Michael, Mr. Perfect, but I'm confident I can at least be average.

I text Jessica and Audrey. "Possible audition this Saturday in Waco. Want to come with? Probably sometime in the afternoon and be back late afternoon. Probably."

Audrey replies almost immediately, "Yay road trip! I'm in!"

Jessica texts back, "Exciting! I have to check tho. Let you know tomorrow?"

I reply, "Yay and sure!"

CHAPTER 20

My second day of nesting goes well and, I hate to admit it, but Michael's growing on me. He's been a big help. I think I'll be able to show Mr. Hernandez some real improvement in accuracy and efficiency. I'm surprised at how excited I am about that.

I decide to stop by my mom's house on the way home. I usually call her every day, but I haven't talked to her since she hung up on me the other day. I'm giving her time to miss me, or at least to not be pissed at me.

Her car's in the driveway, which means she's home from work.

She answers the door in her pajamas. It's five o'clock.

"Are you in your pajamas?" I ask after we greet each other at the door. I don't know why I mess with my mom. I can see she's in her pajamas. The question is meant to let her know that I see she's in her pajamas and it's not even six o'clock.

"Yeah, I got home and wanted to get comfortable. I'm not going anywhere so I figured I might as well put on my pajamas," she says.

When she puts it that way she almost seems normal. I kiss my mom on the cheek, an old tradition and sign of respect I've done all my life. "How are you, Mom? How's work going?"

"Okay. Everything's fine. We're getting a new boss. Mrs. Roberts is retiring in a few weeks."

"Wow. She's been there forever, right?" I remember seeing a picture of Mrs. Roberts when she first started working there. She was a kid. I think she was still in high school.

My mom sits on the rocker recliner she's had for years. It's positioned directly across from the television, the rocker in one corner of the room, the TV in the other.

"Yes," she says, "Mrs. Roberts started when she was seventeen. She hasn't always been in the same office, but she's been at that office, my office, for a while. Fifteen years maybe?"

My mom started at that government office right after Oscar was born and she's been there ever since. At least twenty years. She answers general questions about taxes for small business, regulations, codes, and I don't know what else. Her office is a dull, outdated, dreary place with harsh fluorescent lights and the same furniture and carpet that look like they've been there since the day she started.

"Well, congratulations to Mrs. Roberts. Are ya'll throwing her a retirement party?"

"I don't think so. We'll probably take her out to lunch or something like that."

The local news is on television and the volume's turned way up. I feel like I'm shouting over the news anchor.

"Well, I have some exciting news," I say.

I'm disappointed when her expression doesn't change, but I continue. "Yeah. My weekend was good. Really good." My mom stares at the television. "I was in a talent show at the resort."

"Really? What was your talent?" she says without looking at me.

I juggled flaming pins while standing on my head. Gaw.

"I sang."

"You sang? Wow. You're gonna start singing? Again? I thought you were done with that stuff," she says, looking at the television.

I wanted to tell her about Randy and the audition, too. For some reason I thought she might be happy for me. What was I thinking? She'll shoot it down, for sure. Better to keep my music-related goings-on to myself for now.

"Yeah. It's probably just a one time thing." There's a news report about a firefighter pulling a dog from a burning house.

"Well," she says, "I called you to tell you that your dad came by last week."

"Yeah, you mentioned it on the phone. He came by here?"

My parents have been married almost thirty years. On paper. Do the years of separation count toward the total? If not, cut that number in half. That's how long it's been since the accident that changed my family forever. Since then, my dad has either been somewhere else or wanted to be somewhere else. My mom has been here. Physically, at least.

She sighs, "Yes, he came by." She's looking at the television. "He says he wants a divorce."

I wait a second and resist the urge to say, "It's about damn time," and all I can think is that it's too bad she didn't ask for it first. Finding him would've been the hardest part. I can't tell by looking at her whether she's okay with it or not. She seems to be waiting for some kind of reaction from me, though I don't know what that might be. I've been telling her for years to file for divorce, but she says she took a vow and she won't be the one to break it.

I think about saying 'I'm sorry' even though I'm not, so I say, "Are you okay with it?"

My mom replies almost in a ho-hum voice, "Well, I guess I have to be. If that's what he wants."

She looks fragile and weak with ashen colored skin and dark circles under her eyes.

"Well, it's not like he's been around for a long time. Do you even know where he's been?" I ask. The question sounds harsh and mean.

"He says he's been around." She doesn't turn my way, just keeps looking straight ahead.

I turn to her and say, "Well, mom, as long as you're okay. Maybe it'll be a good thing. It's not too late for you to get back out there and meet someone."

"Ha!" She finally looks away from the television and faces me. "Oh yes, Allison. Because you go out on so many dates, that's how you know?"

Ouch. But she's right. How can I say anything about her getting out there to meet someone? I've never had a serious boyfriend and I'm not sure I want one. Most boyfriends are a hassle. But this is not about me. It's about her.

"Well, Mom, you're only technically married. He's been gone for years. You're better off without him." That gets her attention.

"Allison, he's still your father. And he's still my husband even though you don't believe in the sanctity of our marriage."

Neither does he, Mom, I want to say, but keep that to myself.

"Okay, Mom. It doesn't have anything to do with that. But, he…" I start to say he gave up on both of us a long time ago, but I don't want to get into any of that with her. It never goes well when I try to talk to her about my dad. "… Oh, never mind, Mom. You're right. I gotta go," I say as I stand up.

She looks straight ahead. I wanted to tell her what's going on with me, about the weekend, my job, the audition, and Jessica's wedding, but I leave without another word.

CHAPTER 21

The next morning in Conference Room B, we sit around waiting for our morning brief. Angie's not there yet, but the rest of the group is. Natalie's studying. I'm busying myself surfing the web on my phone. Maya's sitting on the other side of the room talking to Gerald and Todd. I swear, Maya's got no filter between her brain and her mouth. She says whatever comes to her stupid head.

I look up from my phone just as she stands up, squinches her nose, waves her hand in front of her face, and looks at Gerald, "Oh my God, Dude!"

I don't say anything. No one else does either, but she's right. It stinks. And it's Gerald's fault.

Gerald has a problem. It's weird. He's a young guy, but he must have some sort of serious issue with digestion or gastro control or something. He farts. Bad. He must not be able to control it because certainly he would if he could. Right?

And even though she's annoying as heck, I don't blame Maya for her reaction. She's been stuck in training with him for weeks.

It seems more noticeable in the afternoon. But this morning, Natalie brought some "healthy and delicious" muffins for the group. Very high in fiber. It's terrible.

Natalie says Angie's talked to him (that must've been an awkward conversation), but nothing's changed.

Maya says, "God, Gerald! I'm sorry, I need to light a candle or something, 'cuz, Oh my God!"

"Sorry," Gerald says. "I think it was the muffins. Too healthy for my stomach." He's trying to laugh it off. I don't get it.

"What *doesn't* give you gas, Gerald?" Maya asks him.

Normally, a conversation like this would have me laughing out loud, but I feel bad for Gerald. There must be something seriously wrong with him that's causing him to let off these noxious fumes.

Maya pulls a candle out of her very large purse and lights it with a lighter. "I thought I had matches but I can't find them," she says.

"You had a candle in your purse?" says Todd, laughing. "What luck!"

"Luck, schmuck," Maya says. "In my purse for exactly this occasion. How did I know I'd need it?" She gets a can of air freshener from her purse and sprays the room.

Finally, about ten minutes later, Angie walks in. "So sorry I'm late," she says. "I got stuck in a meeting." She doesn't say anything about the candle except, "Oh, it smells good in here."

"I lit a candle because somebody had an above and beyond problem today," Maya says lifting her eyebrows and tilting her head in Gerald's direction.

"Oh gosh," Angie says. "Okay, well go ahead and blow it out now. And sorry, you can't light a candle in the office."

Gerald doesn't acknowledge the conversation. He and Todd are talking about a comic book or zombie show or something.

Maya says, "Gerald, you're too young to be having such a problem. How old are you?"

Gerald realizes she's asking him a question, "Me? How old am I?" he asks.

She nods.

"Twenty-three," Gerald says.

"Holy moly," Maya says. "You better do something about that or you're not going to have any friends when you get older."

"Okay, Maya, that's enough," Angie says.

"Seriously. It's only going to get worse as you get older. Trust me. I know. My fiancee's not even …"

"Maya," Angie says, pausing for emphasis, "that's enough."

Maya runs her mouth in the most annoying way, like everyone wants to hear her personal business. She shares way too much about her fiancee and his habits, likes, and dislikes, and other stuff no one wants to hear.

"Oh, he loves it when I sleep in the nude," she said the other day. "You know it's the healthiest way to sleep." And, my favorite, "You know those medications for older men? You know the ones I'm talking about." She was probably making an obscene gesture, but I don't know because, as a rule, I try not to look at her. "They rock my world."

In the few days I've known her, I know way more than I want to know about that lady. I stay as far away from her as I can. I'm not sure she'll last with the company very long. There are lots of people who get offended with the smallest reference to sex or any amount of cursing and she's got a big mouth.

∽

While I'm walking to my car after work, I see a text from Jessica, "Hey! I'm in for Waco. Okay to hit the outlet malls on the way?" Malls. Plural.

I reply, "Yay! Malls? Sure." Smiley face emoji.

No problem for me. I'm just grateful she's able to come with me.

I call Randy to let him know I'm good to go on Saturday and to confirm we're still on.

He answers the phone, "This is Randy," and he sounds like he's pissed off about something or in a hurry.

"Hi Randy, it's Allison, from the resort talent show?" No sign of recognition. "We talked about possibly meeting in Waco this weekend for an audition?"

"Oh right! Yes, yes," he says. "I'm sorry, my mind was somewhere else."

"It's okay," I say and I smile and nod my head as if he can see me. "Well, if you're still available this weekend, I'm good to go."

"Oh that's perfect. I'm waitin' to hear back from my buddy, for sure, but let's go ahead and plan on it. Can you make it there by one?"

"That'll work for me. One o'clock Saturday. Should I bring anything or have a track recording or how do you want to do this?"

"We can connect your phone or MP3 player, or whatever, into our system and I'll have a mic and that'll be it."

"Okay, sounds good. Will you text me the address and let me know if something changes?"

"Absolutely, I will," he says. "Alright Allison, can't wait to hear you again. I have a good feeling about this. We'll see you Saturday."

I'm glad he has a good feeling about this. I have my doubts. I'm amazed he even called me. I feel like a fake. He'll see that I'm not as good as he thought, and then it'll be over.

At least I have a job. Mr. Hernandez could have fired me. No question. But he's a good guy. Nesting has helped my attitude. I want to do a good job. As much as I can, anyway.

I have a feeling the biggest challenge will be to keep a high level of commitment all day, every day. It's exhausting. And it's not the work or the job. It's me. This is not at all what I planned for myself.

After the accident that wrecked our lives, my brother was gone forever and my dad was absent more and more. Then my grandmother got sick and I did my best to help out however I could. My mom became more bitter and withdrawn.

When I fell on my musical face in college and quit altogether, I believe my mom was pleased. I imagine her thinking that I'd finally settle down, grow up, be responsible, and do what most people have to do to survive. Work. And that's what I did.

But lately I've thought a lot about that moment when I sat in the audience with my grandmother and saw "Maria" on stage. Something was planted inside me that day, like a seed or a glimmer of something that never died.

When I sing at home or occasional karaoke outing, I say I'm just messing around, but I'm really not. For me, that's real. For me, that's truth, even though I rarely have the courage to claim it. Like when someone says, "Hey, you sounded great. You should be in a band!" I brush it off, kind of ignore it like I can't claim it because then it would be real, or I would have to accept it, and do something with it.

It's like tinkering with it is safe, and being at the talent show was also kind of safe, because I'm not a singer. It's not real. I'm an Account Specialist who has a decent voice. That's it. There's nothing at stake for me.

And now this audition. Not that I even want it or anything. They may not even like me. But, let's say I get it. Let's say they want me. Would that change anything? When does it get real?

All I know for sure is I have a job. It's an okay job. I don't love it. Am I supposed to love what I do? Does anyone?

I can only think of one person I know who loves her job—Jessica. She's always wanted to be a teacher. She loves it so much she says, "It doesn't feel like work."

I wonder what that's like.

CHAPTER 22

Saturday finally rolls around and Audrey, Jessica and I are on the road to Waco by eight. We start with coffee and a quick breakfast first, of course, then stop at the first outlet mall along the way.

Jessica details her shopping plan as we pull in to the parking lot of mall number one. She wants to hit Victoria's Secret, Ray-Ban, Nike, and New Balance.

Her wedding planner in hand, she says, "You're appointment's at one and do you need to get there early? Do you need to prep or anything like that?"

"Go to the bathroom, maybe. That's it. So maybe ten minutes early?"

"Already scheduled in. Actually, we're scheduled to arrive at twelve-forty five. So we'll have to leave Round Rock outlet by eleven-thirty." She makes a note in her planner.

"Did you schedule time for lunch or a snack in there, Jess?" Audrey asks from the back seat.

"You just ate, Audrey! And no, I didn't. I made you some trail mix and you can get something when we stop if you want," Jessica says. She hands Audrey a plastic container.

"You did? Oh, Jess. You know what I like," she says in a breathy voice.

Jessica smiles at her. "You're such a weirdo."

I catch a glimpse of Audrey picking out bits from her snack. *Crunch, crunch, crunch.*

"So, how do you feel about your audition today, Allie?" Jessica closes her planner and puts it in the quilted bag we gave her. "I'm just gabbing about all my stuff and we haven't even talked about the reason we're on this trip in the first place."

"Umm. I'm okay, I mean, I have no expectations, really. I actually thought about canceling last night, but..."

"What? I'm glad you didn't."

I shrug my shoulders, "I figure what the hell. We'll make a road trip out of it and go see what it's all about, I guess." It's not that I wanted to cancel, but last night when I was finalizing my song list I felt kind of blah about the whole thing, like I was going through the motions, not loving the idea of auditioning at all.

Jessica says, "Well, maybe you can look at it as being on a journey, kind of. You don't know where the road will lead. Maybe nowhere. Maybe somewhere."

"Whoa. Deep thoughts," I say. She's such a helper. "Yeah, I suppose. At least we get another road trip and you get to do your shopping. Thanks for coming with me. If ya'll hadn't been able to come with me, I'm sure I would've cancelled."

"Of course, Allie," Audrey says.

"For sure. I'm glad it worked out," Jessica says.

She updates us on wedding stuff: her parents' wedding budget concerns, David's high-maintenance family, venue issues, caterer issues, etc.

I tell them about my nesting group. "I feel like I'm on the Island of Misfit Toys."

They laugh.

"I shouldn't say anything because I'm probably the queen of the Misfits. I'm just there because they weren't ready to fire me. They probably think I'm a 'slow learner.'" I hate the thought of it, but that may be true.

"Well at least you don't have a flatulence problem, do you?" Audrey asks.

"No, not usually," I say.

"And you don't have a secret older boyfriend who likes you to sleep in the nude. And if you did, you wouldn't go tell the whole world about it. You'd do the respectable thing and keep it to yourself, right?" Audrey laughs out loud in the back seat.

"If I had a boyfriend, young, old, whatever, I wouldn't go around talking about our bedroom habits. No," I say.

Jessica laughs. "Yeah. *She* sounds like a nutcase."

"And I try to ignore her. These are all details I've picked up incidentally. It's ridiculous."

We're still about ninety-five miles from Waco and decide to hit the next outlet mall on the way back, so we'll have plenty of time and won't have to rush.

We roll in to Waco just after noon, well ahead of schedule and I drive to the address Randy sent me but don't see any cars in the parking lot. "We'll come back."

We find a sandwich shop for a quick bite that we can wrap up and take if we need to. We go through the line for our food and sit at a table by the door.

"You okay?" Jessica asks.

"I'm getting nervous, actually," I say. "I didn't expect to be."

"You're going to be fine," she says.

"It's good to be nervous. That's a good sign," Audrey says.

I take a couple of bites of my sandwich then wrap it up. "I'm going to the car to listen to the music for a few minutes. Take your time."

I play the songs and warm up my voice. I feel pretty good. I have the lyrics, so I don't have to worry about forgetting the words. I drove all this way to sing so here I go. Almost time.

Jessica and Audrey knock on the window and open the door. "Good?" Jessica asks.

"Yep, good to go," I say, but when I pull in to the parking lot and see a couple of other cars there, I feel butterflies in my belly. I keep reminding myself that this audition is for fun. Nothing's at stake. It doesn't matter one way or the other. I'm a wildcard.

. . .

*T*he bar, Waco Tavern, is a little hole-in-the-wall toward what feels like the center of town. The front door is heavy and hard to pull open.

Stepping inside from the hot, bright outdoors I need a second for my eyes to adjust. I hear male voices and see that the guys are at the end of the bar.

Randy looks over, "Hey! You made it! Come on in," he says.

It's dark and cool. The bar's along the right side and there's a small raised stage toward the back. Tables are pushed along the edge of the room with chairs turned over on top of them. A couple of video games and dart boards glow in the dim light.

Jessica and Audrey follow me over. Randy holds out his hand, "Hello again, Allison."

"Hi," I say.

I almost don't recognize him. He looks different in his t-shirt, jeans, and tennis shoes, not jeans and boots.

"This is my friend Brian. This is his place," Randy says, introducing the man behind the bar who's bald with a handle bar mustache curled at the ends. He's very tall.

"Welcome." Brian smiles and shakes my hand.

"And this is Joshua. He's our lead guitarist I was tellin' you about," Randy says.

Joshua extends his hand toward me. "Hi Allison," he says, smiling.

The "picky" one. But he looks like a regular guy, wearing jeans and an Iron Man t-shirt. His hair's light brown and longish, a little shaggy. He's solidly built, muscular, and he's wearing dark sunglasses.

"Hi, nice to meet you," I say. "These are my friends, Jessica and Audrey."

"Oh right! You're getting married soon, right?" Randy says to Jessica.

"Yes," Jessica says. "You have a good memory!"

"Sometimes I do," he says.

Joshua extends his hand toward Jessica and Audrey and holds it there. They each take his hand and smile. "Hello."

A SONG FOR JESSICA

"Okay, are you ready to get started?" Randy asks me. He claps his hands once and rubs them together.

"Can I offer you ladies something to drink?" Brian asks as he rolls his eyes toward Randy. "Please pardon my friend here. His manners took a day off today."

"Oh my gosh, I'm so sorry," Randy says. "Would you like somethin' to drink?"

I look at Audrey and Jessica. They shake their heads. "No thank you, we're good. We stopped for a bite a little while ago," I say. "Thank you, though."

"I'm so anxious to get started," Randy says. "Well, we have a little set up here, Allison," he continues. I follow him and he sets a couple of chairs down in front of the stage. Brian helps him pull a table over and Jessica and Audrey sit at the bar.

I watch Joshua walk toward the table, reach for a chair and sit. *What is it about him?* And then it hits me. Dark sunglasses, no eye contact, feeling for the chair. He's blind. That must be it. Wow. I've never met a blind person before.

"Do you have a track you'd like to play?" Randy asks.

Oh right. Time to sing. "The songs are on my phone."

"Great," Randy says. "And will you turn on the mic and let's check the volume."

"Sure." My song list is ready.

Randy helps me connect to the speaker, checks the volume, then sits with Joshua at the table in front of the stage.

"Whenever you're ready, you're all set to go," he says.

I press play. The intro to my first song, "Angel from Montgomery", starts and I remember what this is about and let the music surround me like moonlight.

What a perfect song. To me it's about realizing the life you've always known isn't what you want. You want something different, if only you could fly away like an angel.

It seems odd that I can relate to it so well. A Hispanic girl from San Antonio, Texas, Catholic, not rich, but not poor, never been to Montgomery, Alabama, don't live in the country. But it sounds like my story. That's the beauty of music, isn't it?

The song ends and there's light applause.

"Good, good," Randy says. "Beautiful."

"Thank you," I say.

"Whenever you're ready for the next one," he says.

"Okay, this is another slow song. I guess I should've mixed up the tempos."

"It's fine," Joshua calls, smiling at me. "Doesn't matter."

I hit play and the next song's a sentimental favorite, "At Last" by the great Etta James. My dad used to listen to all this old music when I was a kid. I thought it was boring then, but now it's the one positive thing I can say my dad taught me. I love this song for its simple message of the life-changing effects of love. How uncomplicated it sounds.

Have fun with it, I remind myself.

"Nice, very nice, Allison," Randy says as he claps.

I look over at Jessica and Audrey and they're clapping, smiling and giving me a thumbs up.

I sing one more, "Heaven, Heartache and the Power of Love," the most country song on my list. I hadn't realized my first three songs have angels, love, and heaven in them. *What's up with that?*

"Very nice, Allison," Joshua says.

Afterward Randy leans toward Joshua and they're talking about me, I suppose.

"Are you up to trying a song you've never seen before?" Joshua asks.

"Sure," I say. *Oh crap. Here we go with the damn sight reading again.*

Randy looks through some papers and says, "I have the sheet music here, I think. I'm assuming you can sight read. Or sight sing, I guess it's called."

"A little," I say.

"No matter," Joshua says. "I'll play it for you and just follow along."

"Sure," I say. Randy hands me the music. At this point it's not about whether I get the job or not. This has been fun. I've had a blast. It's been heaven and love and angels. I don't want to finish it with crap.

Joshua brings his chair with him to the stage and Randy hands him a guitar and a cable and then plugs the other end into a small amplifier on stage.

"Do you want a chair, Allison?" Randy asks.

A SONG FOR JESSICA

"No, I'm good," I say. I look at the sheet music and take a deep breath.

Joshua tunes his guitar, then strums a few chords and starts to play and I read the words as he sings the song about a girl who broke his heart, left him at the altar. When did the trouble start? His heart is heavy with regret, time heals wounds, but surely he won't live that long.

It's upbeat and sounds like a happy song until you listen to the words.

Joshua's voice has a raspy quality and it's deep and melodic. He plays his guitar with it lying flat on his lap, with his left hand over the fret while strumming and picking with his right.

"Got it?" he asks.

"I think so," I say. It's a simple song. I was freaking myself out for nothing.

"Just switch it to female, if you can. If not, it's okay. I'm kind of putting you on the spot here," Joshua says.

"Okay. I think I can do that," I say.

Joshua starts playing and we go through the song. Randy claps when we finish.

"Wow. I'm impressed. You got it in one shot!" Randy says.

"Can we try it again?" Joshua says. "This time sing it like you mean it."

"Sure," I say. Normally a comment like that would make me think he doesn't like me, but I totally get what he means.

"What I mean is, sing it like *you're* that person who showed up to commit your life to the person you love, but he broke your heart and left you standing there alone."

I nod. "Okay."

Joshua strums his guitar, keeping tempo with his whole body. His fingers move up and down the neck of the guitar like he's played it a million times before. He smiles and strums, moving to the beat.

Sing it like I mean it. The pain of lost love, a broken promise, a wound so deep you think you'll never recover. I know what it's like to feel sadness and hurt, but with deep and profound anger, too.

I finish the song loud and strong. *Was that angry and bitter enough?*

Joshua finishes the song and smiles. "That was better," he says.

Our small audience claps. Randy seems happy with it.

"Can we do one more?" Joshua says. "You have time?"

"Sure."

"Let's do 'Far Away'" he tells Randy.

Randy pulls the music and hands it to me. Far away and forever ago when we were kids and the dreams we had, but how beautiful life is because we have each other. We sing.

"Okay, let's do it again," he says.

And this time I sing and Joshua harmonizes and adds background vocals and I think we sound pretty good.

"Alright. Nice job, Allison," Joshua says. He takes his guitar off his lap.

"Done?" Randy asks.

"I'm good," Joshua says. "You, Allison? You okay?"

Fantastic! This was a blast. I've missed this so much. You have no idea. "I'm good too," I say.

I unplug my phone, step off the stage, and hand Randy the music.

"Thank you so much for making the trip," Randy says. "You did good. Did good," he says. Joshua feels his way down the stage steps. "You got it, Josh?"

"Got it."

"Thanks," I say.

Randy says, "We have a few more people to audition, but we'd like to make a decision here pretty quick." Joshua stands beside Randy and nods. "We got some shows lined up toward the beginning of the year. We need to be ready to go by then. A hundred percent."

"Really?" I say. "Okay. Well, thank you so much for the opportunity," I say and shake Randy's hand. I turn to Joshua. "Thank you Joshua."

He extends both hands and shakes with one and covers our clasped hands with the other. He looks at me through those dark sunglasses, smiles and says, "I love what you did to my song."

"Thank you! You gave me a lot to work with. Love your music." He's still holding my hand and it's weird, but when he faces me, I want to turn away.

"You have a great voice."

"Thank you." He lets go of my hand as if he hadn't realized he was still holding it.

Randy walks to the bar to talk to Brian.

Joshua says, "So, Allison, I need to ask you while you're standing right in front of me. What do you think? Do you think you'd like to work with us?" He smiles as he speaks. "I think we might be good together."

That makes me smile. *We might be good together.* Are first impressions always right?

I can't make such a big decision without more details. Sure, I had fun. I like Randy alright and Joshua's intense. Definitely a talented musician. The real deal. But would I want to work with them?

"You know what? I'd need to know details to have some idea about what I'm signing up for, but yeah, I'm interested."

Joshua nods. "Then, we'll be in touch," he says. "Very nice meeting you, Allison."

"Very nice meeting you too, Joshua."

On the way out I wave to Brian and Randy. "Thank you!"

It's nearly two o'clock when we get in the car and I feel giddy.

"Allie, you freaking nailed it!" Audrey says.

Jessica adds, "Oh man, Allie, that was so awesome! You're so good! You sound better every time I hear you. I think you got it if you want it. Would you want it?"

"Think so? I don't know, but that was freaking awesome! I can't even tell you how amazing that felt." I admit I feel good about my chances. I never thought it was possible, but maybe it is. *What about my house? Chewy? My mom? My friends? My life?*

And yet, something about the music got to me today. There was something other-worldly about it, something spiritual and soulful. If we're looking to make connections in this life and that's what makes life worth living, then I think I get that now. Really get it, like I've never gotten it before.

CHAPTER 23

My mom's agreed to come out with me Sunday morning for brunch. After such a great day yesterday, I'm feeling good. I'm ready for this. I don't think even *she* can bring me down today.

I haven't seen her or even talked to her much. I figure I need some focused time to let her know what's going on in my life, although I'm not sure why. I suppose because she's my mom and I feel obligated, even though what I do may not matter a bit to her. It's hard to tell.

My mom is usually distant, distracted, and dismissive, as if she doesn't care. Maybe sometimes she doesn't, but I believe underneath her anger, frustration, depression, grief, and whatever other emotions she keeps trapped inside, she does care.

She's always been a quiet person, but before the accident, she was more kind, open to new experiences, and more positive about life. She used to volunteer at church, dusting the altar or ushering at mass. It seemed to keep her calm and connected.

I'd say she was happy in a reserved type of way, never super optimistic, but able to laugh and show affection. After the accident, everything changed.

I don't remember a time when I heard her laugh since that day my brother left with my dad and never came home.

Grief is supposed to be temporary, like a dark tunnel that you go through, but eventually you should come out the other end, usually with a different perspective.

But my mom has made grief a lifestyle. It's like she's frozen in time, stuck in despair.

I've tried everything I can think of to bring her back, but nothing has worked. And she refuses to seek professional help.

I try to sympathize, but lately, I find myself resenting her grief, impatient with her misery. And then I feel guilty. She's been through a lot. I have to be patient. We have a lot to talk about. Being out for a nice meal might help calm her down. And she's less likely to go off on me in public. That's a bonus.

I choose a new restaurant, a renovated meat-market/grocery store with stone walls, tall ceilings, and hard wood floors. Mario's.

It's a hot morning with not a cloud in the sky, but inside the stone building, it's cool. Industrial-size ceiling fans circulate the air. The place is bustling this morning and the waiters, wearing long white cotton aprons over black slacks and long-sleeve white shirts, buzz around hurriedly. Sounds of laughter and raised voices echo off the walls.

"Is an outside table alright?" the hostess asks.

I wonder if it's too hot outside. I don't want to be sweating on my omelet.

She seems to read my mind. "We have fans and it's usually breezy. It's nice. And if it's too hot for you we can move you inside, but we have a big party coming in and there'll be a wait. Probably about forty-five minutes."

My mom and I agree to try the outside table.

Another girl leads us through the restaurant and outside to a patio surrounded by lots of healthy greenery. It's like an oasis and a lot calmer out here, which will be good so my mom and I can talk without straining to hear each other. We're seated at a far corner of the patio.

"This is beautiful," I say. "I've been wanting to come here for a while, but just haven't. And it's surprisingly cool out here."

"Yes, it's nice. Very nice," my mom says.

"How are you doing, Mom? Feeling better about everything?" I ask, once we're settled and have ordered coffee and food.

"I'm fine. Everyone seems to think it's not a big deal that your father and I are divorcing, so maybe I shouldn't be upset about it."

I've played this conversation over and over in my mind. It's like being in a game show where you have three identical doors and behind each one is a different "prize" only in this case, there's no awesome prize behind any of them, not that I can tell anyway. My choices: 1. Say you understand why she's upset, even though you don't. *Picture my mom and me drowning our sorrows in a box of chocolates, counting the ways my dad's an asshole.* 2. Say it's been a long time coming and tell her to get over it. *Picture me in a badass superhero costume with long boots up to my thighs and a cape - No, no cape - just a badass black outfit and sunglasses, preparing to do badass things.* 3. Ask her why she's so upset about it. *Picture me with my notebook, legs crossed, waiting for my mom's response as she lies on the sofa, tissue in hand, and explains some long lost memory that unlocks the secret of her psyche.*

I choose Door number Two. I love those boots. Only I don't say it quite as bluntly as my imagined scenario.

"Mom, I know it's tough to have it be final, but it's been a long time coming, don't you think?"

"You know what? I don't want to talk about this here. Every one's going to be looking at us. Is that why you invited me, so you could attack me?"

Oh, shit. Here we go.

"No, Mom. I'm sorry. I didn't mean to upset you. I just want to make sure you're okay. That's all."

"Well, no! I'm not okay! There. There's your answer!"

She's raising her voice and now she's scrunching her face as if she's fighting back tears.

Oh hell, are you freaking kidding me? I sit and stare at my water glass. She brings the white linen napkin to her face, dabbing her eyes. She sounds winded, like she's just climbed a flight of stairs. I look away, listening for her recovery, but it doesn't come.

"Mom? Are you okay?" I ask, touching her arm.

She starts breathing loudly and her chest heaves up and down. She grabs the arm of her chair and looks at me wide-eyed. I keep thinking she'll catch her breath. She just needs a few minutes, but it doesn't happen. She gasps for air.

Our server asks me, "Is she okay?"

"I don't know," I say. "Mom, try to relax," but she becomes more distressed with every breath.

The waitress says, "Should we call an ambulance?"

"Mom. Mom," I say. I look at her face for a clue as to whether she needs a doctor.

She pushes her chair away from the table and starts to stand.

"Do you want to walk?" I ask her, but she plops back down in the chair.

Now, I feel panic setting in. A restaurant manager comes by the table, "Ma'm are you okay?" he asks my mom, then turns to me and says, "We have to call an ambulance."

Oh my God. "Okay. Thank you."

"Try to relax, Mom. Can you take a deep breath?" I have no idea how I can help her. It seems like I should be doing something.

"Mom, can you put your head between your knees?" I say, holding her shoulders.

She shakes her head and pulls away from me.

More restaurant staff show up and pull the table away from us. "We have an ambulance on the way. They'll be here shortly," one guy says. "Try to relax. You're okay," he says to my mom.

But she doesn't look okay. Her face is pale. She grabs my arm weakly. Tears are in her eyes and she seems to want to say something. She can't speak.

"What's her name?" the manager asks.

"Fernanda." My head pounds and I don't know what to do. I have no idea what's happening right now.

"Fernanda, can you squeeze my hand?" he says, taking her hand.

My mom looks at him in that same panicked look and then suddenly leans over the arm of her chair and vomits, then starts coughing and choking. She gags loudly.

"Oh my God, Mom!" Her face is red and sweat drips from her hairline.

I hear sirens, first at a distance and then closer. *Hurry.*

"It's okay, Fernanda," he says.

They've cleared out the patio to make way for the paramedics, I suppose. A server offers the manager a towel, but he refuses it.

Just then, the paramedics rush in. One technician kneels by my mom and talks to her in loud, even tones. "I'm going to put a mask on you with some oxygen to help you breath," he says and my mom looks at him shaking her head or nodding at every question.

"Are you her daughter?" another technician asks me.

"Yes," I say.

She asks me for my mom's stats. Name, age, history of heart disease, diabetes, has this happened before, describe what occurred, etc.

"We were just sitting here talking and she started breathing heavy, like she was hyperventilating and then she started grabbing her chest and she couldn't talk," I say.

The other paramedic says something to the one who's talking to me and she asks, "Do you have a hospital preference?"

"St. Paul," I say because that's where my grandmother used to go, but my mom and I have never talked about a hospital preference.

I watch them wheel her away on a gurney and load her in the ambulance. I wonder what the hell happened to her. Is she having a heart attack? My grandmother died of a heart attack. Is my mom dying?

I grab my keys from my purse, apologize and thank the restaurant staff. I walk out by myself and find my car.

I turn the air conditioner on full blast and sob into my steering wheel. All these years I thought she'd come back. I thought I could bring her back somehow, but now I'm out of time. Even though I don't understand her and she frustrates me, she's my mom. I need more time with her. I can't have her die with us this way.

How could I have thought this would be a good idea? I pushed her too hard. She doesn't care about brunch or being out or any of that stuff. I'm not even sure what she cares about. That's pathetic. I'm her daughter. I should know what she cares about. This is my fault. It is. I should have known better. And I wanted to be a badass superhero and set her straight. Yeah, right.

Suddenly, I'm furious with my dad. I wish I could call him and tell him he's a selfish bastard. All these years he's acted as if she were already gone. He just left her, left both of us, without even a little bit of concern. And now, he's killing her by tossing her aside like an old shoe and he's left me alone to deal with everything.

CHAPTER 24

When I get to the hospital, I follow the signs to the emergency room parking lot, but I get turned around and have to circle again. My mom could be dying in the ER and I'm freaking circling the parking lot looking for a parking space. It makes me want to scream.

Finally, I park and try to pull myself together before I go inside. I wipe my eyes and take a deep breath, say a prayer, "God, please send your angels to watch over us. Please don't let her die."

The emergency room is open and spacious, so different from when my grandmother used to come to this hospital.

"My mom came over in an ambulance a few minutes ago," I tell the attendant at the intake desk.

"Her name?" the woman says, looking at her computer screen. Her name tag says her name's Julie.

"Fernanda Deleon."

"Okay, yes. Do you have her ID and insurance card?" she asks.

"Yes." I hand her both.

The clerk types away, asks me more questions about my mom. No, I don't know her doctor's name. I don't know if she has supplemental insurance. I don't know if it's a PPO or HMO. I'm her daughter.

"Can I go back with her?" I ask.

"I'll check." She bangs the keyboard while still looking at her monitor. "Wait one moment." She pushes back from her desk and goes away and comes right back. "Yes, through these doors to room number four. I'll buzz you in."

The big, metal doors swing open before me. The rooms aren't actual rooms, more like stalls with curtains. From a distance, I see my mom lying in the bed, alone in her stall, and surrounded by monitors. She has an IV in her hand and other wires and tubes that must be connected to the machines. Her eyes are closed, her hair's disheveled, and she looks small and weak and old.

"Hi mom," I say and I touch her shoulder.

She forces her eyes open, and tries to focus on my face.

"It's okay, Mom," I say and I take her hand, and even now, the gesture feels awkward. "You better?"

A nurse walks in, "Hello," he says in a sing song voice.

"Hi," I say.

"I'm Harold."

"Hi Harold. I'm Allison. I'm her daughter."

"I figured." He points at me, then at her. "I see the resemblance. Well, mom's doing better. The doctor has ordered some tests."

"Okay, what kind of tests?"

"Primarily to determine if the attack was related to any heart condition." He checks her IV and pushes buttons on the monitor. "I'll let the doctor know you're here."

My mom closes her eyes and breathes steadily, taking a deep breath every so often. Her mascara's smudged. Her lips are pale. One of the machines beeps in steady rhythm.

A few minutes later, the doctor, who couldn't be much older than me, introduces herself. "Hi. I'm Doctor Mata." Her hair is black and shiny and smooth, parted down the middle, and long, down to about her elbows. Her dark features, eyes, eyebrows, skin, make her teeth look incredibly white and perfect when she smiles.

"Hi, Dr. Mata."

"Well, I understand you all were out and your mom started having difficulty breathing," she says looking at my mom.

"Yes," I say.

"We gave her a sedative. She seemed to have a lot of anxiety, but I've ordered a few other tests for her that we'll be doing in just a bit," she says.

"Are you testing for a heart condition? Do you think she could've had a heart attack?" I ask.

"It doesn't seem to have been a heart attack. All the preliminary tests look good. It seems more like a panic attack, but we want to rule out any problems with her heart. Something more serious. We'll know more once we have those results." She looks at a sheet attached to a metal clipboard then looks back at me. "They'll be coming for her in just a minute and we'll get you out of here as soon as we can."

"Thank you."

"You're welcome. It's going to be just a few more minutes." She pats my mom's hand, then nods at me and leaves.

A little while later, Harold, the nurse, rolls her out of the stall and I sit and wait.

My stomach growls. I haven't eaten all day. I have no snacks and no cash for a cash-only vending machine, but I don't feel like I can leave.

I lean my head against the wall and close my eyes. It occurs to me as I sit here, waiting for my mom to get back from a test to determine if she's got "something more serious" going on at the age of fifty-two, that she's all I got. Besides my dad, my mom's my only blood family. I don't have anyone I can call to be with me here. I love Jessica like a sister, but she's got so much going on these days. I'm sure I could call her, but I don't want to bother her.

I think about calling my dad. Is the number I have for him good? Would he answer? I play the conversation out in my head:

Allison. How've you been, Mija. I've been meaning to call you.

Dad, mom's at the ER. She had some sort of attack, possibly a heart attack. It happened when we were talking about you, as a matter of fact.

Oh, that must be why my ears were burning. Is your mother okay?
I don't know, Dad. She might've had a heart attack.
Oh, I see. Well, you'll call me if she gets worse.
You mean like if she dies? Is that when you want me to call you?
Well, before she dies.

I have no idea what he'd say, but I don't imagine he'd care much. I'm not even sure where he's living at the moment.

As angry as I am at my dad, I understand why he left my mom. I don't even understand how they wound up together.

They went to rivaling high schools. My mom was on dance team at her school. Hard to imagine now. Her high school pictures show a different life—my mom smiling, cute, in her dance team uniform, with her friends.

My dad's specialty was shop. His high school pictures were of him with his head under the hood of an old Mustang, or he and Chango, his best friend, standing by an engine block hanging from a tree in his backyard. My dad could fix anything. He was the type of kid who took stuff apart so he could figure out how it worked.

My parents were teenagers when they met at a neighborhood dance, started dating, and got married a year after graduation.

I'm sure they were happy for a while, but what can you say about a marriage? About a lifetime together? When did it all go wrong?

Had their marriage been dying a slow death even before the accident? How would things be different if my brother were alive?

I hope we'd be close. My mom would adore my brother. He'd definitely be her favorite. If he were alive, he'd be here with me. I'd have called him on the way over here and he'd have said the right thing:

Oscar, Mom had some sort of attack. She's on her way to the ER.
Oh my God, Allie! Is she okay?
I don't know. I'm scared, Oscar. What if she's not okay?
It's going to be alright, Allie. What hospital are they taking her to?
St. Paul's
I'm on my way.

. . .

*T*he thought of my brother grown and rushing to be with me makes me miss him.

He would be twenty-four now. I've often wondered what he'd look like. I think he'd be super cute. Dark, curly hair, beautiful smile, not very tall, but strong. He'd be funny and kind. He'd have my dad's charm and my mom's loyalty.

We were close when we were young, but we grew apart. We had such different interests and I thought he was a brat. My parents spoiled him. He didn't have to do chores around the house, like I did. He didn't even clean his room. My parents expected me to do everything for him. I always thought they treated him like a prince and me like the servant girl.

But when he died, I was so sad that he was gone. I felt guilty for wanting my parents to be harder on him. I was too young to fully understand what I'd lost. Now I wish I had a chance to be a better sister to him.

He was ten and I was fourteen when he died. I'd just finished my Freshman year of high school. It was June and I wanted to go swimming with my friends that day, but my mom wanted me to stay home and help her clean the house. She and I spent all morning dusting furniture, mopping floors, and washing windows. I had just lied down to take a nap when my mom came into my room in a panic. She said she was leaving. There had been an accident. She'd be back.

But my mom never came back. The woman who left that day never returned.

Losing a brother. That's really hard. But losing a child? How devastated my parents must have been. I can't imagine the pain they must have felt when they saw his casket being lowered into the ground. So much was buried that day.

I think of my mom. Her attack at the restaurant, gasping for breath, unable to speak, fear in her eyes. I squeeze my eyes shut. I'm not ready to bury her.

Finally, she's rolled back in. She's lying on her back with her eyes closed and she's covered with a white blanket up to her chin.

"Okay, just hang tight here and the doctor will be by to see you," says a guy in scrubs who's delivering her back to ER from wherever she was.

This whole process of checking her in, taking her for more tests, getting her back to the ER has been a lot faster than I thought it would be, but it still feels like it's been a long day.

She opens her eyes and looks up at the ceiling for a second. I stand up and step toward her. She sees me and says, "Oh, Mija. I'm sorry." My mom hardly ever calls me Mija. It means "my daughter" in Spanish (mi hija) and it's a term of endearment.

She's still connected to a monitor and the IV is still in her hand.

Dr. Mata steps in, "Well, Mrs. Deleon, the tests look good. We didn't see anything to be concerned about. Everything checks out, so you can go home. I'd like you to take it easy and I'm going to give you a note to stay home for a few days."

"That's a good idea, Mom. So you can rest," I say.

"Okay," my mom says. Her voice is quiet but still sounds anxious.

"So, it looks like you had a panic attack, which can feel like a heart attack. Who's your doctor?" Dr. Mata asks.

My mom thinks for a second, then remembers. "Dr. Tillman. Janet Tillman."

"Okay, I'm sending the test results to Dr. Tillman and I'd like for you to call her and make a follow up appointment. Okay?"

"Okay," my mom says.

"And we're sending some information about anxiety and panic attacks and what to do if you feel one coming on," Dr. Mata says. "I'm also giving you a prescription for relieving anxiety."

"Thank you," my mom says.

"You're welcome. Harold will be in shortly," she says and she leaves.

Harold, the ER nurse who's been taking care of my mom, comes in to remove her IV and the monitors. He offers to help her dress, but she tells him she can do it.

He leaves and pulls the curtain closed.

I get her clothes that I had folded and stacked and help her get dressed.

A few minutes later, Harold returns with her prescriptions, paperwork, and a wheelchair.

"I'll bring the car around. Is that okay?" I ask Harold.

"Yep. We'll meet you at the main exit," he says.

When I come around for her, she's sitting outside on a bench waiting for me.

"You good?" I ask my mom.

"Yes. I'm okay," she says.

She didn't have a heart attack. That's good news. But that was a heck of a panic attack.

I'm not sure how we're going to get to the bottom of this thing with my dad. I don't even know how this works. Do they have to go to court? Does she have to get a lawyer? If she can't even talk about it, how is she ever going to get through this? How am I?

CHAPTER 25

I'm worn out from everything that happened this weekend, but I wake up before my alarm, shower, and dress, and Chewy and I go for a walk.

Even now, in September, it's almost as hot and steamy as it was in July, but the days are getting shorter. It's still dark and the neighborhood is quiet and peaceful. I wonder how my mom's doing.

Last night, I offered to stay with her for a few days, but she insisted I come home, said she was fine.

I feel bad that she's alone almost all the time and now it's almost like she doesn't know how to be around people. Not even me.

From a practical standpoint, I could live with my mom. She's got plenty of room for Chewy and me. It would save us both a lot of money.

But from a compatibility standpoint, I really *couldn't* live with my mom. I don't even like being over there for more than a couple of hours. I'm afraid she'd rub off on me. I'd come home and watch TV all night, never want to go out, be in my pajamas way before dark and be perfectly okay with being that way forever.

Her house is essentially the same as it's been since I moved out years ago. My room is exactly the same. My brother's too. Not set up like shrines or anything, just not moved, not changed at all. I think she started using the closet in my old room for clothes she doesn't wear anymore. She could donate them, but she can't part with them for some reason. Other than that, the doors stay closed and the rooms are unused.

My mom goes to work every day from 7:30 to 4:00, gets home, turns on the television, watches the five o'clock news for an hour, then watches the six o'clock news while eating her dinner on a TV tray, then watches Wheel of Fortune, then her shows until nine or so. Then gets ready for bed and watches more TV in bed. Hopefully, at some point, she goes to sleep. Then wakes up to do it all again. This is how she passes the time. This is how she lives her life.

I tend to keep my visits short. Even then, she doesn't take her eyes off the television. I want to shake her and say, "Mom! Talk to me!"

When I first moved out, I thought she might experience an awakening. I used to imagine she'd be so happy I was gone that she'd come home, get dressed up, put on some makeup and red lipstick, and go out and meet people. Go dancing, join a bunco club, find an Over-Forty Meetup, go bar hopping. Something. I loved to think of my mom doing something crazy and cool, like becoming a TaiChi master, she in her Gi, shifting from pose to pose in rhythmic motion. Of course, that version of my mom is pure fiction, my cartoon fantasy of my mother.

She didn't do any of those things and probably never will. But maybe when my dad is out of the picture for good, she can get on with her life and find *something* she enjoys doing.

I wish I could help her. I wish she were different. I wish I liked her more. I wish it were easier.

Chewy and I turn to head back home. The sky glows deep orange as the sun rises like fire bursting out over the horizon. It's so beautiful it makes my heart ache.

When I get to work, it feels like a long time since I've been there, but the Conference room's the same as we left it Friday afternoon.

Maya's brought breakfast this morning. Two white, cardboard boxes each stamped with a red ink logo from "The Doughnut Place" are on the table. Yikes. She's brought two dozen doughnuts from the very best doughnut shop in town.

The Doughnut Place has been around forever. My dad used to take us there when we were kids. They only took cash. There was no drive-thru. You had to walk in to the tiny little shop that had a diner-style counter with about four stationary stools. Even five people in that small space meant standing inches away from the next person.

Now they have a drive-thru but still only take cash. Even as inconvenient as that is, cars line the street nearly every morning.

But the doughnuts. Light and fluffy on the inside, golden brown with an ever so slight crunch on the outside, and sweet glaze, light, not overpowering.

I could probably eat a dozen by myself. On a bad day.

Maya's brought two dozen for this small group. That's too many doughnuts in the room.

Angie says, "Maya, thank you for the doughnuts. So thoughtful of you."

"Of course! No problem. This place is right by my house."

Todd takes a doughnut and bites into it. After a moment, he closes his eyes, as in ecstasy. I have to look away. "Ow ma gah," he says with his mouth full, "Ohh."

"I know. Aren't they amazing?" Maya says and proceeds to tell everyone all about The Doughnut Place, its history and recent upgrades. "They have the most amazing breakfast tacos, too. Everything made from scratch, just like grandma used to make. My grandma, anyway."

Gerald gobbles two doughnuts and goes back for more. Hopefully, we'll be out of here before they kick in.

I take a doughnut and savor it as I sip my coffee. "Thank you, Maya. This is a nice treat," I say. She's generous but so annoying.

"No problem. My honey loves this place. It's a wonder he doesn't weigh three-hundred pounds."

As much as I appreciate the doughnut, I don't want to hear about her honey. I'm relieved when Angie asks us to finish up so we can get to work.

I step out to go to the bathroom and wash my hands and decide to give my mom a quick call.

"How are you feeling today, Mom?"

"I'm feeling okay." She sounds half asleep.

"Did you take your medicine? Have you eaten?"

"No, I'm still in bed. I'll get up in a little bit. You're at work?"

"Yes, I'll stop by on my way home, okay?"

"Okay, that's fine."

She sounds okay. Not great but okay.

The doughnuts kick in early for Gerald, who's had more than his share.

Todd says, "Damn, Dude!"

Yeah, it's pretty bad.

Finally, Angie finishes covering the topic for the day and sends us out to meet our Nesting Buddies.

I'm trying hard to pay attention to details as I fill out my reports and compile my bid information. My ever watchful nesting coach, Michael, still picks my work to death—"No. No. No. Not like that."—but overall, he doesn't nitpick as much as he did last week. Mr. Hernandez stopped by earlier to check on me and I was surprised when Michael told him I was doing great.

Finally, it's time for our afternoon debrief. When I get to the conference room, Gerald's sitting in the far corner of the room. The room smells like air freshener and stink. *This is ridiculous.*

I don't understand how he can just keep acting like nothing's wrong when it's very obvious that there's a problem. How can he ignore it? And will he ever do anything about it? Is he hoping no one notices?

I'm grateful when Angie lets us go early.

CHAPTER 26

I pull out my phone after work. I have a voice mail. It's from Randy.

"Hey, Allison. Randy here. Will you call me when you get a minute? I'd like to talk to you about your audition and such. I guess you're at work, but I'd like to talk to you today, if possible. Okay then. I'll talk to you later."

I call him back. "Randy?" Pause. "This is Allison. I got your message. I'm returning your call."

"Hey Allison. Thanks for calling me back."

"Sure. No problem." I start my car, turn on the air conditioner, and sit in the office parking lot.

"Well, I tell you what, we are all done with our auditions. Finished up yesterday. And Joshua and I thought you were outstanding. Outstanding!"

"Oh, wow. Thank you." That makes me smile.

"I tell you, Joshua's not an easy person to please, either. He's a musician's musician. He saw something in you that he thought was special."

"Well, thank you." My mind's eye goes back to Joshua and me singing together in Waco. I thought we were good too.

"He wanted me to be sure and tell you that," Randy says.

"Well please thank him for me. I enjoyed meeting him and I loved his song."

"Now, that was my next question for you." Emphasis on you. "How'd you like the music?"

"I loved it. I was surprised by the mix of country and blues, and even a little folk. I was under the impression that it was mostly country."

"Yes, ma'am. It's a mixture of a lot of things. Josh's got an old soul to be honest with you and I think it comes out in his music, for sure." He pulls away from the phone for a second and then comes back. "Well, Allison, what would you think about workin' with us?"

"Really?"

"Yeah, really!"

"You're offering me the job?" *I can't believe it. This is unbelievable. It's crazy.*

He laughs. "You sound surprised. We thought you were great and we think you'd be a great fit."

They liked me. They thought I was good. They want me. I never thought they'd pick me. Really. Wow. I'm speechless. Oh crap, now what do I do? I haven't taken the time to seriously consider what I would do if they offered it to me. And after the scare with my mom this weekend, I don't see how I could just up and leave. Never mind that I can't quite picture myself being in their band. What would the day to day look like and do I want to leave San Antonio? I've lived here all my life. Would I have to live out of a van? A bus?

It's almost as if I don't need to go any further with it. Someone thought I was good enough. Isn't that enough for me?

Joshua said we'd be good together. He asked me directly. I told him I needed more details. I told him I'd consider it. And now, what should I say?

"Oh my gosh. I don't know what to say."

"Well, we'd love it if you say yes."

I can't say yes just like that. It's too much too soon. I have to be sure I even want this. "Randy, I love the music. I do. I have some questions about, umm, how do I say this? What's a day in the life of a member of the band? What would that look like for me?"

"Well," he says, "I'll be honest with you. We all have other jobs right now. Day jobs I guess you could say. Joshua's a music teacher. I'm a substitute teacher. Steve, our bass player, he works with a cabinet maker. Let's see, where does Doug work?" he asks himself. "I can't remember, but all of us have somethin' to help us pay the rent, especially since we haven't been gigging a whole lot this year. We all have something that makes it so we can go to our gigs, which will be mostly on the weekends, and to rehearse, and all."

"Okay," I say.

"I expect you'll have to do the same, at least for a little while, but there's a good chance we can start making the band more full-time. That's what we're hopin'."

"Okay. Well, I don't know what to say, Randy. First of all, thank you. Thank you for giving me a chance to audition and thank you for your confidence in me. That's amazing."

"Well, sure! I tell you, we've been looking for a while and the way I see it, it was just a crazy stroke of luck that we crossed paths. So, yeah, we're ready to get to work."

"And you said you want to be ready in January? Can I have some time to think it over," I say and I feel like a jerk for wasting his time. "Are you looking for someone to start right away? I have a wedding in October that I have to be here for, and actually, that whole weekend."

"Yeah, that's no problem. We don't have any gigs scheduled 'til early March, so we're lookin' to be ready by then. But we have a lot of work to do, so yeah, we're looking to bring you on pretty quick."

"Okay. Well, I'd like to talk it over with my family. Can I get back to you in a couple of days?" I ask.

"Absolutely. I understand it's a big step. We're askin' you to take a chance on us. I assure you, we're serious. We have big plans for the band, shows, recordings, all of it. And I'm going to have to ask you to just trust us and if it feels like the right thing to do, then we'd love to work with you."

I'm numb. In shock. The chatter in my head comes from all angles: *Take a chance. Stay put. I can't leave. It's too big a risk. It may not be safe. What about the house? What about Chewy? And what about my mom? I don't think I can leave her.*

CHAPTER 27

I told my mom I'd stop by after work. After talking to Randy, I'm psyched. I don't want her to bring me down, but I want to see how she's feeling and make sure she's okay. And I have to talk to her. I have to let her know about all this.

She asked me to pick up a few things for her: chicken soup, crackers, sweet tea, orange juice, cookies, milk.

I let myself in with my key. "Hi Mom," I say as I walk through the living room toward the kitchen. "How're you feeling?"

I put the grocery bag on the edge of her small dinette table. The rest of the table's covered with mail, store flyers, plastic containers and cardboard boxes.

"Okay."

"Are you hungry? Want some soup?"

"Okay."

Dishes, appliances—blender, toaster, toaster oven, can opener, smaller blender—and about twenty plastic grocery bags, some empty, some not, a cereal box, a package of cookies, soap dispenser, dishwashing soap, a box of hair color, and various other items cover the kitchen counter and stove.

I open the can of soup, the brand she used to buy when I was little, and find a saucepan in a low cabinet where she's always kept them. I clear pans, a shoe box, and more plastic bags off a burner on the stove.

While the soup's heating, I look through plastic bags and boxes to see what I can put away or throw away. My mom calls from the other room, "Just leave it."

"I'm just going to pick up a little, while the soup's on," I say through the wall cutout from the kitchen to the living room.

My dad cut the wall out and built a bar-style counter on the living room side. We used to have barstools that spun all the way around and my brother and I would spin and spin and then jump off the stools, wobbly, walking like Frankenstein bumping into each other with arms held up in front of us, and finally falling to the ground. Oscar used to laugh so hard and I'd tickle him to get him to laugh even harder until he peed his pants. He had a great laugh, this hilarious, infectious giggle. He'd gasp for air, shouting, "Allie! No!" between wild bawls of laughter. My brother.

I stuff some bags, mostly from fast food drive-throughs, into one bag. I look to put the cereal box and cookie box in the pantry, but it's full too. She'd never be able to find them, so I put them back on the table where they were.

I serve the soup in a bowl and put it on a plate with some saltines and set it on her TV tray.

"Thank you, Mija," she says.

"You're welcome, Mom."

The news is on. She stares at the television screen and asks, "How was your day?"

"Fine." I sit in the other living room chair and look at the television to see what's so interesting. The weather. "You're feeling okay, Mom? Did you take your medicine?"

She's in her green and pink floral housedress, an oversized smock that snaps up the front. Her hair's flat on one side of her head.

"Yes, but I'm not going to take it anymore. It made me sick this morning."

"It did? Sick from your stomach?"

"Yeah, I was in bed all day. I just got up a little while ago." She raises the spoon to her lips and sips.

"Oh no. Had you eaten when you took the medicine?"

"I had a few cookies with milk, but it didn't help."

We watch the news together.

"Did you get cookies?" she asks.

I put a few iced oatmeal cookies on a napkin for her.

I look at the television screen too. "It's supposed to rain tomorrow? Thank God. Maybe it'll cool us off a bit," I say.

"I know. It's been so hot. Is it hot outside?"

"Very hot."

After the news and when she's finished her cookies I pick up her dishes and move the TV tray.

"Mom, I need to talk to you about a few things." I get the remote and turn the volume down on the television.

"If it's about your father I don't want to talk about it," she says staring straight ahead.

"No, it's not about that." Although we're going to have to talk about the divorce at some point, I don't want to talk about it now either.

"Oh. Something else?"

I haven't talked to her much since the trip to Louisiana. Even though I kind of want to talk to her about my job troubles, I don't want to hear what she might have to say about it, so I decide not to mention it. But I definitely want to tell her more about the talent show and the audition. I decide not to tell her about Randy's offer just yet.

The whole time I'm talking, she keeps her eyes on the television and doesn't say a word. When I'm done, she still doesn't speak or even look at me, so I say "That's all."

I shouldn't be surprised that she hardly even blinks in response. Her silence twists my stomach, but I wait for her to say something.

Finally, she says, "Aye, Allison. Why did Jessica do that to you? Make you be in that talent show?"

Of all the things to say. "She didn't *make* me, Mom. I could've said no."

She shakes her head, still looking ahead in the direction of the television.

"I mean, even though I didn't want to at first, I'm really glad I did it," I say, looking at the television too.

"That's good, I guess," she says.

C'mon, Mom. Throw me a bone. Something. But what did I expect?

When I was going through that nightmare year with Mr. Whatshisface, I kept most of the details from my mom, partly because I didn't want to hear her reaction, which in my mind would have certainly been: "Oh no, Allison. Get out of that. I don't know why you even started that. What can you do with that?"

Part of the trouble with me and music in my mom's eyes was that it was something my dad introduced me to, something he nurtured in my early years, and then after the accident when he split and came back and split and came back, my mom resented it all even more.

She sold my keyboard, which didn't matter that much to me. I had quit lessons by then, but still liked to mess around on it and figure out how to play songs by ear.

I liked the keyboard, but I preferred guitar. I had picked it up in middle school, sixth grade. My friend Laura played and taught me some basic chords. I was pretty good at tuning the guitar by ear, but I struggled getting my fingers to stretch, and curl, twist in the correct spot.

When my middle school choir teacher, Mrs. Cook, saw that I liked playing, she opened up a class for whoever was interested and gave us lessons one day a week after school. Free. Only two other kids showed up, but we had a nice little thing going there. Mrs. Cook had an old guitar and case that she let me borrow. She said, "It sounds good and it's got new strings, but it's old. I trust you to take good care of it."

When I came back to school from summer break starting eighth grade, Mrs. Cook had moved to another school. I didn't get a chance to thank her or say good-bye. We heard she got a job at a high school across town.

That's how I got Mrs. Cook's guitar. I asked one of my other teachers to contact her to see if I could return it to her. She said Mrs. Cook wanted me to keep it as long as I promised to play it, and she was sorry she didn't get to see me before she left. And, of course, the other stuff teachers always say, be good, keep playing, keep singing, etc.

I made sure I never played when my mom was home. She didn't like that I'd gotten a guitar from a teacher. She said it wasn't right, but when Mrs. Cook left, she didn't help me get it back to her. "She shouldn't have 'lent' it to you in the first place," she said. "If she really wanted it she could've gotten it from you. She knows where you go to school."

Once I heard back from Mrs. Cook that I could keep it if I kept playing, I accepted it as a gift and I still have it. I've never even thought to buy my own, for some reason. I've been practicing a lot lately, since Jessica asked me to sing a song at the wedding. My fingers were out of shape. My hands cramped, my fingertips throbbed, but when I heard that rich sound of Mrs. Cook's guitar, I remembered her generosity and encouragement.

My mom looks straight ahead at the television. I want her to hear me.

"Mom, can I turn off the television, please? Do you mind?" I ask.

She raises an eyebrow. "No, go ahead," she says.

"I just want to make sure I have your full attention." I turn it off and face her again. "After the talent show, a guy approached me and I got to talking to him. His name is Randy and he wanted me to audition for his band. I called him and met him in Waco on Saturday. It went really well. He and the guitar player seemed to like me."

She looks at me expressionless. No smile, no frown, nothing.

I can't tell what she's thinking. I feel my heart thump in my chest.

"Why are you telling me?" she says.

I lean forward. "Because you're my mom and I want you to know."

She stares at me. "Why did you have to go to Waco?"

My mom's dark, brown eyes look so sad. Do they always look like that? "Well, they're from Dallas. That's where the band's based, and he has a friend who has a place in Waco, which is about half way between here and Dallas, so…yeah," I shrug, "that made it easier for both of us."

"Are you telling me you're moving to Dallas?" she asks.

"They haven't offered me the job, yet, Mom. I don't know if I'd take it if they did, but it was really cool to audition. That's all." I can't come out with it. I can't tell her the truth: *I have a chance to sing in this band, but I'd have to move to Dallas. I want to do it. I want to take a chance. What do you think?* I regret holding back.

She looks at her hands in her lap but says nothing.

I wait for her to say something. Anything. But she sits in silence. Finally, I say, "Well, what do you think?"

"Well, if you want to leave me too," she says.

Why does it have to be like this with her? Why can't she ever be happy for me? "Actually, I'm not sure what I want." I try to read her face. She seems calm. "Either way, the talent show and the audition have me thinking about getting back into music."

She shakes her head. "That's a hard life and there are lots of people who are very talented and a lot younger than you struggling to make it."

I want to tell her what I'm thinking, how I truly feel, but I think she's fragile and I don't want an episode like the other day, so I just say, "I know, Mom. That's true."

"You can watch that show, *America's Most Talented*, and those people are good. I mean, you're good, but they're *really* good. And most of them don't make it." She gestures toward the television. She looks past me.

I roll my eyes. *Right.* My mom has never told me I was good. Ever. I feel my throat tighten. How can I explain it's not about winning a freaking contest or being on TV? Why would I want that? So people like my mom can sit and say, 'Oh, she's terrible' or 'Wow she's so fat' or 'Eww, I hate her'? No, thanks.

"When you couldn't make it in college, you were so depressed after that. I don't want to see you go through that again. People are mean." She frowns and shakes her head.

"Yeah, I know." *People are mean, Mom.*

"Besides, I didn't know you were thinking about singing again. I mean, for a career."

"I wasn't. It just kind of happened, I guess." I lean back in my chair and cross my legs.

She mimics me, "I guess," she says.

Now, why does she have to do that? Yes, Mom, people are mean.

She makes me want to cry, to just curl up in a ball and cry. "It's a long shot, I know, but it's something. Anyway, I just wanted to let you know what's going on with me," I say as I stand up to go to the kitchen to wash my hands.

I know she's upset about my dad. And about my brother. And about life. She's given up. Maybe she wants me to give up too. I don't know.

When I'm drying my hands, I realize I've left the orange juice on the table. I go to put it in the refrigerator and, shocker, the fridge is jam-packed with take out and plastic food containers. "Mom, do you want me to come over this weekend and help you clear out your pantry?" Maybe she'd feel better about things if her house wasn't so cluttered. I can't give up trying to help her get it together.

"I don't need your help. I can do it."

"Mom, let me help you. I can help you. We can work on it a couple of hours. We'd clear out a lot in a couple of hours."

She glares at me through the cutout from her rocker recliner in the living room.

"Fine," I say. "Just offering."

"No, you want to come over here and tell me what *I'm* doing wrong and criticize the way *I* live and you're not perfect, either, Allison! You always think you're better than everyone, but you're not."

After all I've tried to do to help her even after she puts me down and makes me feel like I'm not good enough. Even though I know she's not speaking rationally right now, she sets me off.

"Right, Mom." I raise my voice at her through the cutout. "I think I'm better than everyone. Than who? I just want to help you, Mom! I can't even talk to you about what's going on with me because you start criticizing me. Mocking me! Why can't you ever just be happy for me? You sit there in your chair doing the same thing every day and you're…" I stop myself and take a deep breath. My face feels hot. I don't want to fight with her.

I say in an even voice, "I'm not trying to tell you what to do, but this is not healthy. It's not good for you, Mom. There's not even a spot for a cereal box in the pantry, it's so full of crap."

She mumbles, but I hear her, "No, you're full of crap."

There's nothing else I can say. I have to go. "Okay, fine. I'm leaving. You're welcome for the soup."

"Oh right! Leave! You're just like your father!" She leans forward in her chair.

I look at her again through the cutout. "Yeah, he's such an asshole. But you damn near have a heart attack because you can't handle the fact that he's finally doing it! He finally got the balls to leave you for good!" And as soon as I say it, I wish I could take it back. *Shit.*

I hear her crying. *Oh no. I suck. I made her cry. What's wrong with me? I can't leave her like this.* And just as I turn the corner from the kitchen to the living room, something hits me right on the bridge of my nose.

"Oww! Dammit!" I grab my nose. Tears come to my eyes. I double over and squeeze my eyes shut.

After a few minutes, as I'm holding my hands to my face, I stand up and see pieces of the remote on the ground. I go to the bathroom to see if it looks as bad as it feels.

The skin's broken, there's a small cut, and I can see a bump forming. My head starts hurting and I walk back to the kitchen, find a plastic bag in the pantry and fill it with ice.

"Well, don't talk to me like that!" she says. "I'm still your mother!"

"Then act like it, Mom. I'm trying to talk to you about what's going on with me. That's all. Why are you mad at me? Because I try to help you?" I sound like I have a cold.

She says something else that I don't hear, then she says, "You always acted like you were so much better than me because of your friends. 'Ooo, Jessica.'" More mocking.

I can't believe this. "You know what? I'm going to ignore that because I know you like Jessica and you're just being rude as hell because you're upset." I pick up the remote pieces from the kitchen floor. The back popped off and the batteries are scattered.

I slam the pieces on the coffee table in front of her on my way out. "Here's your stupid remote. Sorry I broke it with my nose."

CHAPTER 28

I get home and Chewy's sitting by her leash which is hanging on a hook by the back door.

"Oh, Chewy. Not today."

I make myself another icepack and go to the bathroom to look at my nose again. It's tender and only slightly swollen. It looks fine, except for a small scratch right on the bridge. In a way, I wish it looked worse so I could send my mom a picture of it, swollen and purple, with a message, *"Look what you did, Jerk!"*

Yeah, I wouldn't do that even if I do think she deserves it.

I can only take the icepack on my nose for a minute or so at a time.

I look in the mirror once more. Dammit. It doesn't look that bad.

"Come on, Chewy. I guess I'm okay."

I hook her leash on and pick her up and snuggle her close. "Thank you for loving me so much, Chewy. You're the best."

She starts to wiggle out of my arms. I put her down.

"Got my phone and headphones? Okay, let's go."

Chewy and I walk on the sidewalk on the shady side of the street.

I listen to music and try not to think about anything. Not my mom. Not the band. Not what it would take for me to move to Dallas. Not the wedding or Jessica or which of us will move away first.

By the time I get home from our walk, I'm hot and my bra is damp with sweat, so I change out of my work clothes into a t-shirt and shorts.

I find a bag of sweet-salty snacks in the pantry, stand at the kitchen counter, and eat out of the box. I stop to pour myself a glass of water and gulp it down without stopping, then gasp for air.

"Okay, close the box and walk away," I say, taking a couple more handfuls.

Finally, I wrap the liner, close the box and put it back in the pantry.

I sit on the sofa. The house is quiet. My grandmother's house. My house. Could I sell it? What would my grandmother say?

She'd probably say, "It's a house. Wood and nails, pipes and a roof. Get what you can for it and move on."

My grandmother would listen. She'd understand. She was born in Falfurrias, Texas, "a small town between nowhere and no place," she used to say. Her parents had moved to San Antonio for work when she was a girl and spent her whole life here. She married my grandfather when she was eighteen and he was nineteen. My grandmother was one of those people who was easy to love. She had lots of friends, people she'd known for years and she could call on the phone and they'd laugh and visit. When Oscar was a baby, I was chasing him around the living room, crawling. He had that crazy laugh and he squealed and tried to get away from me. I said, "I'm gonna get you." I bumped a pedestal table in the corner of the room and her small tiffany lamp came crashing down to the ground.

I cried and cried. I felt terrible about breaking my grandmother's lamp. She said, "Don't cry. It's just a lamp. I can get another one. Thank God, it didn't fall on your head."

It took a lot for my grandmother to get upset and when Oscar died, that was the worst I had ever seen her. Even when she wasn't crying, I could tell she was fighting back tears. She was heartbroken. My grandfather had died just two years before and, of course, she mourned his death. She would miss him, but for her to bury her grandson was a different kind of sadness.

Yes, she was devastated, but she knew she had to get back to living her life. Her friends made sure she got out of the house. It took time, but eventually she didn't cry for Oscar every day even though she still missed him and was still sad. I guess you could say she healed her broken heart.

My mom never healed. For a long time, she stayed in her room and refused to leave. My grandmother, my dad, even her work friends tried to persuade her to do something as simple as go for a walk or to the grocery store, but she wouldn't.

After a while, she went back to work and would come straight home where she'd close the door and not come out until the next morning. My grandmother tried everything to get her through those dark days and even threatened to take me away from my mom. It didn't matter.

Even up until the day she died, my grandmother never stopped trying to help my mom through her grief. "It takes time," she'd say. "She has to want to, and right now she doesn't want to."

She still doesn't want to, Grandma. Will she ever?

By the time my grandmother had her first heart attack, she and my mom were speaking to each other, at least. They weren't close, but they were cordial, talking about the weather or doctor visits, but nothing in depth, like how they felt or how much they meant to each other or anything like that.

I don't know if my mom had any regrets when my grandmother died. It's almost like she was so numb she couldn't feel the loss. I imagine it was like when the dentist numbed my mouth to fix a cavity and I chewed the inside of my mouth until it bled, but I didn't feel a thing.

Or maybe she didn't care that much, though that seems worse. Maybe it was something in between. I don't know. We've never talked about it. All I know is I never saw my mom cry about losing her mom.

Now as I sit in this house, I can't imagine I'd ever turn my back on my family and leave my mom completely alone. I don't think I could do it.

CHAPTER 29

The next day at work I have a hard time focusing on my reports. I'm thinking about the band and Randy's offer. My Nesting Buddy, Michael, keeps me in check. Only a few more days and I'll be back out there on my own.

On my way home from work, I think about calling my mom, but I don't want to talk to her yet. She probably didn't go to work, or maybe she did. I'm sure she's okay. Tomorrow. I'll call her tomorrow.

I start to call Jessica, but remember she's got something with school every night this week. I'm on my own for this one.

After dinner and a walk, Chewy and I go out to the backyard and I look up at the sky. The sun's been down for a little while, but it's still warm. The sky's clear and I make out the Little Dipper, the North Star, and another object that shines very bright, maybe Mars. And lots of other twinkles of light, stars I can't name, that shine brighter than the ones I *can* name. Are they further away? Is it an illusion? My perspective?

I wonder what it's like up there. It looks so calm and peaceful from here, but really, it's a fiery storm, molten lava flowing, and explosions all over the place. Or maybe the light source no longer exists. Isn't it possible to still see light from stars that have been dead for thousands of years?

Chewy sits on the patio chair beside me and rolls on her back with her paws in the air. I rub her belly.

My phone rings from a number I don't recognize, "Hello?" I say.

"Hello, Allison? This is Joshua Robinson, from River Rangers."

It takes me a second to realize who I'm talking to. Joshua. Guitar player. Blind Joshua. Held my hand for a long time Joshua.

"Oh, right! Hi Joshua."

"I hope it's not too late to call." His voice is relaxed and calm.

"No, it's fine."

"I got your number from Randy, is that okay? I totally understand if you don't want to talk to me. Is it okay that I call you?" he says.

"No, no, that's fine. I don't mind. Really. It's fine. Thanks for asking though." I frown and shake my head. It's weird when you're on the phone and you realize you're making gestures even though the person you're talking to can't see you.

"Okay, I wasn't sure about calling you and I tried not to, but I couldn't stop thinking about you and your audition. And Randy said he talked to you so I figured I'd see if I could get your thoughts about the band. Maybe answer any questions you might have."

I smile, "Oh, well, yeah, it's fine." Chewy stands up, shakes, and jumps off the chair.

"I know you asked for a couple days to think about it and I respect that, so I'm not gonna try and pressure you for a decision, but I do want to give you something to think about as you mull things over," he says.

I don't really want anything else to think about. I feel like I have enough and he doesn't even know the half of it, but I say, "Okay."

"First of all, I think you have an amazing voice."

Gee thanks, I think and smile to myself.

"It's just beautiful and has such a rich quality that's just unique," he says.

"Thank you. I appreciate that." I admit I love the compliment.

"Randy doesn't even know this, I don't think, but I've been looking for a singer for a long time. Years probably. When he said he heard you sing and you might be a good fit for us, I thought it was just another dead end, but when I heard you, I thought 'Oh my goodness. He's right! For once.'" Joshua laughs.

"Really? But, how'd you know? I mean, what made you think I was what you've been looking for?" I really want to know because I thought maybe I was imagining it.

"A few things. Of course, your voice. Your approach to the music. And it was also your choice in music. When I heard 'Angel from Montgomery', I could hardly believe it."

"Yeah, that's a great song."

"Oh yeah. Better than great. It's… I don't know. That's the kind of music I want to write. So when you picked *that song* and you sang *that song*, I felt an immediate connection."

I laugh. "Yeah, I know what you mean. That's one of my favorite songs of all time. And I was thinking that it was perfect because it's a little country. And, honestly, I like country music okay, but I grew up with rock and blues. But 'Angel from Montgomery' isn't really country. And your song wasn't really country."

"Yeah, that's true. I grew up with blues mostly. But, it's all music. They're all children from the same mother. That's it."

"Huh. I've never heard it put quite that way before, but, yeah, you're right. That makes sense."

"My granddad told me that. He'd be mad if I didn't give him credit for it, so I'll give it to him. He's been dead a while, but he's the kinda guy that'd make sure I knew he knew." I can hear the smile in his voice.

"Was your granddad a musician?"

"He was the best blues guitar man I've ever known, but he didn't play in a band. He played to play and nothing more. Well, that's not true, he taught me. Tried to teach all his grandkids, but it only took with me."

"Yeah? How long have you been playing?"

"Since I was about eight."

"Why do you think you took to it?" I'm interested to hear his story, but don't want to sound like I'm interrogating him.

"Only thing I can think of is that I'm a patient man. And I was a patient kid when it came to music. My granddad used to play a lick and then I'd play it, awful, and then he'd play it again, then I would, until mine sounded like his."

"That's cool. You learned by watching. And do you read music?"

"Well, Allison, it's hard to read Braille and play the guitar at the same time," he says.

"Oh, right!" *Stupid!* There I go putting my foot in my mouth. "Sorry, that was a stupid question."

He laughs a deep, throaty laugh. "Not at all! It's a great question. I'm just messin' with you."

"Oh, I see." *He's teasing me.*

"There actually is such a thing as braille sheet music and I can read it, but I play mostly by ear."

"Yeah, me too. But there's such a thing as Braille sheet music? I don't think I've ever even thought about that."

"Oh yeah. There's Braille everything. I didn't learn Braille when I first started school."

"Oh no? When did you learn?"

"I started losing my sight when I was ten or so and my mom took me to a doctor who didn't know what he was doin' where I was concerned. Not saying' he was a dumb quack or anything, but he never figured out what was going on with me, so I didn't start learning Braille until I was fourteen or so."

"Really? Do you think it would've been easier to learn if you'da started sooner?"

"Maybe, but by the time I started, it wasn't hard. I picked it up pretty quick. I can't complain. I had a good teacher."

"Man, I can't imagine. I don't know what I'd do if I ever lost my sight. I don't know how I'd handle something like that." I come inside to charge my phone. Chewy follows.

"You know, sight's just one of those things that makes some things in life a little easier, but you can live without it. I didn't think I'd adjust very well either, even as a kid. I thought, why me? But I got over it. Learned to live without it. And ever since then, it's been more of a blessing than a curse."

That's hard for me to imagine. I'm almost positive I would never be able to see something like losing my vision as a blessing.

"Well, good grief, Allison, I didn't call you to tell you my life's story and here I am runnin' my mouth."

I laugh. "Oh no, not at all. I'm sorry. I'm being so nosey asking you all these personal questions. But, thank you for telling me. Your story's inspiring."

"Well, I guess." He laughs. His voice is light and melodic. "And you? You're in San Antonio?"

"Yes."

"Come to think of it, I've never been to San Antonio. I hear it's beautiful."

"I like it. I was born and raised here. Never lived anywhere else."

"I've been as far south as Austin. Loved Austin. It was a quick trip but very cool."

"Yeah, you'll have to come to San Antonio. Come visit the Alamo." I say it more like one of those things people say that you know will never happen, like 'Yeah, we gotta get together.' It'll never happen.

"Definitely. The Cradle of Liberty."

"Yeah. I'll go with you if you ever come to town. Lived here all my life and never even been to The Alamo."

"You've never been to The Alamo?"

"Actually, that's not true. I've seen it from the outside, but never been inside."

"Then I'll have to set up some time to come down and visit. You'll show me around?"

"Sure. I'd love to," I say.

"Excellent. Well, shoot," he says in a more serious tone. "Actually, let me focus, on what I'm supposed to talk to you about. Why did I call you?"

"Questions about the band? The audition?"

"That's right. That's right. I called to tell you about what I thought at your audition. Did that. And I also wanted to tell you a little about the band and our plans and all."

"Definitely. I'd love to hear it."

"I know it's a lot to ask a person, you, to drop everything you're doing to come and sing with us, but this is a project that's been in the works for a long time. You're the last piece of this puzzle."

He says they've covered country and blues in the Dallas area for about two years and have slowly introduced originals. Their singer wasn't working out so they parted ways. Randy's a new manager and even though he seems a little bit of an old cowboy, Randy's good at bringing people together and he's got connections and a good business sense. Randy's not afraid to get out there and meet people. He used to manage a band years ago and got out of it because of where his family was at the time.

They're going to be recording next year, singing at some music festivals and hopefully that'll lead to more touring. They travel by van right now and have a trailer. They've all known each other either from school or family connections. His middle name is Joseph and he rattles off his social security number in case I want to do a background check. Do I have any other questions?

"I do have a question. I have a dog. A little dog. If I decide I can do this, can I bring her?"

"Sure, bring your dog," he says. "Does she like to travel?"

"She does. She loves the car."

"What's her name?"

I tell him about Chewy, that she was a boomerang dog at the shelter and I named her Chewy because she looks like Chewbacca the wookie. "She knows I'm talking about her. She's looking at me, wondering what's up."

"Do you dress her up and put bows on her?" he asks.

"No. Tried it once. Got her the cutest Wonder Woman costume for Halloween one year. I thought she was adorable, but she was not havin' it. Not at all."

He laughs. "Well, good for her. She made her position clear. She sounds like an awesome girl," he says.

"Yeah, she is." Joshua sounds like a great guy. I have to be honest with him. I'm flattered that they liked me and they want me to sing with them. I never would have thought I'd even have a chance to do something like this, but I have to face facts. There's too much going on here. I can't leave my mom. Heck, she went nuts about the audition. She's going through too much right now for me to put this on her too. It wouldn't be right for me to leave her. Not now. *I have to tell him.*

"Joshua? I need to tell you something."

"Sure. Anything."

"When I went up to Waco, I didn't really think much of it. And *never* considered actually doing this. Like, I was kind of going through the motions and invited my friends for a road trip because they wanted to shop at the outlet malls anyway, so we made a day of it. I'm not sure why I went, to be honest with you."

"That's okay," he says.

"Well, it is and it isn't. I mean, I'm grateful for the opportunity. I am. It's just that…" God, I'm such a jerk. He's so nice. And he needs somebody and I put myself out there like I wanted it, but now I can't go through with it. This sucks, but the sooner I tell him the better.

Joshua doesn't say anything.

I take a deep breath. "It's complicated, I guess. There's a lot going on with my family right now and for me to up and leave? I don't think I can. Plus, I've lived here all my life. I live in my grandmother's house and I'm not sure what I would do about the house. My mom's not well. She's my only family." I feel my throat tightening up.

He says, "I understand, Allison. It's okay. And again, I'm not trying to convince you here, but can I ask you something?"

"Sure."

"You say you were going through the motions, but I didn't see it that way. I heard something in your voice that day. Was that my imagination? Wishful thinking?"

Now, tears come to my eyes. "No. It's just that it's been a long time since I've felt that kind of … I don't even know what to call it, joy, I guess. Singing on stage these past few weeks has been…I don't know. It's been amazing." I want to tell him I never expected another chance, that I'd given up, that it was something I used to do but never thought I could do again. And then, there I was.

"Yeah?"

"Yes. And, honestly, the fact that you picked me to sing with you… It's unreal. But I had a feeling that day like I was where I was supposed to be, like I belonged there." After all these years of feeling inadequate, of feeling ashamed about what I can't do, to have someone see something good in me is almost unbelievable. I choke back tears. "It's just that…I feel bad that I'm kind of backing out on you now, but… I don't know. I feel like a jerk…"

"No," he says. "You're not a jerk." I can tell he's smiling and I hope he can't tell I'm blubbering like a stupid kid. "This is a big decision. I understand. I want you to know we want you. Really, *I* want you."

That makes me chuckle even though I'm in tears.

"I respect you wanting to take some time to look at it every which way, but in the end, I want you to know you're my first and last pick. There's no one else."

How can I say no to him? "Thank you. That means a lot to me. It does." I sniff and dab my eyes with my t-shirt.

"You know what? Take the weekend. You think about it. If I call you in a few days, you think that'll be enough time for you to sort it out?"

When we finally hang up, it's after midnight. The pressure's off for now. Time for me to put my big girl pants on and decide. *Stop being such a chicken-shit.*

CHAPTER 30

Over the next couple of days I take every opportunity to listen to the River Rangers' music and the more I hear it, the more I want to be part of it. I sing along and imagine what it would be like to be on stage with the band.

I've been away from music so long. I've missed it. The singing, of course, but also the chance to collaborate with people. There's nothing like it. To be on a team with like-minded people, talented musicians. There's a special kind of synergy to that. An attractive, mysterious force.

As I think about this and listen to the music over and over, I've thought about Joshua a lot too. He seems strong. Stable. Funny. And honest. Is that real?

It's impossible to say you know a person after speaking to them for just a few hours, isn't it? Would twenty hours be enough? It might help, but there are no guarantees. I know that.

Still, I've thought about calling him several times to get to know him a little better. But I've talked myself out of it every time. I want to make this decision on what's right for me, not be persuaded by someone I hardly know.

There is *one* thing about accepting Joshua's offer. I wouldn't miss my job. Maybe because now I have at least one other option, the job seems more boring. Or I'm just restless. After today, we have two more days of nesting. That means two more days of morning brief and afternoon debrief.

The new group gets their new team and desk assignments today and I'm praying to God that Gerald does not end up on my team or anywhere near me. His flatulence problem would drive me right out the door.

I want to feel sorry for him, but I don't understand how he can live like that.

Last week's doughnut incident put him over the edge, I think. Todd teases him and they do their guy thing and make crude jokes or comments or who knows what the heck they're saying to each other, but Todd must have gone too far. Gerald looked hurt and angry. They ignored each other and Gerald moved as far from Todd as he could, and they didn't speak to each other at all during the morning or afternoon sessions.

Of course, Monday morning it was all forgotten and they were back to their normal guy selves. Mumble mumble mumble. Hahahaha.

I wouldn't mind Natalie being on my team, even though it won't be for long. She said she's a student, but it turns out she's graduating in a few months. She's already looking for an accounting job, with or without the company. Natalie's like Super Woman. She's a single mom, a student, works full-time. I get tired just listening to everything she does before I've even gotten out of bed. She wakes up at four-thirty to run on her treadmill for an hour. I have a hard time rolling out of bed at six-thirty.

Todd would be an okay teammate too. Not great, but he'd be alright. I probably wouldn't talk to him much, so that would be okay.

Then there's Maya. Oh Maya. That lady. Where do I begin to tell the troubles with Maya? She says whatever fool thing comes to her head.

"Allison, you're so serious. Lighten up, girlfriend. Got a lot on your mind?" she said one day. I'd just met her. She doesn't seem to understand that not every one's like her, telling the whole world her business.

Plus, the way she dresses. It's like she's in costume most of the time.

She looks like a throwback from some sort of hippie commune—frizzed out hair, a headband sitting on her head like a crown, big, floppy, flowery tops, and shoes that look like men's house slippers. One day she looked like a disco queen—red glittery top, banded at the waist, tight, black stretchy pants, black platform shoes, hair curled in swoopy waves. "I like to liven things up sometimes," she said.

Maya's strange, for sure, but she's not all bad. She's generous. She's brought food for the group several times since I've been with them—brownies, tacos, those damn doughnuts. One day she brought Gerald a video game controller key-ring she'd bought at a garage sale for a quarter. She's nice, but there's something about her that makes me cringe, something that's actually repulsive to me. I can't put my finger on it.

I've always thought I was a "live and let live" kind of person, but maybe as I've gotten older I've become more intolerant of certain things. Or maybe I've always been this way. I don't know.

Sitting by Maya every day wouldn't be good for me.

The woman can't whisper. One day, she was telling Angie about a condition she has and says she may have to step out of the room frequently, but it's not because she's trying to get out of work. She has a doctor's note and something's going on with her uterus and she wants to have a baby and she's almost forty and her new boyfriend's sperm may not be very productive so she has to step out to make sure she keeps her bladder empty but at the same time she needs to drink lots of water.

All this she "whispered" to Angie at the front of the room instead of stepping outside. Angie tried to stop her several times and Maya just kept "whispering" more personal details.

And here's the kicker about Maya, she talks about her boyfriend all the damn time. He's old. He loves to have sex. Erectile dysfunction pharmaceuticals have changed his life. They met at the grocery store in her neighborhood. He loves her loud voice and crazy outfits.

At first I thought she was funny in an odd way, but after only a couple of days, she was too much.

On our second to last day of afternoon debrief, Angie says, "Allison, I'll be giving them their team assignments, so you can stay with us or go back to your desk until four o'clock."

I go back to my desk and log on to read my email and re-organize my work space.

A little while later, I hear her, "Oh, hi Mr. Hernandez. It's great to meet you."

Maya. Are you freaking kidding me?

I hear their footsteps approach. "This will be your desk," Mr. Hernandez says and he's on the other side of the partition, at the cubicle directly opposite me.

I stand up.

"Oh yay! I get to sit by you, Allison. Maybe some of your shyness will rub off on me," she says.

Today, she's wearing a long, oversized blue paisley dress. She opens and closes her desk drawers and all the cabinets. "Nice," she says. "I have a lot of pictures I want to put up. Do you have a lot of stuff at your desk, Allison?"

I shake my head. "No, I don't."

"You don't? Well I have a lot. This is great!"

Mr. Hernandez says, "Yeah, that's fine. Feel free to make yourself at home."

You don't know what you're saying, Mr. Hernandez.

~

After work, I text Jessica: Hey! How are you? Call me when you have a minute.

I call my mom. I haven't talked to her since she chunked the remote at me.

"I'm on my way home. Can I come by?"

"No, you don't need to. I'm fine."

"I'd like to come by, Mom, if that's okay."

"Fine!"

When I get there, she's in her pajamas, sitting in her chair, watching the news. It's 5:30.

"How are you?" I ask.

She looks at the TV. "Fine."

"How was work?"

"Good," she says without looking at me.

I look at the television. Traffic report. No major incidents to report. Traffic is moving slowly. Engrossing news.

I lean back in the swivel rocker. She sits in her recliner. "Mom, I'm sorry about the other day." I can't tell if she's listening because she's not looking at me. "I didn't mean to upset you. I hadn't had a chance to tell you about my audition and I wanted you to know. I'm sorry it got outta hand."

She stares straight ahead and doesn't look at me.

"How are you feeling, Mom? Feeling okay?"

"Yes, I'm fine. Why do you keep asking me?" she says.

Because you don't look fine, Mom. You look bad. Depressed. Are you going to spend the rest of your life in that damn chair? Staring at the television? Day after day?

"Because I'm concerned about you, Mom. I want to make sure you're okay."

I've talked to my mom about seeing a psychiatrist many times. She won't. She says she's fine. She's been depressed since Oscar died. Maybe even before that, but when Oscar died, my mom was consumed with grief. It settled in and dug in deep. She couldn't move on without him, and maybe she felt she owed it to him to stay sad, like it was the only thing she could do for him. I don't know.

She finally looks at me and says, "I'm fine. You don't need to worry about me. I have what I need. I don't need you coming over here checking on me."

I take a deep breath and sigh a little too loudly, I guess.

My mom exaggerates a sigh, mimicking me and then glares at me.

"Do you need anything? I'm going to the grocery store later," I say.

"I told you I have what I need."

You mean no thank you, mom? Rudeness.

I stand up to leave. "Okay. Well, if you want to continue to be mad at me, I guess that's up to you."

She stares at the television, ignoring me like a bratty little kid might ignore her older sister.

When I get home, I sit on the sofa with Chewy and scratch her ears.

"Oh Chewy. Grandma makes me crazy."

Would my mom care if I weren't here? Would she even notice? She seems extra bitter and angry lately. I know she's mad at my dad, but I think she's probably mad at me too.

I don't blame her. It's hard dealing with change. Even when it's change for the better.

CHAPTER 31

The next day in our afternoon debrief, Angie covers a few more of the office methods and procedures and how and when to ask for help if we need it.

"You're going to have questions, but if you have anything that maybe's a little different from training or any concerns, those are the things you can ask me," Angie says.

These past few days I've felt like I don't belong here with this group anymore. It's overkill. I know what I need to do and I should have gone back to my regular work assignment last week. Not that I'm not enjoying it as much as I can. In fact, I'm milking it now.

I met with Mr. Hernandez before lunch today. "How do you think the nesting has gone. Has it been helpful?"

"I think so." That's the truth. "Michael has helped me get organized. I think I'll be more efficient." Also true.

"Excellent, Allison. I've heard nothing but positive things from Angie. She says you've been coachable and receptive to development. And you've provided great insight for the new folks." He nods his head. "So thank you for staying positive and agreeing to work with Angie, and Michael, too."

"They've been great. Thank you for not firing me."

He squirms and raises his eyebrows as if to say, "Well, it was close."

At the afternoon debrief, Maya says to Angie, "I have a question. Actually, it's more of a suggestion."

"Okay," Angie says.

"Let's do a group happy hour tomorrow after work. It's TGIF, last day of training, and we can invite our Nesting Buddies, get to know them a little better in a more relaxed setting. Maybe we can get out a little early and we can go out for a drink or two and a few snacks," she says.

"Great idea!" Angie says. "We may be able to leave an hour early. Let me see if I can get it cleared now. I'll be back," she says and leaves the room.

Maya, Gerald, and Todd huddle together to talk.

"So, Natalie, how's school going for you?" I ask her.

"Oh my gosh. I'm so ready to be done."

"Oh, I bet," I say. "It's incredible that you've almost finished school. How do you do it? Single mom, working full-time."

She shrugs. "Once I decided I was going to do it, it was just a matter of keeping at it. One semester at a time." She smiles and looks off in the distance. "Gosh, when I started I thought I'd never finish and now, here I am, at the end of the road."

"Yeah. Really awesome. Huge accomplishment!" I don't know how old Natalie is, but she couldn't be much older than me. People like Natalie make me feel like a slug.

She starts to ask me something, but Angie comes back.

"Okay," Angie says. "We're cleared and I'll email your mentors inviting them to join us." She motions quick and silent applause. "Thanks for the idea, Maya. We usually do something like that but I totally forgot to get it together."

"You rock!" Maya says, and starts clapping. She high-fives the guys. *Geez, it's not all that. Calm down.*

"We'll meet at Charlie's, just down the street. We're approved to leave the office at three tomorrow and from there you can go home, but you have to stay at least until four."

We're all okay with that.

I get home from work and listen to Joshua's music as I scan the news and social media on my phone.

I've talked myself out of calling him again because it might make things more confusing for me. Better to keep my distance, I guess.

It feels like it's been forever since I've talked to Jessica, but our road trip to Waco was just last weekend. The beginning of the school year is a busy time for her with all their back-to-school activities. Plus, the wedding's just a few weeks away. Incredible. I'm sure she's got a lot going on with that and getting ready for family coming in from out of town. Yeah, I don't want to bother her.

Maybe Audrey's available for dinner. I text her: Hey! You busy? Want to grab a bite?

Audrey: Just leaving work. Call you in 10?

Me: K

I log on to social media to kill time. Nothing interesting. I'm more of a social media voyeur. I rarely post and never check in. I don't want to report every mundane detail of my life. How can I be frustrated with my mom for never doing anything when I do *almost* less than she does?

I could take a picture of a bowl of popcorn and say, "Time for dinner!" instead of those beautiful, gourmet, perfectly plated meals most people post. Or, another favorite, a bowl of granola and ice cold milk. Could I make that look beautiful and perfect?

My phone rings.

"Hey Audrey. How's it going?"

"Good. *Now* I'm leaving work. I'm down for dinner if you want to meet. That'll keep me from going home and binge watching *Grey's Anatomy*."

We decide on a Mexican food restaurant with a shady, outdoor patio and it's dog-friendly so I can bring Chewy. And margaritas for Audrey.

"Meet on the patio in thirty minutes?" I ask.

"I'll be there."

Thirty minutes later, Chewy and I walk up the ramp to the restaurant's back patio.

"Hey Allie," Audrey says when she see us. I hug her. She crouches down to Chewy, "Hey, Chews! I haven't seen you in forever. Remember me?"

Chewy drops to the ground and rolls on her back to expose her belly for Audrey to scratch.

"You do! Aww, what a good girl," Audrey says, smiling.

"Of course she remembers you! You're unforgettable."

"Well, thank you," she says. "I think." She stands up and pulls on her denim dress.

It's breezy and pleasant on the crowded patio.

"Look at that. Live music too," I say. He's set up in a corner of the patio with his guitar and singing "Margaritaville". I clap when he finishes. He nods at me.

"Thank you. Time for a short break, but don't go away. I'll be right back," he says.

"That's what I'm talkin' about. Margaritaville." Audrey opens the menu. "Why am I looking at this? I know what I want."

"I don't."

Audrey leans back in her chair. "Oh my goodness, this is nice. I am so glad you called."

"Me too. Glad you could make it, so last minute and everything."

I close the menu and look under the table at Chewy sleeping with her front paws crossed under her chin. A waiter puts a bowl of tortilla chips and salsa on our table.

"How's it going? What's new?" Audrey asks. She crosses her legs and rests her chin on her fist.

"It's good. Pretty good. I do have something pretty major on my mind." I grab my hair and twist it behind me.

Audrey's eyes widen. "What?"

"The audition in Waco? For the band?" I dip a chip in salsa.

"Yeah?"

"They offered me the job." I eat the chip whole.

She leans forward with a look of surprise. "What? Oh my God,

Allie! That's fantastic. Congratulations!" She reaches over to hug me. "Honestly, I'm not surprised. You were so good."

"Well, thanks. It was a good day."

Our waiter takes our order and our menus.

A group of servers, the leader holding a blue-velvet sombrero, surrounds a big group at a nearby table. The sombrero is placed on a little boy seated at the head of the table. It must be his birthday. It looks like the whole family's here. Parents, grandparents, aunts and uncles, cousins, at least twenty people. "Josh, smile," a man (probably dad) with a camera says. Josh smiles so hard I can see he's missing his front teeth. *What a cutie.* The lead waiter announces, "We have a special celebration in the house tonight. This is Josh and today he turns six." His family claps. So do we. The waiters begin clapping in rhythm. We, and everyone else on the patio, clap along. *Clap, clap, clap.* The clapping continues when they start to sing: Happy birthday to you. (To you, to you) and they sing a festive Happy Birthday Song. The crowd on the patio applauds. The servers shuffle back to their work.

I say, "Aww, how sweet." The waiter is posing for pictures with Josh before going back to his work. He leaves the sombrero on Josh's head.

Josh has dollar bills pinned to his shirt. I think it's a Mexican tradition (I'm not sure) that lets everyone know it's his birthday. An older man, probably around seventy, who's seated at a table next to theirs, speaks to Josh's father, then walks over to Josh and hands him a dollar bill. Josh looks confused at first, then he smiles and takes it from the man. A woman sitting next to Josh reminds him to say thank you.

How awesome is that? That little boy is surrounded by so much love. Of course I'm sure they have issues. Every family does. But he seems like a sweet kid. Cute and happy. Something about the scene gets to me. I get teary-eyed. For some reason it makes my heart ache.

I pull a dollar bill from my wallet for Josh.

A waiter delivers our drinks. Chewy comes out from under the table and we deliver the dollar to Josh. "Here you go, Josh. Happy birthday," I say.

He takes the dollar. "Thank you."

"You're welcome."

Josh holds the bill up to his mom. "I see that, Mijo. Isn't that nice?" He nods.

"Thank you," his mom says to me.

"You're welcome." Chewy and I head back to our table.

Audrey says, "Okay, so, Allie, they offered you the job? Yes? Continue."

"Oh right. Randy called on, gosh, was it Monday? Yeah, I think it was Monday. I said I needed to think about it. And then, Joshua, the guitarist called me."

"Oh yeah? Okay. What did he say?"

I tell her Joshua and I talked for a long time about music, but also our families and life and all kinds of things. "He said for me to take my time to decide. That he'd call me Sunday."

"He sounds like a cool guy, Allie. Do you like him?"

It's a simple question on the surface. I cock my head.

"C'mon, Allie. You can say you like him. You know he likes you." She sips her strawberry margarita.

"I don't know if he *likes* me like what you're suggesting, but yeah. I like him."

Audrey stirs her drink and smirks. "Well, at least you said it."

The musician gets back from break and the music starts again. *Take It Easy.*

"Let's not complicate the issue. I think I'd like working with him, let's put it that way."

"So, are you going? What're you gonna do?"

I'm not sure how much Audrey knows about my family situation. "I don't know. It's a bad time. You probably know a little about my parents."

"A little."

"My mom's having a hard time right now. My parents have been separated for a long time and my dad finally filed for divorce. She's not taking it well. She's freaking out. That's part of it."

"I'm sorry you're going through that, Allie. That's rough." She looks into her slushy drink as she stirs.

"Plus, I have my grandmother's house. And, I don't know, something about just up and leaving doesn't feel right."

"What would *they* say about it, your grandmother and your mom. They're your two main reasons for staying, right? What would they say about that?"

I sit back in my chair and look at Chewy, who's lying on the ground beside me, napping.

"My grandmother would probably say go. She'd probably say 'If you want to do it, do it now, while you're young.' I don't think she'd tell me to do it or not do it. She might worry about me playing with a bunch of guys, maybe.

"She had an adventurous spirit. She loved to travel and learn about different places and people." I shake my head. "It's so weird. She and my mom are so different." When I think about how full of life my grandmother was, I wonder how my mom turned out the way she is. There must be something I don't know about. Something that happened even before Oscar died that caused her to be so depressed all the time.

"Your grandma sounds like a fun lady."

"Yeah, she was. She taught me a lot about how to squeeze the most out of life." I realize the irony of what I just said. "Ha! She was a good teacher, but I must not have been a very good student."

Our food arrives. Tortilla soup for me, chicken tacos for Audrey.

We eat without talking. Chewy sits up. "People food, Chewy. Not for dogs." I take a chew bone out of my purse and hold it for her to grab. She sniffs it, then bites it and lies down again, holding the treat with her front paws and gnawing away.

"Oh my gosh, this is so good," Audrey says. "How's the soup?"

"Really good," I say.

"I don't see how you can eat soup when it's hot. I don't get it," she says.

"I like soup." I sip the hot, salty broth from my spoon.

"Well, Allie, it's a big decision. You're right to take your time and make sure it's something you really want to do."

"I guess. What do you think I should do? What would you do if you were me?"

"Girl, I'd be at home packing, not sitting here eating dinner, handing over cash to some kid I don't even know."

I laugh and shake my head. Audrey's a free spirit.

"But, it's not me. It's you. I get that you have concerns. Do you think your grandmother would say anything about the house?"

"You know, she'd just want me to be happy. She'd never want the house to be a burden."

"What about your mom? What would she say?" Audrey asks.

"I don't know." I stir my soup. "She's been through so much. And she's got a lot on her mind these days. I think she feels alone, my dad being gone and all. I think she's depressed and I'm afraid it's making her sick. She had an panic attack on Sunday."

Audrey looks confused. "A panic attack? What happened?"

"We were at brunch, and for her to even go out in the first place is a shocker. And she starts talking about my dad, or not even talking about him, but she's mad at me for not being more sympathetic that he filed for divorce and I was trying to tell her, essentially, it's been a long time coming."

"How long have they been separated?" Audrey asks.

"On and off since my Junior year. Not long after my brother died."

"Oh my gosh. That is a long time. That sucks. I mean, that she had an attack and all."

"It does. All of it. Part of me is furious with her, like I just want to shake her. I want her to snap out of it. I don't know how to get her unstuck. And I just feel like I need to be here for her," I say.

"So, what does your gut tell you?"

"I don't know. These guys seem like the real deal to me." I'm dominating the conversation and Audrey's playing therapist. I hate to be a pain in the ass talking-about-myself-all-the-time kind of friend.

"That's enough about me. I'm sorry! I'm doing all the talking and dumping everything on you," I say shaking my head. "What about you? What's new with you?" I move my plate to an empty spot on the table.

"Allie. I'm your friend. You got a lot going on right now and it's fine. That's what friends are for," she says. "No apology needed. At all."

I smile. Audrey always seems so, I can't think of the word, not happy exactly, but okay, like sometimes she's really happy, but sometimes she's just okay and she doesn't seem to carry a lot of baggage. And her personality is so carefree. Maybe that's it.

"Thanks," I say. "I know. I think part of the problem is that my family issues have been going on for a long time. Nothing's changed for years. How long has it been?" I do the mental math. "Almost fifteen years?"

"Yeah, hang in there, Allie," she says. "I know you want to take care of your mom because you're a good daughter, but you gotta take care of yourself too. You're important too. Don't forget that."

"So, enough about me. Really. What's happening with you? Seeing anyone?"

"Eh, kind of. There's a guy at work and he's great and fun to hang out with, but, I don't know. With the wedding coming up and all. Plus I had kind of made a promise to myself that I wouldn't," she pauses, "well, two things. One, I wouldn't date anyone I work with ever again. Not a good idea." She gives me a cautionary frown. "And second, I wouldn't date anyone *at all* for a whole year. And it's only been like four months."

"Wow, two strikes on the nice, fun guy who's probably drop-dead gorgeous too," I say. "Eh, no worries. Another one'll come around when you're ready."

She smiles, "Yeah, my heart's not in it, I guess. I'm just not that interested in dating right now. I want to focus on me for a while. Be super selfish and do what I want when I want. For a while, at least." She pauses. "Well, I might as well tell you since we're baring our souls. You're the first person I tell… I applied for a job in Chicago."

"Chicago? Really?"

"Yes! A friend from school called me about a job opening in her marketing department. I figured, what the heck. I got nothin' to lose. We'll see if anything comes of it."

"Good luck! That sounds exciting."

"It was funny because I got so excited about it and the idea of something totally different and I thought, you know, what the hell? I can go anywhere I want, take a position with lots of travel if I want. Now's the time, like your grandmother said."

"What about your parents?"

"They love Chicago. I think they'd love to have an excuse to come visit."

"That's awesome. And your house? You're renting, right?"

"Yep. My lease is up this month and then I can go month to month. It's a little more expensive, but we'll see."

I'm excited for her but also jealous that she can pick up and go. No attachments.

"Have you talked to Jess?" Audrey asks.

"No, I haven't even called her. I know she's been crazy busy with school. Parent conferences, meetings. I think she has a PTA meeting tonight, too. It's nuts."

"Yeah but she has summers off. Don't feel sorry for her, Allie." Audrey snickers.

I shake my head at that "they get summers off" comment that sets Jessica off. She's always working, takes work home, spends a ton of money on her kids and her classroom and people seem to think that having summers off is the reward for being overworked and underpaid. Or something like that.

"Last I heard, they're going on their honeymoon over Thanksgiving break, but what about the week after the wedding? Would she go back to school that Monday? Did they decide?" I ask.

"I saw her this weekend at my dad's birthday dinner and she said she's taking a couple of days and they're driving to New Orleans for a long weekend, then she'll be back at school. She doesn't want to miss that much school even though she could. She wants to get back," Audrey says.

"Can you believe the wedding's three weeks away?" she says.

"I know. It's incredible. Time flies," I say.

I'm glad Audrey was available tonight. This has been tons better than staying home alone.

"Thanks for listening, Audrey," I say when we leave. "It helps to talk it out."

"Anytime, Allie," she says. "I say trust your gut." She hugs me. "Sounds simple, doesn't it?"

CHAPTER 32

I volunteered to bring breakfast tacos to work this morning, our last day of nesting, so Chewy and I walk earlier than usual. The neighborhood is quiet and dark when we start, but by the time we get home, the sun's rising, shining crimson on the cloudy sky.

"Look at that, Chewy."

I think of Oscar. He's been on my mind since seeing little Josh at dinner last night—his big smile, happy face, celebrating a birthday. Josh reminded me of my little brother. I imagine Oscar's in the clouds, looking down on me, light, free, and happy. Ten-year old Oscar, skinny, dark curly hair, big teeth, big smile. "Allie!" he'd shriek when I'd grab his video game remote. "Mom said I could play!"

"He can play," my mom used to say, "but you better make sure his homework's done by the time I get home. And you need to help him," she'd tell me.

"Don't be mad at me! I'm not gonna get in trouble because you haven't done your homework. You can have it back when you're done," I'd tell him.

My brother was getting to that awkward stage, the tween years. He needed braces. My parents said he'd get them eventually, but he didn't want them.

"No, they hurt. I don't want braces. My teeth are perfect just like this. God made me this way, Mom. I'm good," he'd say.

I smile remembering my brother. *Was I a good sister to him? Did I love him enough?*

These are the questions I ask myself. Who's to say and how would I know? My memory's sketchy when it comes to life with my brother.

We tormented each other, like most siblings do. Kid rules. You got to take it if you give it, especially when you're younger. His specialty was bursting out of a hiding place when I least suspected and scaring me half to death. He knew I'd get him back. He'd have been disappointed if I didn't.

If he didn't know I loved him then, I hope he knows now. Somehow.

"Okay, Chewy. I'm leaving. I won't be late," I say gathering my purse and keys. "Love you! Be a good girl."

When I get in the car, I see that I have a text from Jessica. I forgot I texted her yesterday. "Hey Allie! How are you? This week's been nuts and so happy it's finally Friday! (happy face emoji) Happy Friday!"

I text back, "TGIF! How about coffee tomorrow? 8am?" I hope she can make it. It'll be nice to sit for a relaxed conversation with her.

"I'll have to let you know. Mom's keeping me v busy. (Stressed face emoticon)."

"K. LMK. Have a great day!"

"You too!"

~

"Awesome," Gerald says as he looks in the brown paper bags I picked up before work. He brought juice. Todd brought grocery store cinnamon rolls.

"Just put 'em all out," I say and I get a bag and flip it over, aluminum foil wrapped tacos, marked with a black marker to identify the contents of each: bean and cheese, potato and egg, bacon and egg, chorizo and egg. The large conference room table serves as a buffet table today.

"Yay! Breakfast!" Maya says when she steps in the room.

Angie and Natalie walk in together. "Good morning, everyone," Angie says. "Wow, lots of food."

"I brought enough for our nesting coaches, in case they want some," I say.

"Excellent," Angie says. "I'll let everyone know, but I'd like to cover a few things before that."

Angie covers the details of a change in the workflow process. "And this afternoon, we're okay to leave the office at three and head to our mixer at Charlie's. We need to stay until at least four and after that, you're free to go. You're on the clock 'til four."

"Can we invite people to join us?" Maya asks.

I resist the urge to roll my eyes. *Oh, Maya, we don't want to see your "honey."*

"After four is fine," Angie says.

Before long, it's lunchtime and I'm not hungry at all. I find a shady spot outside and consider calling Joshua. Just to say hi.

I go over what I'll say, kind of like a script. I'll ask him how he's doing. I can ask him about the shows they have scheduled. I never asked him about that and that's something I need to know. Although, what if he makes the shows sound amazing and that makes it even harder for me. Or what if he thinks I'm ready to sign up. That would be awkward.

Never mind. I better not call him.

I sit and surf the web instead, then get bored with that, put my phone in my pocket and sit and listen to the birds chirp.

The afternoon goes by quickly. Michael hardly pays attention to anything I'm doing. He takes a break, comes back, asks about my dog. (Michael's a huge Star Wars fan and loves that I named my dog Chewy.) He asks about working for Mr. Hernandez, takes another break, etc. I didn't think he had it in him to relax a bit.

I ask him to look at a bid before I send it through.

"Perfect. You're fine, Allison. You totally got this," he says.

"You think so?"

He squinches his face. "Please. You're fine."

"Okay then."

He leans toward me. "I don't think you needed to sit with me two weeks, but whatever." He rolls his chair back and puts his hands up in surrender.

"I thought it was a little much, myself. But, it's okay with me." I'm finishing up a bid and I turn toward him and whisper, "He could have fired me."

"Oh well. It's been great for me. Super easy. At least you don't argue with me."

"Why would I argue with you?" I say turning back to the keyboard.

"I've had brand new people assigned to nest with me and they think they know more than I do. They correct me and say, 'That's not what we learned in training.' God, that's annoying."

I smile. Michael's grown on me. "Are you going to Charlie's this afternoon?"

"Oh yeah. I love Charlie's. Besides, it gets me out of the office a little earlier."

"Well, thanks for working with me. And for your patience. You've been great." I get a card from my purse and hand it to him.

"For me?" He opens the card and smiles. It's a Star Wars themed card with a ten-dollar gift card to Charlie's. "Thank you, Allison."

We sit and chat until three o'clock, then close our files and shut down the computer. Michael and I walk out together. "See you there," he calls.

When I get to my car, before I head over to the restaurant, I see a text from Jessica: Coffee. 8am. Be there.

I reply: Excellent!

*C*harlie's is a "casual dining restaurant" just a few blocks from the office. They're known for their massive onion rings. One order is a stacked tower of thick, golden-brown rings deep-fried to perfection.

Todd and Gerald are sitting near the hostess station when I walk in, and within a few minutes, everyone else arrives. It's between lunch and dinner crowds and the restaurant is mostly empty. We're escorted to an area in the back.

Our table's long to accommodate twelve with extra space to add chairs so guests can squeeze in. Michael and I sit near Angie, who's sitting at the head of the table.

The other mentors introduce themselves and the conversation naturally turns to work. Angie orders onion rings, and two appetizer sampler platters. The waitress takes our drink orders.

Angie stands to address our group. "Well thank you all so much for all your work this week. Especially our mentors who graciously agreed to work with you all."

Maya claps. "Here, here," she says.

Michael whispers to me, "Oh my God. She's so loud."

I turn to him and smile as if to say, I know.

Maya tells everyone about a long conversation she had with one of her sales reps and how he was furious when he first got on the phone, but when they hung up, "We were laughing and joking around. He was happy as a clam. We're best buds."

"That's awesome, Maya. Well done," Angie says.

Maya flips her hair in Michael's direction and he leans toward me to avoid getting whipped with it.

The waitress comes with our drink orders.

Angie asks Michael about someone named Bob who used to be with the company. I don't like when people talk over me like that. I think about offering Michael to switch places with me, but then I'd be by Maya. I don't say a word, just listen and sip my iced tea.

Then I hear Maya say, "Oh hi, honey! You're a little early," she says. It's the fiancé. The old guy. I don't look over. "He's early. Is that okay?" she asks Angie. I already know Maya and her boyfriend are a train wreck. I don't have the kind of morbid curiosity that makes me have to see them together.

Angie looks up from her conversation with Michael. "Sure. That's fine," she says.

Maya presents him to the group, "Everyone, this is my fiancee, Joe. Joe, this is my work group. I guess I'll just go around the table and introduce you to everyone."

"Hello," he says. "Hi. Nice to meet you…"

That voice. Maya's boyfriend. I know that voice. *Oh my …. No.* My feet go cold. *It can't be.* I strain to listen to him over Michael and Angie's voices.

"Hello," the fiancé says.

They're almost to me. I shift in my seat to catch a glimpse of him before they get to me, to confirm what I already know. And there he is: thick, wavy hair, dark skin. It's a kick in the gut. Of all the men in the world, Maya had to hook up with my dad? Are you fucking kidding me.

She gets to Angie. "And this is Angie, the greatest trainer ever."

Ohmygodohmygod! My hands tremble. I fish around for something in my purse, then push my chair back and put my head under the table as if I've dropped something I desperately need.

"Allison? Yoohoo, Allison. I don't know what she's doing under the table, but that's Allison. Then there's Michael. Right Michael?"

"You got it," he says.

"And that's everyone," Maya says.

Michael looks under the table at me. "You okay? Did you drop something?"

"Yes, I'm fine." *Where can I go? I gotta get outta here.* "I'll be back," I tell Michael.

I duck out of the room and from the corner of my eye I see him see me.

I go into the bathroom stall and think about what to do. I want to leave. Is it time? Almost. I can hang out in here and I'll text Angie and tell her I got sick and have to leave. Do I have her number? I check. Yes, I do. Crap. Should I say something to him? Confront him? That might cause a scene. That's all I need. Better to just get the hell outta here.

Me: Angie, I'm not feeling well. I have to go home. I'm fine but I have to go. I'm in the bathroom right now.

I wait a few minutes. No reply. Screw it. I return to my seat and tell Angie I'm not feeling well. I have to go.

Angie says, "Oh no. Okay, well, I hope you feel better. I'll see you Monday. Have a good weekend."

Michael says, "I got your drink. Don't worry. Go home."

"Thanks," I say.

I can't stop running it over and over in my mind. Maya's boyfriend. My dad. The guy Maya's been talking about, the one who likes her sleeping in the nude and takes drugs for … *Stop. Stop thinking about it!* That's why he wants a divorce after all these years. How long has it been since I've seen him? Three years? Longer?

My keys in hand, I unlock my car and rush to open the door. I see my dad by the front door. He followed me. Is he going to try to talk to me? What's he going to say? What will I say to him?

One thing comes to mind for sure: You want to have a baby with her? You're not qualified. You suck. You're an asshole. No kid wants an asshole dad. And I know all about your personal problems, Dad. Wanna know how I know? Your loudmouth girlfriend's told everyone, so you can go back inside and meet all those people and know that everyone's as grossed out as I am.

That's a lot more than one thing, but it doesn't matter. He doesn't follow me, just stands outside by the door and watches me. I should say something. I should tell him what an asshole he is. But I don't. I get in my car and close the door. Lock it. Start it. My tires screech as I pull away.

Now I really do feel like I might be sick. Tears well up in my eyes and I pull off the road into the big, vacant lot of a shut-down hardware store. My heart pounds. I turn the air conditioner on full blast and lean my forehead on the steering wheel, angry at myself for crying.

CHAPTER 33

Chewy greets me at the door when I get home. At least *some*one loves me.

I sit on the sofa and pat my lap, "Come on, Chewy."

She leaps up and I scratch her ears and her brown eyes are pure love. "Thank you for loving me, Chewy. You're a good girl."

She jumps down and we go out to the backyard and sit on the patio under the cover. It's too hot to stay out, so I come inside and put on shorts and a t-shirt and flip-flops.

"Oh Chewy, you won't believe who I saw today."

She's her usual quiet self.

The house is still and I can hear noise from outside: a lawnmower, a dog barking, trucks passing the house, and the inside noise of the refrigerator buzzing. I slouch down on the sofa with my legs on the coffee table and think about my dad.

It was him. He didn't even try to talk to me. He didn't come after me. He's not wondering about me. Why should I waste my time wondering about him?

Great. Now he's connected to this person from my work world. And stupid Maya sits right across from me. I have to hear her annoying voice every day. And now, when she talks about her honey I know she's talking about my asshole father.

No. Can't do it. Can I get away from her? Is there anywhere else I can go?

I'll ask Mr. Hernandez if I can switch desks. I'll switch with Todd! Yes, that's it. He can sit by Maya and ooze his charm on her every day. That would be perfect. But she's such an obnoxious freak, he won't want to sit by her.

Will Gerald? Maybe.

No. Natalie! She won't care. She'll probably be leaving anyway.

Great. First thing Monday morning I'll ask Mr. Hernandez if I can switch desks with Natalie and then ask Natalie if she'll switch with me. No, the other way around.

Okay, maybe that won't be so bad. And maybe I can ask him to talk to Maya about appropriate office talk and let her know no one wants to hear about her personal life and her old, wrinkly boyfriend. *"I went to bed early but I got to sleep late, if you catch my drift."*

My phone goes off. Text message. I don't recognize the number. Could it be from him?

No, it's Joshua: Hi Allison. Just got done with lessons for the day and wondering if you might have some time to talk tonight. Lemme know.

I save his number in my phone.

Me: Hi Joshua. I will. Just got home and it's been a hectic day so unwinding a little. Around 7?

Him: Sounds good.

I get my guitar from the stand in the corner of the room and strum and tune. The sound fills the empty space. When Jessica asked me to play guitar and sing at the wedding, I started practicing and it didn't take long for my fingers to get back in shape, though those first few weeks I felt clunky and uncoordinated. Now, I strum with a guitar pick and play various chords to warm up.

I play one of the first songs I learned years ago, *Amazing Grace*. Three chords. Simple.

I've always loved the song. It reminds me of the power of love and forgiveness, like when you've made a serious mistake and some one forgives you and gives you another chance, not because you deserve it, but because they love you. Serious stuff.

I don't remember where I first heard the story about *Amazing Grace*, but the way I heard it, it was written by an Englishman who worked on a ship in the slave trade in the 1800's. The song is about the moment he realized slavery was pure evil and, not just that, but what a wretch *he* was for being part of it, for allowing that evil to continue. That revelation changed his life. He could no longer rationalize slavery or pretend he didn't know it was wrong. After that, he became a minister and an abolitionist. He says he was saved by Grace.

The story's always stayed with me. I wonder if he ever imagined that we'd still be singing his song a hundred years after he was dead and gone. Probably not. How could he?

That's a testament to the power of music. I think so, anyway.

When I'm ready for a break, I stop and look for dinner.

Popcorn sounds good. Needs butter, of course, and salt. Lots of salt.

Now's one of those times I'm glad I can't drink because I'd want to drown my sorrows in a bottle of some type of hard liquor and probably wind up passed out on the kitchen floor.

I'll binge on massive amounts of popcorn instead.

I pour myself a glass of iced tea, grab the large bowl of popcorn and head toward the back door. Except, the sun's going down and the mosquitos will be feeding. Not good for me, not good for Chewy.

I turn on the television and sit on the sofa, mindlessly munching and watching.

Before long, I reach the bottom of the bowl. "Geez, I ate it all, Chewy. Can you believe that?"

I put the bowl in the sink and open up the freezer for a quart of rocky road ice cream I know is in there somewhere. "There it is." I get a spoon and return to the sofa. I hunt for chocolate chunks and stir the ice cream until the stiffness is gone and it's the consistency of cookie dough. Yum. Sweet, rich, creamy.

Now, I feel full, huge and stuffed to my ears. We need to go for a walk.

Did I say it out loud because Chewy is sitting by the front door.

"Yes, yes. We're going," I say and I clip on her leash.

Across the street and a few houses down, the crazy family in the neighborhood is out. They moved in when our old neighbor, Mr. Ramon, died and Mrs. Ramon sold the house and moved in with her daughter. I'm not sure how many kids are in that family. Four maybe? I think they all still live there. One of them, Dolores, is my age. She's got two kids now and they live there too.

Their front yard looks like a car lot. There are two cars in the driveway, one in the yard, and about three in the street. The father stands on the dusty yard and shouts something to a guy getting in one of the cars in the street. "Cuidado, mijo," *(Be careful, son.)* he says as he watches his son drive away. The old man waves to me. I wave back.

I went to Catholic school through eighth grade and they went to the local public school, so I never knew any of them. When I got to high school, I'd see them on the bus and talked to Dolores sometimes, but I wouldn't say we were friends. She hung out with the kids who got in trouble and skipped school. When we graduated from high school they threw Dolores a huge party with a live band in the backyard. Cars lined up and down the street.

My grandmother never said they were a bad element, but she always had a look that said, "Watch out for them." She'd raise her eyebrows and purse her lips slightly as she looked away. I've only ever seen them from a distance and they seem to be in a cycle that will never end. Have kids, struggle raising kids, those kids have kids, struggle raising kids. It's the same thing over and over.

I suppose as long as they have each other, they'll be okay. What do I know?

The walk helps my food digest and when I get home, I pop a few antacid tablets.

It's almost seven and Joshua will be calling.

I feel like a dork waiting for him to call me. It's kind of ridiculous, but I can't wait to talk to him, especially since I was going to call him the other day and talked myself out of it.

7:00.

7:05.

Was I supposed to call him?

7:10

7:15

God, I'm an idiot. Sitting by the phone waiting for a boy to call me. Stupid.

7:20

Never mind. What's showing at the movies? I'll go to a movie.

7:22 The phone rings. It's Joshua.

I answer nonchalantly, as if I haven't been sitting by the phone waiting for his call for twenty-two minutes.

"Sorry I'm late," he says. "I was on the phone with a parent discussing her son's progress with lessons."

"Oh, that's okay. Yeah, it's fine. No worries. I'm just here. I was thinking about checking out a movie later. Maybe," I say.

"Oh yeah. What movie?"

"I don't know. I was just looking up what's showing," I say. "How've you been?"

"Me? I've been good." I hear a smile in his voice. "How about you?"

"I'm fine. Had a hectic day. I'm glad it's Friday."

"You had a hectic day? What's a hectic day in the life of Allison…" His voice trails off.

"Oh, God, Allison. I forgot your last name. Oh man, I'm so sorry."

I laugh. "It's okay. Joshua Joseph Robinson." He told me his full name the other night.

"Oh, now I feel worse." I can almost see his face turning red.

I laugh. "No, it's fine. Don't feel bad. Really. My last name's Deleon."

"Deleon! That's it. Oh, I can't believe I forgot your last name."

"No problem. It's fine."

"I'll try this again. What's a hectic day in the life of Allison Deleon?"

"Oh nothing. Just a little family drama. That's it," I say.

"You mentioned your mom, right?"

"I may have, but today it wasn't my mom."

"And I know you have a dog. And do you have any other family?"

"Not really. I mean, I have a father, but he's not around. Well, he is, but he isn't. Anyway. My younger brother died when I was fourteen," I say.

"Oh I'm sorry to hear that. How old was he?" he asks.

"He was ten. He'd just turned ten."

"Oh that's a tragic loss." I hear real sympathy in his voice.

"It was. My mom still hasn't recovered. Her life is in two time periods: before Oscar died and after Oscar died."

"That's a devastating thing, to bury a child. I had a younger sister who died when she was a baby and if it weren't for the rest of us kids, I don't know how my mom would've handled it. But she had four other kids to raise so it was a tough thing for her. She still remembers my baby sister's birthday every year."

"How old was she?"

"Less than a year old. Four months? Five months? Something like that. SIDS. My mom says she put her to bed one night and was happy that she had slept through the night, only, she never woke up."

"Oh. That's terrible. My brother died in a car accident. He was in a pickup that got rammed by one of those big gravel trucks. Killed instantly. Probably. The accident devastated my family. Gosh, how did we start talking about all this depressing stuff?" There are very few people I would talk to about my brother's death.

He laughs. "I have a way of doing that to people. To me, it's not depressing, especially if it happened a long time ago. It's just something that happened."

"Yeah."

"I just feel like death is part of life. Some of us get to live a little longer than others, that's all. But life is short for all of us, don't you think?"

"Honestly, I don't think about it much. Which is weird given my family history, I guess," I say. I don't think about it much because when I do, it seems so unfair. Why do some people live to be a hundred and other people don't make it past infancy?

"Oh, I've thought about it a lot. Too much probably."

Why would anyone think a lot about death? "Do you think about dying and, like, how you're going to die?" I ask.

"No, not like that. It's more in a broader sense. Well, to start with, I think of time as a man-made thing. It's just our measurement of earth cycles, really."

"Okay."

I can hear the smile in his voice as he continues. "So if you take all the earth cycles since they started, that's billions of years. Billions. So, if my baby sister lived six months and your brother lived ten years and you live to be a hundred and I live to be seventy, those are all a fraction of a sliver of time compared to billions."

"And that doesn't depress you?"

He laughs. "Not at all! It's uplifting!"

I can't see how any of this could be uplifting. "How is that uplifting? You're saying that our lives are an insignificant speck of existence. How could anything you do in life matter?" Is this why he seems so relaxed? Because nothing matters?

"Ahh. There's the rub. My baby sister, Carol was her name, lived about two-hundred days, but her passing changed my mom, just like your brother's loss changed your mom. Their short lives made an impact on people who loved them. That's not insignificant."

That's true, Joshua, Mr. Deep Thinker Guy. "Okay. I see what you're saying, but my mom's life changed for the worse. It hit her hard and knocked her down. She never got up. At least your mom recovered. Maybe that's why you see it that way."

"Maybe. But consider this. Let's say you're right. My mom's attitude affected the way I see death and living, and I'm sharing this with you now, and my attitude could affect your attitude and your attitude might affect your mom's attitude and your mom's attitude might affect your dad's attitude, and so on. So it becomes this never-ending ripple effect that goes on indefinitely. We're connected. We, people, not you and me, necessarily," he says.

"Uh-huh. I get it."

"And that's the uplifting part. Thanks for hearing me out because I almost tripped over myself just now. I've thought about this for a long time but never said it out loud to any one before."

"You're welcome." Maybe it's stupid, but I think it's cool that he shared his philosophy with me. The World According to Joshua. "But I have a question. What if people, like my mom, for example, never recover. She was never much of an optimist, but since then, she's extremely negative. I don't know. I mean, sure, we impact each others' lives and especially those closest to us, probably, but … I don't know what I'm getting at. Never mind." I want to hear what he has to say about my mom's grief consuming every part of her, but it's not right for me to paint such a negative picture of her.

"No, I get what you're saying. I think there are times when it's a negative impact. It's not always positive. So, could the terrible tragedy of my sister's death have been a negative in my family even now? Absolutely. My mom could have blamed God or herself or someone else. Sure. I might be a different person had she handled it differently," he says.

I don't know if my mother blamed God. Maybe so. She stopped going to mass after that, but she's never said she blamed God. She blamed my dad and I heard that a few thousand times in my life. She always beat to death the idea that my brother would be alive had my dad done things differently that day, though she's never explained how because she won't talk about it.

"I suppose you're right." I want to ask him about other family, but it would be mostly to sound courteous because I don't want to know. It sounds like he's got a big, well-adjusted family.

"So, I'm going to change the subject, if that's okay," I say.

"Sure."

"Actually, I have a couple questions for you."

"Okay."

"How many songs have you written? That's the first question. And what's your writing process?"

He's written hundreds of songs of which, according to him, only a few are keepers. He records songs and has a friend transcribe. And that's it.

We talk about music and movies until it starts to get late. I remember that I'm meeting Jessica early tomorrow.

I tell him I have to go. I feel drained and exhausted from a long and emotional day.

"Allison, it's been great talking to you."

"Same here, Joshua. Thank you for sharing your perspective about losing a sibling, burying a child and all that. I didn't realize you're a philosopher too. Songwriter, musician, philosopher. You're a regular Renaissance Man."

"I like the sound of that."

It's not until after I've hung up that I realize he never asked me about my decision or if I'm leaning toward taking it or turning it down.

CHAPTER 34

It's a sticky, muggy, drizzly Saturday morning and I drive toward downtown to meet Jessica at Petra's, our favorite coffee shop.

Petra's started as a tiny little place, no bigger than a two-car garage. Now they're in a place three times the size in the art district. The music selection is always interesting and indie, most I've never heard of. That inspires me in a way.

Even if I don't join the band—which, the more I think about it, the more unlikely it seems—if I can figure out some way to get back into performing again, it may not be too late for me. I can start with acoustic sets in coffee shops and restaurants, like the guy on the patio the other night, and then, you never know. Maybe that'll open some doors, put some people in my path who can help get me to the point where I can play more. Record, even.

Could that happen? Sometimes it seems like just a crazy dream. Realistically, I'll never be anything but a small-time musician, but so what?

I could keep my job and play a few nights a week. Coffee shop gigs could work. I'm not doing anything else. Why not? At least it's a start.

Jessica's looking at the menu board when I walk up. She turns and sees me.

"Oh my God! It feels like forever," she says as she hugs me.

"I know! I was just thinking the same thing," I say.

We get coffee and breakfast, me a muffin and fruit, her oatmeal.

"You look great!" she says.

"Oh, thanks. Do I look different? It hasn't been that long since I've seen you." She makes me laugh.

"I don't know. Your hair maybe?"

My hair does what it wants and today it looks full and curly. "You caught me on a good day. How are you? They've been keeping you busy at school, huh?"

"Ugh. It's been crazy. We've had something pretty much every night since school started. And at home my mom's driving me nuts with wedding stuff. I'm to the point where now whatever's done is done and what's not done is okay because it's enough."

We stop for napkins and utensils before looking for a seat.

"Yeah, definitely. You have all the major stuff ready to go, right? Flowers, caterer, dress, what else do you need?"

"Need? Nothing. My mom's trying to set up four star hotel service for my family coming in from Cali. She's rearranging furniture, buying new linens, getting new drapes installed. And we're all still working so we don't have time for all this. She's stressing out. *I'm* stressing out."

We find a table against the wall toward the back. "Yeah. Hang in there. It's not long now. You can always come to my house if you need a break. We'd love to have you."

"Aww, thanks. I actually stay at David's when he's in town, and hopefully we'll be able to move into the house soon." She gives an exasperated look. "He should already be moved in by now."

"Oh right. You were supposed to move in before the wedding. What happened?"

"It's not ready." Jessica and David are renting a house from a friend who bought it as an investment property, but he wanted to do some light remodeling and the contractors are behind schedule. "They re-did the floors, and it's an old house, and all the wiring had to be re-done. And I don't even know what else. Supposedly, they'll be done this week and we should be able to get the keys by next weekend. We'll see." She shrugs.

"Cuttin' it close, people," I say.

"I know. So, most of my stuff is in storage, but, y'know, I'm using my old room. My mom's like, 'When do you think you'll be leaving?' and I'm like 'Are you freaking kidding me? No, you cannot use my room.'"

Jessica's mom is great, but she's wound a little tight. And Jessica's not like that at all.

She shakes her head. "And she knows the situation. She knows I don't know. I'm not sure why she has to keep asking me. I'm seriously about to lose it on her." Jessica sips her coffee. "Like today, coming here, she's like, 'Where're you going?' and I say 'Coffee with Allie.' And she says, 'We have things to do!' I didn't even answer. I just left. She's going overboard."

"Whoa. That's a lot. Well, just think, Jess, soon, it'll all be done. And everyone will be talking about how great it was."

"Oh my gosh. I can hardly wait." She stirs her oatmeal.

"And when is his family coming in?" I peel the paper back from my blueberry muffin. "Jess, you want some?"

"Ooo, sure. Just a little." I put a small piece of muffin on her plate. "His parents get here the Tuesday before."

"And are they staying with ya'll?" I ask.

"Please. No. They rented a house somewhere around here. Yeah, they haven't been as, I don't know, accepting, of the way we've planned everything. His mom especially. She just kind of turns her nose up at things. I don't think she likes me very much."

"What? There's no way she doesn't like you. She must be jealous of you," I say.

Jessica smirks. "No. That's not it," she says. "She's just a manipulative meany."

I laugh.

"No, really, Allie. She's not nice. David says that's just the way she is. He's used to it and that's why he stays as far from her as he can. And, get this, I don't know if I told you, when she insisted that we have the wedding in October and I wanted to make it easy for them since they're traveling so far to be here, David was like, 'It's fine. They'll figure it out. Summer works out better for you and we need to stick with that.' But no, I wanted her to like me. And now I realize she doesn't like anybody. She duped me for sure."

"Well, now you know. I can't wait to meet her." I feign excitement.

"I know. Yay." She sips her coffee. "Oh my gosh! I've been running my mouth but I want to hear about you and the band and all that. Thank you for letting me vent, by the way. I hate when I do that, but, whew, I feel better. Thank you." She forces a smile.

"Yeah, of course. Umm. Me? Oh, wow. Well, gosh, where do I start? Okay, well I told you that my dad finally filed for divorce?"

"Yes, we'd just come back from the trip?" she says, thinking about how she knew.

"Right. Okay, well I'd been to see my mom a couple of times and she was just super pissy so I thought, she's upset. Understandable."

Jessica nods. "Sure."

"So I thought, do something nice for her. And we never go out. I was kind of surprised she was willing to go when I invited her to brunch at Mario's," I say.

"Oh yeah. I hear Mario's is nice."

"It is. Nice place. So, we're sitting on the patio and she gets mad because she says I don't think it's a big deal that my dad's asking for a divorce." I try to remember the particulars about the conversation that day, and all I can remember is when it all went to crap. "But I say something that sets her off and she starts breathing hard, clutching her chest, and I think 'Oh my God! She's having a freaking heart attack right there at the restaurant.'"

"Oh my God, Allie!" Jessica's eyes widen. "Was it?"

"Well, no, thank God it wasn't a heart attack, but we didn't know. The manager called an ambulance, cleared out the patio, my mom puked all over him. It was bad," I say.

"Allie, that's awful."

"Yeah, so she was in the emergency room and they ran some tests and then let her go," I say.

"Why didn't you call me?" she asks.

"I didn't want to bother you. She was fine."

"Allie," Jessica says, taking my hand, "promise me that you'll call me when something like that happens. Promise me." She looks serious.

"Jess, you have so much of your own stuff to worry about," I say.

"Screw all that stuff. I mean it. Please call me," she says looking in my face and waiting.

I remember thinking about calling her. "Okay, I promise."

"Thank you. Well, thank God she's okay."

"Yeah, well. Something else. I don't even know how to say this."

Her eyes widen. "What?"

"Remember I told you I met with my boss at work. He could have fired me but instead he had me go to this remedial nesting…"

"Uh-huh."

"So this woman in the group I was with. Her name's Maya and she's a weirdo, I won't get into that, but she's also a loudmouth and kept talking about her new boyfriend, who's some old guy, and saying shit about their sex life and other stuff that was way too much information."

Jessica nods. "Yeah, I remember you mentioned that."

"Well," I say taking a deep breath, "come to find out, her boyfriend," I pause, "her boyfriend? Is my dad."

"Her boyfriend's your dad?" she asks. "Her boyfriend's your dad!" Jessica brings her hands to her mouth and holds them there for a second. "No," she whispers.

"I know," I say, nodding my head. "Yep."

"Oh no!"

"Yeah, the guy she talks about all time and won't shut up about is my dad. *That's* why he finally asked my mom for a divorce. He wants to marry this annoying woman. And, oh my gosh, I left out the worst part," I say.

"How could it be worse than that?"

"Well, it's not worse but it's a kicker," I say. "She got her new desk assignment."

Jessica's face is all sympathy.

"Exactly. She sits directly across from me, so I'll get to hear her all day long."

"Oh my goodness, Allie. How did you find out? How? I mean, did you just piece it together?"

"We had a work happy hour and she invited him and that's when I saw him. Actually, I heard him before I saw him."

"You saw him? What did he say?"

"I didn't talk to him. I went to the bathroom 'cause I couldn't speak. I was shocked."

"He didn't try to talk to you?" she asks.

"No, not really."

"Are you sure he saw you? Knew it was you?"

"He saw me," I say. "He watched me drive away. And really, it would've been horrible to talk to him. I haven't seen him or even spoken to him in probably more than two years,"

"Yeah, but he could've said something. Oh, Allie. I'm sorry," she says. "How's that gonna be at work?"

"I don't know. It should be okay. I'm gonna ask to switch desks with another girl so at least I don't have to be right there by her. My soon to be stepmom," I say.

"Oh wow! That's true," she says. "But what about the band? Have you heard back from them?"

I haven't even told her about the band. "Well, I wanted to talk to you about that too." I tell her that they offered me the job.

Her jaw drops. "What? And you didn't tell me?"

"I'm sorry. There was so much going on this week. I figured I'd fill you in today."

"Well, congratulations." It sounds like more of a question than a statement. That may be because of my lack of enthusiasm.

"Thanks. I'm sorry I didn't tell you sooner." I should've left her a message

"It's okay. I'm excited for you. You don't seem very excited, though."

"I don't know. As much as I like Joshua…"

"Joshua?" She perks up.

"Yeah, the guitar player?"

She cocks her head to the side. "Did you skip part of the story? I think you left that part out."

"Oh, it's nothing. I've talked to him on the phone a couple of times." I shrug it off.

"Yeah? He's just calling to talk to you about music and songs and the business, or what?" She's teasing me.

"No." What's the point in talking about Joshua? We get along, and maybe we'll stay friends, but probably not. It's not realistic. "We talk about everything and we get along well. I mean, he's an awesome guy. But, whatever. As much as I'd like to just leave everything and go…" I shake my head. "I can't."

"Why not, Allie?"

I've thought about this a lot. "It's a few things, I guess. Mostly, everything going on with my mom," I say, "I just don't see how I can leave her. I'm all she's got."

"Have you told him?"

"I have to let him know tomorrow. I'm gonna have to tell him I can't do it."

Jessica's thinking about what to say. "Allie, you're my best friend." She sighs. "I love you and I want the best for you."

"Thanks, Jess. I know you do." I wonder what she thinks of me. Does she think I'm weak?

"I just want to give you something to think about. The band, whatever. It doesn't matter. You're not gonna do it? That's fine. Whatever. But…"

Does she want me to leave my mom? Would she leave her mom? "Well, I can't just leave her. She's sick, Jessica. I have to take care of her," I say. "It wouldn't be right for me to leave her."

"I'm not saying you should leave her, Allie. I'm not. I understand why you can't. But what about your life?" She looks directly at me. "I mean…" she searches for the right words. I think I know what she wants to say.

I picture my mom sitting in her chair, staring at the television hour after hour. How does she get through the day? How does she manage at work? Does she ever smile? How does she treat her co-workers? "I get what you're saying, Jessica," I say.

"Well that's good because I'm not sure I know what I'm trying to say," she says.

I smile.

"No, I get it. She could do better. She's made her choices and I need to make mine."

Jessica's slow to respond. "Yeah, it's that. But it's more than that, Allie. I understand. You had a bad experience and that's soured you on your dreams. You turned your back and," she says looking up from her empty bowl and looking at me, "that professor was wrong. He was a teacher. He should've been helping you, but he didn't. He was an asshole. Some teachers are assholes, Allie. And the worst thing is that he crushed something you loved and you're great at. What he did was horrible."

I wince at her exaggeration.

"No, really, Allie," she says. "You know why?" I don't respond. "Because he silenced you. You have a gift and instead of bringing it out like a teacher's supposed to, he smothered it. He robbed you, yes. But he robbed me too. He robbed every one who needs to hear your voice." She's dead serious.

"Jessica, I'm not that good."

She takes my hand and makes me look at her. "Allie, you are. And you know what? I know this all sounds a little dramatic, and maybe because it's the teacher in me, but you can do it." She lets go of my hand and sits back in her chair and says, "Maybe not with the band or anything like that, but don't give up."

I've thought about this over and over for hours. Nothing changes the past. What's dead is dead. Can't be revived.

"Thanks, Jess. Really. Maybe something will change. I just don't know what. I was thinking, just on my way over here, about doing acoustic sets at coffee shops or restaurants. Something like that." It feels strange to say it out loud, even to Jessica.

"Really? That would be cool." She sips her coffee.

"Yeah, I've been practicing my guitar, of course, to play at the wedding. Excited about that. So that's helped a lot," I say looking at her. "I guess you're right. Little by little, maybe. I'll have to see how it goes."

"Well, sure."

I smile at her. "Thanks for talking to me about it, though. I appreciate it."

A guy picks up our empty dishes.

"You're welcome," she says. "I'm sorry the band thing isn't going to work out. I don't know why, I was excited about you going on tour."

"Yeah, not this time."

We talk about other things and I know Jessica's got a busy day ahead. "Well, I know you have to get back," I say. "Are you ready?"

"Yeah, I left my phone in the car. My mom's probably blowin' it up," she says. "How 'bout we meet next Saturday too. Same time, same station."

"Sure," I say. "That'd be great."

We walk out to the grey, misty morning. "Gosh, I wish it would just pour down rain," she says.

"I know. This is a mess."

Jessica opens her umbrella and we huddle under it. "Well, wish me luck with my mom today."

"Good luck."

"Thanks for being so awesome, Allie. Y'know, it's all gonna be okay."

"Yeah, I know."

"Let me know what happens. At work and with the band," she says.

"I will."

We hug under her umbrella.

"Great to see you," she says.

"You too."

I watch her walk down the street toward her car.

"Love you!" I call to her.

She turns toward me and waves, "Love you too!"

CHAPTER 35

Coffee with Jessica is the highlight of my weekend. The rest of the time I stay home, clean house, do laundry, re-pot plants, and mop floors.

Sunday afternoon, after bathing Chewy, I take Mom a bowl of chicken soup I made that turned out delicious. She's up and moving around. She looks good.

"Thank you, Mija," she says and hugs me.

"You're welcome, Mom."

She clears off two spots on her kitchen table and piles the mail into a stack and puts the other bags and stuff on the other end of the small table.

Even though we don't talk about our argument or about my dad and the divorce, things seem back to normal between us. I wonder if and when she'll want to talk about those things, but until she brings it up the subject is taboo.

So we talk about the weather. "It's been so hot," she says. "And it's already going to be October."

"I know," I say.

"Well, we live in Texas. What do we expect?" she says.

"That's true. Still. It would be nice to have it a little cooler. Although I don't like when it's cold."

"Me either. I can't stand the cold."

She asks about Chewy.

"She's good. Keeping me on my toes."

She leaves her spoon in the bowl after her last bite. "That was very good," she says.

"Thanks, Mom. I'm glad you liked it."

"I don't cook too much anymore. It's too much trouble just for me."

My mom was never much of a cook. She used to make us a lot of those boxed meals with noodles and powder, or boxed macaroni and cheese or canned food. Now she mostly eats frozen dinners and take-out.

"Will you have some ice cream?" she asks. My mom is dressed in an old pair of khaki pants and one of my old t-shirts. She's been going through closets and drawers for anything that reminds her of my dad and has piled it all on the living room sofa.

It may not be much, but it's a start.

"Sure, I'll have some ice cream, Mom."

She gets the ice cream, I get bowls, spoons, and the ice cream scoop.

"Oh, Mom. It's soft. Is your freezer working okay?"

"I don't know. I think it might be going out."

"Did it just start or has it been like that?"

"It's been like that. When it completely breaks, I'll get another one."

Why wait for that, Mom? You know it's not working. Either get someone to look at it and fix it or get another one now. You could get sick if you don't keep your food cold enough. That's what I want to say, but I keep all that to myself. "You might be able to get it fixed. Do you want me to see about getting someone to look at it for you?"

She crosses her arms and looks at the refrigerator, as if she's considering what to do. This is the kind of stuff I don't get about her. I want to say, "Mom, the damn thing's not working. You have two options. Pick one. It's not complicated, Mom. It's a freaking refrigerator. Why is this so difficult?" But it's been a nice visit so far so I keep my mouth shut.

"No, it's okay. I'll just wait."

I don't understand what she's waiting for or why she can't do the simplest thing to help herself. I don't get it, but it's not worth getting upset over either.

We sit and eat cookies and creamy ice cream. "I like it soft like this," she says.

"It's good," I say. I want to talk about her getting my dad's stuff together. I want to ask her if he's coming by for it or what she's doing with it. I want to tell her I saw him. "Are you donating all the stuff you've cleaned out?"

"I called him and told him he can come by tomorrow and pick it up if he wants it. If not I'll donate it."

She called him? Did she talk to him or did she leave a message? Did he tell her he saw me? "When did you call him? Did you talk to him?"

"I called him yesterday. Yes, I talked to him. He said he would try to come by." She looks at me over a spoonful of ice cream. "That's it."

What a jerk. He doesn't even mention that he saw his only living child for the first time in years. I don't expect anything from him. I don't. I'm disgusted with myself for feeling disappointed.

She seems better with the whole situation. "You're very nice to get his stuff together."

"He asked me to. I told him I would." She sounds resigned, but sad. She scrapes her bowl for the last bit of ice cream. "I found so many things that remind me of your brother." Tears come to her eyes.

It's been so long. Will she ever be able to remember him without crying?

I finish the last of my ice cream. "Yeah?"

"I found his fishing pole. He used it that day."

"Where was his fishing pole?"

"Stuffed in the back of the closet. Your dad must have put it there." She sniffs and wipes her nose with a napkin.

I want to say something to help her be okay, but I don't know what to say. It's a landmine. If I encourage her to talk about it, she may resent me for it. If I talk about Oscar and how terrible it is that he died so young, that may make it worse. It's hard for me to sit in that awkward silence, but I do.

Finally, she stands up and picks up our bowls and carries them to the sink.

"Well, Mom, I'm going to go. I have to get ready for the week." I stand and push my chair in. I feel like I need to acknowledge what she said. "I'm sorry you're going through all this, Mom. I know it's hard for you."

She turns to me and forces a smile. "It is." She crosses her arms and leans her hip against the kitchen counter. She looks at the floor, then at me. "I know I don't tell you enough, but thank you."

I smile. Even that little bit of emotion coming from my mom feels huge. "You're welcome, Mom."

When I get home, I decide to call Joshua to tell him what I've decided.

"Allison! So good to hear from you." I can hear the smile in his voice.

"Good to hear you, too," I say. "How are you?"

"I'm good. How 'bout you?"

"I'm fine." He sounds like such a happy person. And so nice.

"So tell me something good, Allison."

Oh shit. I'm such a jerk. "Something good? Chewy had a bath today and she's soft and fluffy."

He laughs. "That *is* good."

I have to just tell him. There's no way around it. "Yeah. But I didn't call to tell you that." I close my eyes and see him in his Iron Man t-shirt and jeans, the way he looked the first day I met him. I open my eyes and scratch Chewy who's sitting right beside me on the couch. "I called to tell you…" I squeeze my eyes shut, "I can't move to Dallas. I can't join your band."

"Okay?"

That's all he says. I wait for him to say something else, but he doesn't.

"I'm sorry."

"No, Allison. It's okay. You have to do what's right for you," he says and he sounds so understanding and soothing. Not at all like I expected.

"Well, I'm not sure it's what's right for me, but it's what I have to do." Does anyone ever do what's right for them? Don't most people do what they think they *need* to do?

"I understand. Is it some of the stuff you were telling me about the other day? Like with your mom?" And then, as if he regrets he said it, he says, "Never mind. That's none of my business. You don't need to explain yourself. I didn't mean to make it sound like that."

I want to tell him. I want to explain how I'd love to go. I'd love to work with him and sing and be part of his group and create music and get to know him better and learn from him but I feel obligated to be here and leaving my mom would be selfish and leaving my home and my life and my family feels irresponsible.

"No, it's okay. I want to tell you. First of all, I'm sorry for wasting your time. I feel bad about that."

"Not at all. Something good's come out of it. It wasn't a waste at all."

Is he talking about meeting me and getting to know me? I don't ask. "God, I feel like such a jerk. You're so nice! This would be so much easier for me if you weren't so nice about it." I'm teasing him, but it's also true.

I imagine he's smiling. "No. I wouldn't do that to you. I can hear the struggle in your voice. I know part of you wants to do it."

At least he understands my predicament. A little. "That's true. It's my mom. Of course, she's a big part of it. But, it's also…" *the uncertainty of the band and whether I'm good enough.*

"Allison, it's okay. You don't need to explain. I'm disappointed, I admit. But, I understand."

"Joshua, I loved singing with you. It was amazing and fun. I loved it. It was just… I don't even know how to say it. It was great. And I know it wouldn't always be that way, of course. I tried to imagine what it would be like every day and I imagine long days, late nights, and not all of it loads of fun, but making music…" I shouldn't have started down this path. Why did I? Tears well up in my eyes and I struggle to continue. "…I know for sure, now I know for sure, I need to sing. Even if it's just playing at a coffee shop or deli, or whatever. I know I need to sing. So, thank you for helping me see that." I feel stupid for getting emotional about this, but I'm glad I told him.

"See? There's nothing wasted. I'm happy that you've re-discovered that passion."

I smile and wipe my eyes. "Thank you."

"Allison, I'd like to keep in touch, if that's okay."

"Sure. I'd like that." *I'd love it if we could stay friends.*

"Me too."

When I hang up the phone I put my head in my hands and cry. Am I making excuses? Could I just go and see what happens? Would my mom be okay? At what point is it time for me to take care of *my* life and focus on *my* happiness?

This is my chance. He wants me. He saw something in me. That's no small thing. But it's not enough. Am I just stuck? How can I get mad at my mom for being stuck when I'm stuck too? Is that what's happening here? Am I going to wind up like my mom?

I cry harder. What a horrible thought.

CHAPTER 36

When I get to work Monday morning and walk into the building a sick feeling settles in me. My hands tingle as I walk toward Mr. Hernandez's office to ask about switching desks. I hear Maya talking and I cringe. *Oh my God! Shut up!*

He's at his desk and I knock on the panel wall.

"Hi Mr. Hernandez," I say.

"Oh hey, Allison. Good morning."

"Got a minute?"

"Sure! What's up?" He swivels his chair toward me.

I hesitate. "Is there any way we can talk in private?"

"Sure." He stands up and I follow him to an empty conference room. We sit at the table.

"Mr. Hernandez, I hate to be a pain, but is there any way I can move to a different desk?"

"A different desk? We can see what's available." He leans back in his chair with his hands behind his head. His pink dress shirt and pink tie look very stylish. "Sometimes there's not a lot available and there's another group coming out of training, besides the group you were with." He leans forward with his hands on the table. "Is everything okay?"

"Yes, it's fine."

He nods his head. "I think they're marked if they've been assigned. Let's walk out to the floor and see what's available."

"Oh, I don't want to be difficult."

"No, it's fine. Let's go see."

"It's okay. Never mind." I'm shaking my head.

"It's fine. Really," he says. "What's the problem?"

"It's kind of personal, but just between us."

"Of course," he says.

"Well, Maya, the lady who was assigned the desk right across from me."

"Maya. Yes. She's new to our team."

"Yes. Well I just found out on Friday that Maya's boyfriend. He's an older guy." I look at Mr. Hernandez who looks as though he's trying to keep up.

He raises her eyebrows and nods his head, "Okay?"

"That's my dad. My estranged dad," I say.

He's connecting the dots, I think. And then says, "Oh." He gives me a look of understanding.

"Yeah. And she's such a blabber mouth and so loud and broadcasts all her personal business," I say. He looks surprised. "I mean, I shouldn't know about her sexual habits. That's not workplace appropriate at all." I should stop talking, but he doesn't stop me so I keep talking. "I don't care what they do. I really don't. That's not the point. But honestly, no one else blabs their personal life to the whole office." He nods his head.

"You're right about that, Allison. I'll keep an eye on her. Would changing desks make things a little easier for you?"

"I don't know. I hope so. At least I won't have to hear her every minute of the day." Mr. Hernandez is willing to work with me yet again. "I don't know. It may be fine. She's on my team so I can deal with it. It's just that I was totally shocked when I found out Friday afternoon."

"Oh, I bet. That's understandable, Allison. But you're right about appropriate office behavior. That shouldn't be happening."

"She's just one of those people who has no filter. She just says whatever comes to her head. She's fine, just loud."

"Well, let's go see what's available. If there's not an empty seat, then maybe someone on the team will be willing to switch with you. As long as it's fine with them, it's fine with me." He stands up and walks toward the door.

We walk around the office looking for an empty desk, but every one is either already occupied or reserved.

"It looks like we're going to have to see if we can get someone to switch with you. It shouldn't be a big deal, but hang tight for now," he says.

Maybe I should just deal with it. On my way back to my desk, I pass by Natalie's new desk. "Hey Natalie? Are you on Mr. Hernandez's team?"

She looks up from her computer screen. "Hey Allison. How are you? No, not on Hernandez's team." She turns to me.

"Oh, fine. Just looking for a new desk."

"Yeah, I thought you might be," she says.

"What? Why? Wait a second..."

Natalie nods her head. "Yeah, cat's out of the bag. It's a small world, Allison. Too small sometimes."

Oh no. Are you kidding? She knows? Well of course she knows. With Maya's big mouth, everyone knows. I cringe. "How'd you hear?"

"She brought doughnuts this morning. They're on her desk and she invited her new team to come get a doughnut. When they do, she tells them all about it. Says she's going to be your new stepmom."

I shake my head in disgust.

"So, at least a dozen people in the office heard it from her. Everyone else heard it from them," she says.

I'm dumbfounded.

Natalie grimaces. "I'll be happy to trade desks with you if it's okay with my boss."

"I'll have to check. Thanks though."

I walk over to my desk and don't even look in Maya's direction. There's a white envelope on my keyboard. "Allison." My dad's handwriting.

I put the card in my purse. I may not even read it.

Mr. Hernandez must have talked to Maya because I don't hear her the rest of the day. I stay seated at my desk and try hard not to listen to anything she says or does. It seems the more I try, the more I hear her.

I see Michael in the break room at lunch. "That's kind of a strange situation," he says. "You just discovered you're working with your new stepmom."

"Kind of," I say, trying not to make a face.

"Well, you'll get through it. It's a stinker when work and home worlds collide like that, but," he shrugs, "everything happens for a reason."

Everything happens for a reason? Is that what he said? What kind of crap is that? There's no reason here. Reason means it makes sense. Reason means there's a natural progression of occurrences. No reason here. Just dumb freaking luck. Stupid Michael.

CHAPTER 37

When I get home, I change from my work clothes into shorts and a t-shirt. Chewy waits by her leash.

I open the card: *Allison, I would like to talk to you. Please call me so we can meet. Love, Dad* He includes his phone number.

I sit on the sofa and look at Chewy and out the back door. A large grackle bathes in my grandmother's bird bath. It's flapping its wings, splashing up water, but barely fitting in the small bowl.

I've always considered grackles ugly birds with their obnoxious cawing, bullying other birds, and crapping all over my car. Is it wrong to hate them, maybe not hate, hate's a strong word, dislike them because they're rude assholes? Does the grackle bathing in my grandmother's birdbath have any redeeming qualities? Are they all worthy of contempt? Are there any sweet grackles? God probably thinks so. And their mothers. He ducks his head in the water and flaps his wings, oblivious to my bitterness.

Chewy sighs and lies down on the floor by her leash.

"Yes, Chewy, we're going," I say.

I take my phone and headphones and call Jessica. Voicemail. I decide to text instead. "Hey Jess. Call me when you get a sec. Not urgent."

On our walk, Chewy takes her time and stops often. She sniffs at spots where there must be something very interesting. She's engrossed.

We're just to the end of the block when Jessica calls back. The wedding's coming up so fast and I imagine she's getting buried under all she has to do for school and the wedding, but she told me to call her and I need to talk this out.

"Hey Jess. Are you still at school?"

"Just leaving," she says. "I had a conference with a parent."

"Do you ever leave on time? Like right after school?" I ask.

"Of course!" she says, laughing. "Haven't in a while, I gotta say, but it happens sometimes."

I shake my head. I wonder if she'll still spend twelve hours a day at school when she's got her own kids. I don't know how she does it. Or why. She works at a school in a good neighborhood. Not rich, but not poor. If there's anything I've learned from her is that you can't tell by looking at someone what they're about. You'd never think by looking at them that some kids have serious issues, like no food at home, physical or emotional abuse, homelessness, drug use in the home, parents incarcerated. You name it. Jessica will do everything she can to help her students. I once told her, "Jessica, they're not your kids." And she said, "Oh, but they are."

"How're you? Everything okay?" she asks.

"I'm good. Pretty good. Chewy and I are walking."

"Hi Chews!"

We turn the corner. "She says hi." Jessica laughs. "Actually, I called to talk something out. I got a note from my dad. He wants me to call him to set up a time to meet."

"Oh wow. Are you going to call him?"

"I don't know," I say. "I think it may be good for me to sit down and talk to him, but really, what's he going to say? Is there anything he can say that'll make any of this any better?" I turn down a street off our regular route.

"Well, I know you're angry, but it might help to hear him out. I don't know," she says.

"I don't know if it's anger or disgust or what," I say. "Honestly, I can't help thinking about my mom and all he's put her through."

"Yeah. Both of you have had a lot to deal with. And now it's kind of spilling into your work life, right? How did it go with the girlfriend? Did you see her today?" she asks.

"I saw her, but I didn't talk to her. I'm sure she put my dad's card on my desk because it was there when I got to work this morning. On my keyboard."

"Oh, that sucks," she says.

"Yeah, but my boss said he'd help me find a new desk so I don't have to sit right by her. Soon, hopefully." Chewy and I are back on our regular route and head home.

"Well that's good," she says.

"Yeah, the bad news is she told everyone in the office she's gonna be my new stepmom."

"She didn't."

"Yes, she did."

"Oh Allie, I'm sorry."

I appreciate Jessica's sympathy. I'm not sure why, but it makes me feel better knowing at least *someone* feels my pain. "Thanks," I say. "It's not the end of the world. It'll blow over soon enough."

"You're probably right," she says. "Hang in there, Allie. Try not to let it stress you out."

"I won't. It's fine."

"And what did you decide about the band?"

"I turned it down. I called him yesterday. Told him I couldn't do it."

"You talked to the guy?"

"Yeah. Joshua."

"How'd that go?"

"I don't know. I felt like such a jerk."

"A jerk? Why? You're not a jerk. You're just not ready. That's all."

I can hear her blinker in the background. *Click. Click. Click.*

"He was great. Really understanding. And I guess I wish I could do it." I consider how I feel about my decision. "I wonder what I'm passing up, I guess."

"Allie, if it didn't feel like the right thing to do, then you made the right decision. Something else will come up."

"I guess."

"It will. I know it will. Don't let it get you down." It sounds like she's not driving anymore.

"I won't," I say even though it's already getting me down. I don't want to be someone who walks around with a dark cloud over her head, but it feels like I'm becoming that girl.

"Well, listen. I have to make a stop on my way home, but let me know how it goes and what you decide about your dad."

"Oh crap! Jessica, you're getting married in like ten days!"

"Twelve. I know. I'm ready to be married already." She laughs.

"I bet. Okay, well I'll let you go," I say.

"Also... I almost forgot to tell you... the rehearsal and rehearsal dinner's next Friday and I was going to mail invitations, but that's not gonna happen after all. Friday at six at Saint Joseph's, then dinner at my parents."

"Yay! Can't wait." Jessica's the one who has a lot going on. "And Jess, thank you so much for listening to my sob story. You're the best," I say.

"Of course," she says. "I'm glad you called to talk it out."

Just as I hang up with Jessica, a big, brown dog across the street lifts his head, sees us, and bolts toward Chewy and me.

"Chewy!" I scoop her up just as the dog gets closer, barking and baring his teeth.

I hold Chewy tight and stand very still.

He's from the crazy neighbors' house. Two boys shooting baskets in the driveway stop and call the dog, "King! King!"

One of the boys finally comes after him. "He won't bite," he says.

The dog stands his ground and barks, lunging slightly every few seconds. The boy takes him by the collar. "He's big, but he won't bite," the boy says. "King, how did you get out?" he asks the dog as he leads him to the backyard through a rickety gate at the side of the house.

The other boy continues to shoot the basketball and looks over at me like *"What? Get over it. He didn't bite you."* But he says nothing.

"Oh my goodness, Chewy! That was close," I say as I put her down. I'd heard the dog bark before but had never seen him until today.

My heart races and I feel shaky and unsteady until we get home.

CHAPTER 38

When I get home, I turn on the television and keep the volume low. Chewy sits by her bowl. I give her a scoop of kibble and fill her water bowl. The adrenalin from that dog charging at us finally starts to wear off.

I think about what Jessica said and wonder how I can get past my anger toward my dad. I think I want to hold on to it. If I let it go, I let him off the hook and I'm not ready to do that.

I sit on the sofa with my guitar. I strum and sing and think about him. Before the accident he was a good father to Oscar and me. He was my biggest fan, the one who encouraged me, signed me up for piano lessons, and always had time to listen to me play.

He taught my brother about cars and tools. Oscar followed my dad like a shadow. Oscar was just in kindergarten and he already knew the difference between a wrench and a pair of pliers, and a bolt and a screw. Things *I* didn't know.

My brother tried to teach me. "Allie, do you know the difference between a Phillips and a flathead?"

"No, Oscar. What's the difference between a Phillips and a flathead?"

"A flathead is flat. And a Phillips isn't. See?" He shoved the screwdriver tips close to my face and held them there until I looked at them.

"Oh. I see."

He smiled proudly. "Yep," he'd say as he put his tools back in his "toolbox" which was just my dad's old lunch bag.

My mom didn't want him learning about cars and tools. She said she wanted something better for him, but my dad always insisted. "He wants to learn," he'd tell my mom. "What am I supposed to do, tell him to go away?"

I try to remember when my dad changed. Of course, it was after Oscar died. His son was gone, but *I* was still there. How did he slip away until he disappeared?

That seems like a lifetime ago.

My dad. The man who buried a son he loved more than life, the man who ran from my mom, and ran from me.

He must not have understood how much I needed him or he wouldn't have left. He loved me. Didn't he?

Didn't *I* need a father? Didn't *I* need a family? Wasn't *I* good enough for my parents? I couldn't fix what happened. I still can't fix it. I can't fix anything.

I pick up a photo album that sits on my coffee table. On the outside, gold embossed letters "Family" and the photo on the cover is one of all of us at Oscar's last birthday. His overdone grin, narrow eyes, and chin pointed toward the camera behind his cake. I stand behind him, head lowered, looking at the cake or something else. My parents smile.

I turn the pages looking for pictures of my dad. I know I have a few.

There's one of the two of us. We're dancing. My grandmother's birthday party. I smile at the memory. I felt so small. He was so strong.

And a picture of Oscar and dad working on Chango's truck. Oscar must have been standing on a chair. He's looking under the hood holding a wrench and my dad's pointing at some part of the engine.

He was a good dad. And then he wasn't.

Looking at these pictures helps me remember, and remembering makes it all worse.

I wish I could say, "Screw you! You *and* mom! I don't need you! I'm a grown woman now. I don't care that you abandoned me. I don't care that you didn't love *me* enough to make an effort, to try even a *little* bit. You can't hurt me anymore. I grew up without you. See? You suck! You aren't the only one who lost someone that day."

I've never told them that. My mom or dad. I don't think I've even allowed myself to think that, to let myself be angry at them for forgetting about me when Oscar died. That's how I feel.

I realize I'm fighting back tears, overcome with sadness for all that we lost so long ago. For what *I* lost. My mom used to say, "Don't be so selfish."

Is it selfish to want someone to love you?

It's time to say what's on my heart. I need to unload this. I'm tired of carrying it. Will it ever be okay? Will I ever get over it?

When I finally get to bed, I lie awake desperate for rest. So many thoughts running through my head until at last I drift off to sleep.

I'm sitting at the kitchen table, in my school uniform, and a guy walks in and he's holding a baby. He says something to me and I look up and it's a guy that I know somehow is my brother, but he's grown. What are you doing? I ask him. I came to take the car, he says. And when I look up again, the baby's gone. Come on, he says. We have to go. I get my purse and my keys and go outside with him. I'll drive, he says. I hand him the keys and now I look like I'm dressed for work. And suddenly I'm on a merry go round, sitting on a stationary wooden horse on a carousel and I can't see my brother. I'm going round and round and I hear a deep, terrifying laugh, and I'm screaming, Oscar! Oscar! and the carousel goes faster and faster, and I'm crying and hysterical and I can't get off the carousel. I yell, Stop! Stop! and I start to panic. Suddenly, I'm in a car again, and the car's going very fast up a steep hill and it's so steep that it's going straight up to the sky. And then the car slows down and starts falling back, off the road. I feel weightless, suspended in the air.

I hear my own low cry as I wake up. My face is hot and I sob into my pillow. It feels good to let it out. I cry harder.

When the tears finally stop, I go to the bathroom and splash my face with water. I move in the dark rather than facing the stark light, and sit on the edge of the bathtub with my face in a towel.

I've had versions of the dream before, but tonight was different. Oscar's always a little boy, never grown. And tonight, he felt so close, like he was really there beside me.

I go back to my room and Chewy's standing by the bed.

"Come on, Chewy. It's okay."

I lie down and she snuggles at my feet.

CHAPTER 39

*B*efore leaving for work, I text my dad. *I'll be at City Coffee Shop on San Pedro 6:30 today if you want to talk.*

I'll be there even if I don't hear back from him. This is it. His only chance and it doesn't matter to me if he takes it or not.

When I get to my desk, I see that he's texted back. *Okay.*

"Whatever," I say to myself, even though I feel assured by his response. Assured of what? I don't know. Because I don't care. Let's see if he shows up.

I keep to myself at work. I don't feel like talking to anyone. I think about taking time off but decide to stick it out. Mr. Hernandez lets me know he's talked to Maya about practicing discretion. Right. And that for now, he'd like me to stay where I am. Fine.

At lunch, I need a break from the office and head east on the freeway. I figure I'll drive twenty minutes out and then back. I turn my music up—Aretha Franklin, Billie Holliday, Mary J. Blige, Beyonce, Shakira, Alicia Keys, Selena—driving along, singing, or just listening, grateful for the time away, grateful for the music.

I stay at my desk, without even getting up for a drink of water, and listen to music while I work on bids, contracts, and administrative reports. My mind wanders to good things, to thoughts that take me away from this desk. The wedding, Jessica, the talent show, the band, the audition, Joshua.

I get home and water my grandmother's roses and freshen the water in the birdbath in the backyard while Chewy explores.

"Okay, Chewy, let's go inside," I say and she sniffs around a little more until I call her from the door, "Chewy!"

She runs inside and drinks from her bowl, sniffs her food and sits under her leash.

"We'll walk when I get home, okay?"

I get to City Coffee Shop at six-fifteen and order an iced coffee. The shop is a bright and open design. Art deco? Urban? Not relaxing and comfortable like Petra's, much less intimate and homey. Not suitable for long hours of conversation. Perfect. There are only a few other people in the shop at this hour.

6:30. He's not here yet. No text either. I decide I'll give him fifteen minutes, like we used to do for our professors. After that, I'm out.

6:35. I half expected this and resign myself to being stood up by my own father.

6:37. He walks in and looks around.

My heart stops for a moment. It's him. I didn't look at him very well the other day, and now that I see him again, he looks old. He wears a long sleeve denim shirt tucked in to faded jeans. He's smaller than I remember, thinner. His hair is graying, but still mostly dark and still thick and wavy.

I wave, like I'm calling a waiter. He pops his head back in recognition.

I stand up to greet him, "Hi Dad."

"Hi Mija," and he reaches to hug me. Awkward hug. He doesn't seem to realize I'm pissed at him. Or maybe he doesn't care.

"Did you get something?" he asks and then sees my drink. "Okay, I guess I'll get water," he says as he stands and approaches the counter.

He returns, sipping from the straw, "Ahh. Thirsty." He looks at me. "You look good, Mija."

"Thanks." I look at him the way you look at someone when you're playing the staring game. No inkling of a smile.

Awkward silence.

"So what's up, Dad?"

"Well, thank you for calling me and for meeting me," he says and he's looking at his cup of water. "Uhh, well, I wanted to talk to you about a few things, and see how you're doing."

"I'm fine," I say straight-faced. "Working, but you know that, of course. Just, the usual stuff, work, home, mom. You know, the stuff you left me to deal with."

I don't want to be sarcastic and rude, but as much as I try to restrain myself, I pounce. Jab and dig.

"I don't blame you for being upset," he says.

"Don't blame me? Okay Dad, really, I'm fine. Say what you want to say. How are you gonna make this better? What can you possibly say to make any of this okay?"

He squirms a little in his chair and looks at his hands, as if he's thinking about what to say or how to start. He seems small and old, unsure of himself. I admit it. I'm glad he's uncomfortable.

"I want you to know," he says and I see that he's struggling, but I can't muster sympathy. I feel like a bully who keeps kicking when she's already beat down her victim. I look at him expressionless.

"After your brother died, it was very hard for your mom and me," he begins. "We tried to get through it but it was very hard. I blamed myself for what happened. And your mother blamed me. A day did not go by that she didn't remind me, somehow, that the accident was my fault," he says.

His deep voice used to comfort me. It still sounds familiar even though now he's more like a stranger.

"After your brother died…" he says.

"Oscar, Dad. His name was Oscar," I say. I want to scream right now.

"When Oscar died, your mother left me. Not physically. She was there, but she wasn't there. I missed him so much and I felt that it was my fault and," he sighs loudly and looks at me. "She always told me to leave, but I never would. And we had our troubles for a while, but I knew she needed me. And then one day, I was tired of feeling bad and sad. So I did what she asked me to do and I left. And every once in a while I'd come back and try it again, try to make her love me again, see if she'd forgive me, but she never did."

I saw all this from the outside, with the focus on my mom going through the motions of living. Going to work, coming home, closing her door. She shut herself off and sank further and further into her pit of grief. I thought it would get better. Time heals all wounds. Except this one.

I know it was hard. It must have been awful for him, but what about me? I needed at least one of them. "You both acted like Oscar was your only child." I've played this conversation over and over in my head, and now that I have a chance to say it, it sounds weak and I hate it. I sound like a selfish brat, but it's the truth. "Grandma was the only one who remembered *I* was still alive."

My grandmother adored Oscar and his death devastated her too. For months, she was as depressed as anyone, but my grandmother understood that life goes on. You have to keep moving forward instead of getting stuck wishing things were different. You have to love the people right in front of you, too.

I continue, "It's not fair that you left me when you left mom. Like you forgot you had a daughter."

"I'm sorry I left you too. There's no excuse for that. I should've made sure you were okay. I'm sorry," he says.

Silence.

"Where were you all those years you'd come and go? Were you here? In the same city with not even the decency to let me know you were here this whole time?" I ask. Somehow knowing he was in town maybe just miles away makes me furious.

He holds onto his cup of water and looks past me. "Most of the time, I was here and I'd stay with friends, but sometimes I worked around Austin, or near Corpus. That's it."

I want to get to the bottom of this and be done with him. "So you finally want to settle down and that's why you filed for divorce?" I ask.

"Pretty much. I figure it's time to move on," he says.

I snicker at the remark. It sets me off. "That's pathetic. *She's* pathetic. And now you're together? It's seriously fucked up. Not that I think you planned it or anything. You couldn't have, but your girlfriend talks a lot. A *lot*. About your personal life and about you. Talking about your sex life and how often you take 'medicine' and all kinds of crap. And now she's told everyone at work that she's going to be my stepmom?" I shake my head. "I don't understand your attraction to her at all, even though that's not my business. I don't fucking care. But seriously! Can't you do something about her blabbing your business to anyone and everyone?"

"I didn't know she was doing that. To her, nothing's a secret. She's different that way. I'll talk to her," he says. His hands are on the table and they tremble a little.

Stop being so mean. Look at him. He's trembling! Ugh. Stupid. "Actually Dad, I think it's about time you filed for divorce. It's been a long time since you were together. I know mom can be hard to live with, but I didn't know she asked you to leave and the other stuff."

He says, "Other stuff?"

"I mean, I knew she blamed you because I heard her say it a million times. I thought it was just general anger towards you. She's struggling."

He nods. "I'm probably not helping, either," he says.

"No, you're not. But the divorce is long overdue. I think so, at least. But that's not my business."

I pause. I've thought about this for years and wonder what it would do to know, how it might help, and I figure this is my chance to ask. "I have a question and you don't have to answer if you don't want."

He nods. "Sure."

"Mom blamed you and you said you felt that it was your fault. But why? It was an accident. How was it your fault?"

My father sips his water. "Yes, it was an accident, but it could have been prevented had I done some things different."

"Like what?"

"That day Chango, my friend, you remember Chango?"

"Yeah, your best friend you grew up with. Oscar was with him in the truck that day."

"Yes, well, Chango wanted to go fishing at the pond we always went to, and Oscar wanted to go. Please, please, he said. You know how he used to do that?"

I nod.

"Your mom didn't want to let him go, but he finally wore her down. He was so excited to be with us and be out there fishing." He smiles. "It was a beautiful day, kinda cool in the shade and breezy. Perfect day. Oscar said he was hungry and I kept telling him we'd be leaving soon and we'd eat on the way back into town. We had just had breakfast so I didn't think he could be hungry. But he kept on. I was catching fish and he wasn't catching nothin' so he got bored. He kept bugging me to take him to the store. I kept telling him no.

"Finally, Chango said 'Let me take him.' And before I could say yes or no, Oscar was in the truck. I said, 'Well, I guess he's going.' Chango said 'We'll be right back' so they went.

"A little while had passed and I was still there fishing. Then I thought they should have gotten back already. And I waited and waited. But Chango, he always took a long time for everything, so he must've been distracted by something. That's what I thought. Then I heard sirens and I thought, 'Oh no' and in the back of my mind I wondered if something happened to them. Of course, I didn't have a cell phone or any way to get a hold of 'em.

"By this time I had packed the fish and was ready to go, just waiting, and I hear more sirens, and then I knew something had happened. I ran out to the road and tried to get someone to stop to take me to the store. There was only one store near the pond and someone finally stopped for me. I must've looked desperate because I was waving my arms, almost jumping in the road. I needed to get to my boy.

"And when we got close, there were police cars and fire trucks, flashing lights and in the middle of all that, I saw the grill of Chango's truck. I ran toward it," he says.

"I see the truck. Smashed and twisted metal. I see the gravel truck on its side in the middle of the road. Dust everywhere. Gravel spilled all over the road. I start screaming 'My boy's in there! My boy's in there!' and the cops held me back.

"Finally, they let me see him. They pulled back the sheet. And there he was. Cuts on his face, but he looked the same, like he was sleeping. What started off to be such a great day, turned out to be the worst day of my life," my father says.

This is the first time I've ever heard this story. "Why didn't you ever tell me this before?"

"I always wanted to, but your mom didn't want me to tell anyone. Every time I tried to talk to her about what happened that day, she'd get so angry. I didn't want to make it worse. If that's possible. She never wanted to talk about it. I always wondered what Oscar was doing when they got hit. Were they laughing? Was he happy? You know, right at the moment it happened," he says.

Why would he think about that?

"All these years later, I still think about that day and how it could have been different."

"It was an accident. That wasn't your fault," I say.

"I shouldn't have let him go. I should've made him wait. We had just eaten. Something told me to not let him go, but I let him go anyway. I should've stopped him. I was responsible for him. I should've made him stay with me. It *was* my fault."

For years after the accident, at various times, especially, Oscar's birthday, the day he died (June first), Christmas, and Independence Day (Oscar's favorite time of year), my mom would start her rant of blame toward my father. What he should've done differently, how life would be different had he done what he was supposed to do, how her son would still be here had he just taken care of Oscar like he said he would.

My father continues. "For years after that, I didn't deserve anything good. My son was dead. I should suffer for that. For a long time. It wasn't until I met Maya that I felt hope again. She helped me see that I can't go back. I messed up. I wish he was still alive. I wish it hadn't happened, but it did. It took me a long time, but I finally understood that."

I think of taking his hand, patting his arm, some kind of gesture to comfort him, but I don't move.

We sit in uncomfortable silence.

"So you look good," he says finally. "You look just like your mother."

I don't want to chit chat. He doesn't know me. I don't want to give him even the smallest opening.

"She used to keep her hair long like that. It was beautiful. How is she?"

"She's okay. Not really, but she'll adjust. She says she's fine."

"That's good. She deserves to be happy too."

I express neither agreement nor disagreement.

"Are you still singing?" he asks.

What would make him ask that after not knowing anything else about me? "A little."

"Yeah? That's great. You were always so good. I loved hearing you sing. It made you so happy."

He missed all my high school performances. Didn't make a single one. "Yeah," I say.

We walk out together and he walks me to my car.

"Thanks for calling me," he says. "I wasn't sure you would."

I hold on to my anger. Stubbornly.

"You know, the accident wasn't your fault. But leaving me? That was all you."

He looks at the ground. "I know. I shouldn't have left," he says, looking at me.

"No, you shouldn't have. I needed you. But I wasn't good enough to stick around for? You figured, well, since Oscar's gone, you're done? What a chickenshit thing to do, don't you think? You weren't done. And now, you're back and what do you want? Why are we having this conversation?" I ask him. And as I often do when I'm frustrated and angry, I start crying.

He stutters. "I...I wanted to explain what happened. And why I left."

I wipe my tears with the inside of my shirt. "Well, you've done that."

"Yes, I have. I understand if you don't want to talk to me."

I smirk. So clueless. But the anger. I can't hang on to it. I have to let it go. I feel as if I'm forcing myself to loosen my grip on the anger I've held on to all these years.

"You know. I'm not a little kid anymore. I'm a grown woman. I've made it without you. I'm angry. I am. I needed you and you didn't love me enough to even try." I raise my voice. "For all these years *that* hurts more than anything. But I'm not going to let you hurt me anymore. You had your reasons for doing what you did. You figured it was okay to leave me. And you didn't think it was a big deal. That's fine. I don't need you anymore."

"I'm sorry," he says.

"I know."

CHAPTER 40

*A*s much as I dreaded seeing my dad, he offered me something today. I can't put my finger on exactly why, but I feel better. It's about my brother. I finally know what happened that day. It's been fourteen years since Oscar died and I'd never heard the whole story and how one thing done differently would have changed the outcome. One thing done differently and I'd have a brother. Flesh and blood. But Oscar wanted a snack.

"Oh, Oscar." I say out loud. "You have no idea…"

My dad lost his son and his best friend that day. Chango was a true and loyal friend. They grew up together in the same neighborhood. How horrible it must have been for my dad when he raced to the store looking for them and saw the crushed cab in the midst of police cars and fire trucks.

Poor Oscar. He was just a kid excited to be out there with the guys. We lost him that day, and that's huge, but we lost our family too. My mom pushed everyone away. She hoarded her grief and made it hers alone.

How could she ever recover by keeping it to herself? She couldn't. She can't.

I don't know why, but I want to see my mom. I feel like I understand her in a way that I didn't before, and maybe now I can help pull her out of her grief.

I go into the store, pick out a quart of chocolate chocolate chip ice cream, pay at the counter and I'm back in my car in a few minutes.

I dial my mom's number. She answers.

"Hi mom. How are you?"

"Fine. I'm fine," she says.

"I'm on my way home. Can I stop by?"

"No, it's okay. Not today."

"Why not, Mom? I have ice cream for us."

"I don't want ice cream. I'm fine. It's late. Are you just getting home from work?"

"No, I had something to do after work today."

"Oh, I see," she says.

"You okay? What's wrong?"

"Yes, I'm fine." She sighs. "Nothing's wrong."

What can I say to her? I imagine her sitting on her chair in her pajamas watching her show. Is that it? Am I disturbing her?

"What are you doing, Mom?"

"I'm watching my show. Or I was. Watching my show." Now she sounds irritated.

Why is she like this? *Okay mom, I get it. I'm bothering you. I wouldn't want you to miss your crappy show.*

"Okay, I'll let you get back to it."

We hang up. I was hoping I could talk to her about my brother, to tell her how I felt when he died. The truth is, I'm not sure what I would say to her, but it makes me wonder if I'll ever be able to get past the wall she's built around herself.

When I get home, I put the ice cream in the freezer and text Jessica: Hey Jess. Update: I met w my dad and it was ok. Ttys.

I plop on the sofa and turn on the television. Chewy sits by her leash, ready to walk.

"Oh, Chewy. Not tonight."

She comes over to the sofa and jumps up and looks at my face. I scratch her ears and say, "I know. It's been a long day for you."

She wags her tail.

"Okay, we'll both sleep better if we go." I turn off the television. "Come on. Let's go."

I force myself off the sofa, make sure I have my phone and my headlamp. It's dark now. I'm always extra-cautious walking in the dark.

"C'mon Chewy, we're not going far."

I try to remember a time when my parents were happy, at least a time they looked happy through my child eyes. They always seemed a little mismatched. My dad was such an easy-going guy. Nothing bothered him. If Oscar or I got in trouble at school, which we both did occasionally, we always opted to tell dad. He was a pushover and, most of the time, he wouldn't tell mom.

She always made a big deal about the smallest mistake, making it seem like we were the worst kids ever, like she wanted us to be perfect. I always thought she was harder on me than she was on Oscar.

My phone rings and it's Jessica.

"You already met him?" she asks. She sounds groggy, like she's half-asleep.

"Yeah. It was short, but it went well."

"I'm glad it went well, Allie."

"Yeah, I feel some resolution. And I asked him to talk to his stupid-ass girlfriend about having a little discretion," I say. "He said he would. We'll see."

I don't want to get into everything with her, partly because I feel worn out and partly because I'm just not ready to tell her about it yet. Besides, she sounds exhausted.

"Are you okay? You sound wiped out."

"Oh, yeah. I'm fine. Stomach bug's going around at school."

She doesn't sound like herself at all. "Maybe you should go to the med clinic, Jess. You can't afford to be sick right now. And you're *never* sick." There's always something going around at her school.

"I know, but I'm fine. If I'm not better tomorrow I'll go. I promise."

"Are you sure? Cause I can take you. I'm not doing anything."

Finally I hear a smile in her voice. "I'm positive. I'll be fine. I came home right after school and got in bed." She never does that.

"Wow, you *must* be sick. Well go back to sleep. Sorry I woke you."

"Actually, I needed to tell you something." She seems to be thinking about it, then remembers. "Umm, David and I are planning a night out on Saturday. Not sure where yet, but just to get everyone together before the wedding. If you can make it."

"Sounds great. I'll be there. Text me the details." I want to get her off the phone so she can get some rest. "Okay, Jess. Go back to sleep. Take it easy this week."

"Yeah, I will."

The night sky is dark and clear. The moment Chewy and I turn around to head home, a flash of light followed by a glowing, green streak bursts in the sky. *Whoa! Was that a shooting star?* What should I wish for? So many possibilities. I wish for what I always wish for even though I don't believe wishing on a shooting star will make a difference.

CHAPTER 41

*J*ust as I'm getting home and hanging up Chewy's leash, my phone rings. It's Joshua.

"Hey, Joshua. How are you?"

"Hi Allison. So glad you're answering your phone tonight."

That's funny. I almost always answer my phone unless I'm at work. Not very many people call me.

"Yep, your lucky day," I say, smiling. "How are you?"

I go to my bedroom to put on my nightshirt and pajama shorts. I slip off my work shoes and slide my slippers on.

"I'm good. Just wanted to call and check on you."

"Me? I'm fine." Why would he need to check on me?

"Well, the other night you seemed a little upset and I just want to make sure you're okay."

Oh right. How could I forget? When I told him I couldn't take the job and started crying out of nowhere. "Thank you for checking on me. I appreciate it. I'm fine. Yeah, it's been a little hectic, but I'm fine. Getting ready for my friend's wedding. And you? Have you started looking for another singer?"

"I guess that means you haven't changed your mind, huh?" He laughs. "No, I'm kidding. Kind of."

I smile. "No. Nothing's changed on this end."

"Thought I'd ask," he says. "No, we haven't yet. Not really. We'll start back up this weekend. We have a few leads."

"That's good." I wish I could've jumped at the chance to work with real musicians who've already done a lot of the work to share their music with the world. There's no looking back, I guess. I'll just have to ease into it as best I can.

"And when do you start touring?"

"It was going to be February, but we had to push back on some of the dates and find another band to fill in for us."

"You can do that?"

"We can. We don't like to because we don't want to burn our bridges. We aren't on contract, so it was just a matter of finding a good replacement. But not too good, if you know what I mean."

I see my guitar in the corner. "Yes, I do," I say. "Well, I can't go on tour with ya'll, but I have been practicing my guitar."

"Yeah? Let's play something."

"Can we do that? Over the phone?"

"Sure, why not? There are apps for that, but let's keep it simple and just play."

"Okay. I'll give it a shot. Go easy on me," I say.

And he starts playing a riff and I try to follow along. He sings and I recognize it, the song I sang at my audition. "I don't remember the words," I say when he stops.

"Can I email 'em to you?" he says.

I give him my email address and in a few minutes, I get the lyrics and read over them.

"Okay, got 'em," I say. "I'll try to keep up with you. I need to go slow." He said he was a patient guy. He's going to need to be.

"You got it," he says.

"Can we do face to face instead of just voice? Skype, FaceTime, hangouts?" I ask him. Even though this isn't the most ideal situation for playing together, it's better than nothing. And seeing would be better than just hearing him.

"Video? You can do that?" he asks. "I have no need for it," he says with a smile in his voice.

"Oh, right," I say because I knew that, but the idea didn't fully connect to my brain. "Okay, never mind."

"You can practice blind today. See how you do," he says.

"Not very well, so far, but I'm doing my best," I say.

I play the song and he listens, "Yep. That's it," he says. I play tentatively and he encourages me along and I fumble on a few of the chords, looking closely at the image on my phone and I stop to scroll.

The set up is awkward and frustrating. "I need to write down the chords so I can see them," I say getting up for a paper and pen. It's almost ten o'clock. Darn it. I have to go to work tomorrow. "Okay, I'm writing the chords," I say. "Oh, it's only five. Why did it seem like more?" I say out loud.

"Yep, it's only five," he says.

"Hmm. It sounds like more," I say.

I play them again and again, strumming easily and humming as I play. "Okay, I think I got it," I say. "How do you want to do this?"

He starts playing and I imagine his hands moving nimbly on his instrument, sliding along the neck and picking strings, the guitar sitting on his lap the way he played that day in Waco. The music comes so easily for him, flows from him like it's from the center of his soul, like juice from fruit, the good stuff.

"Well, let's just play," he says. He taps his guitar so it sounds like a drum, "On four. One, two, three, four," and I follow along. He keeps it simple for me and when we get through it once, he says, "Again. From the top."

We play it three times through and by the end of it, I feel more comfortable with it.

"You good?" he asks.

"Yep, I think I got it."

"Yeah you got it," he says in his simple, reassuring way. "Okay, let's go to regular tempo so it'll be a little more like this," and he plays it again, slightly faster and I play along with him and I'm surprised that I can keep up.

He stops. "Do you remember the words?"

"No, I don't, but I have them here."

"Okay, girl, let me have it," he says and he taps his guitar again—one, two, three, four, and we begin.

I strum as I had been and he plays something else that sounds like a bass or some other sound filling in the music, and the sound of my own guitar along with the small distant but still beautiful sound coming from him, somehow strengthens my voice, so I'm not afraid or hesitant and I sing out. Maybe because he's not with me in person or maybe it's because I know he likes my voice and that makes it easy for me to sing unafraid, putting myself out there, just going at it and if I mess up, it's okay. The music takes me and I sing out this song about a girl who screwed up, who had a man she loved and then messed around on him and now she's alone. And I tap into my well of regret, the pain of loss.

And the song ends with Joshua playing a few chords of magic and a final strum.

"Wow, that felt good," I say.

He laughs. "Yeah, it was!" he says. "Really good."

"What a great song, Joshua," I say and I wish I could see him. "Powerful."

"Oh my goodness, Allison. I'm going to be honest with you right now," he says.

Please don't make it weird. I tend to keep my guard up when I don't know a person very well. I tend to hold back. But today, I didn't. With Joshua, I don't.

"Okay?"

"Allison, you breathed life into this song."

"Well, thank you." He's ignoring my imperfections. That's a good thing.

"No, Allison. You make it come alive. I mean it. I've played this song a hundred times and it's never been that to me. Never. I'm not kidding. I have goosebumps, and tears in my eyes."

There's an urgency in his voice that's a little scary. I admit, something comes over me with him. I don't know what it is. I feel strong, different, appreciated, brave. How can that happen with a song? What would it be like to live like that? To have something that takes you beyond the regular into the supernatural, into superhero status, like Wonder Woman, having superhuman powers, but I'm still just me? It's confusing and intense. And it wouldn't even matter what people think because it's not from them. It's from me. My soul. Something in my soul that's wanting to get out after being pushed down so long.

Joshua's praise feels good. It's empowering. I feel unstoppable, until that little voice inside me says, "Yeah, but for every person who likes it, there'll be a thousand who say it's nothing special." No amount of praise can shut her up.

"Thank you. That means a lot to me," I say. "It really does."

"No, Allison. I don't think you're getting what I'm telling you."

I finger the chords on my guitar and strum lightly, then stop. "No, I hear you and I'm serious. I appreciate it. A lot. I'm happy that you like my voice. Really," I say looking at the phone, raising my voice.

"Allison," he says and pauses.

"I'm here." My fingers are sore. I lean my guitar against the sofa and pat on my lap to call Chewy.

"You know that song? This little light of mine, I'm gonna let it shine," and he sings a few bars.

"Sure I know it. It's a Sunday school song about Jesus. Jesus is the light, I'm gonna let Him shine," I sing, as I scratch Chewy behind her ears.

"Okay, then not that one," he says.

I laugh.

"What I mean is," he says, winding up to make his point, "your voice is your light. And you didn't create that yourself. That's a gift, Allison. You can choose to let it shine or not."

He sounds like Jessica.

"Are you there?" he asks.

"Yes, I'm here," I say. "I get what you're saying."

"Okay, you're with me, so just hang on 'cause I'm not done."

"Alright." Joshua, the philosopher.

"Music is your gift, the expression of which is needed in this world. The way you take my music and put it out there," he says and I imagine him throwing his hands up in the air, "I hear something in you that pulls out that essence, that anguish, that pain people feel and puts it out there and says, 'Yep, there it is. And you're not alone!'" he says excitedly. "That's it. That's the message," he says almost to himself.

"Are you still talking to me?" I ask, even though I'm pretty sure that last part wasn't for me.

"I was circling the landing strip and wasn't sure it'd come to me, but it did. Okay, so, *yes*, that's it right there. People need to know they're not alone. People need to know that. Yes. Love is hard. Life sucks sometimes. And it's ugly and people can be hateful and rude, but look at all the amazing beauty that surrounds us. Your voice, oh my God, Allison, your voice! It does that."

I can't speak. I think of my mom. Stone-faced, unmoving. I'll never reach her.

"Can I tell you something?" I say.

"Of course."

"First of all, thank you," I say and I hear him say 'You're welcome.' "I'm very flattered that you like my voice but I gotta tell you, I know a lot of people won't." The tears start to come and I hate when I'm trying to say something and I'm crying because I sound like a baby and I hate that. My throat hurts and I could just stop, but I don't. "I've never thought of it that way," I say. "Sorry, I sound like a baby."

"It's okay. You don't sound like a baby at all."

I smile.

Just then I get a text from Audrey. It's eleven-thirty. I'd normally be in bed by now. "You up?" her text says.

"Yes," I text back.

I continue my thought, "I had a bad experience in school with a teacher who made it his mission to keep me from pursuing a vocal performance degree, mostly because I can't read music. I mean I can read it, but I can't seem to develop that skill, for some reason. Anyway, since then, I've felt completely inadequate, musically. He was successful, that's for sure. He wanted to put me out and he did."

Joshua is slow to respond, "I'm sorry that happened. Sometimes people think they're doing good when they aren't. That's people."

"I agree," I say. "I suppose I let him get the best of me. He put out my light, I guess you could say."

"He mighta tried, but he didn't put it out. No Allison. He doesn't decide. A little fan to the flame, a little fuel to the fire. That's all you need."

"Well, thank you for adding fuel to my tiny little glow."

"Allison, you can make it a raging fire!"

I laugh hard, but I'm still crying. And now my head hurts. He laughs too.

"You know what?" he asks.

"What?"

"I believe you'll figure it out. You're going to find a way."

"Thanks, Joshua." We've been on the phone a long time. The phone display reads: 'Joshua 2:25:20'

Just then my phone buzzes with another text from Audrey: Call me.

"K," I text back.

"You're welcome, Allison. I loved jamming with you tonight. Let's do it again sometime."

"Definitely."

When we finally hang up, I'm spent, but I call Audrey back. No answer.

"Come on Chewy. We have to get to bed. It's late." I slide the door open for her to go out to the backyard, but she hesitates. "Go Chewy. I'll be back in a minute," I say and she steps out into the dark.

As I wash my face and brush my teeth, I think I hear a knock at the door. I listen again and check the time. It's after midnight.

I rinse my mouth and go to the front room. Loud knocking. "Who is it?" I call.

"Allie, it's me. Audrey."

I open the door and Audrey's standing there. Something's happened.

CHAPTER 42

"Audrey, what are you doing? What's wrong?" I say, opening the door wide and standing back to let her in.

She steps inside and faces me. Her hair's pushed behind her ears, red eyes, red face, no makeup, gym shorts and a t-shirt, tennis shoes.

She doesn't seem to be able to speak. She's been crying.

I face her and hold her at arm's distance to get her to look at me, but she's looking at the floor. "Audrey, what's going on?"

Chewy barks twice. *Oh Chewy!* I rush to open the back door to let her in, then stand in front of Audrey again, waiting for her to tell me what the hell's going on.

"Audrey, what…?" I give her a minute to collect her thoughts. Something must have happened with Jessica and the wedding. Something bad. It has to be. Is it David? Did something happen to him? Did he call it off? Oh no. Jessica. She'll be devastated.

Audrey's still looking at the floor. I stoop a little to try and see her face.

Finally, she says without looking at me, "Allie, something's happened to Jessica."

I freeze. "What?"

She doesn't look at me.

"Audrey." I ask slowly and deliberately, "What happened?" Oh no. She wasn't feeling well. Did she drive herself to the hospital? Was she in an accident? "Audrey, where's Jessica?" I feel my heart thump.

Audrey seems to wake up, like she'd been in a daze, but now she's suddenly conscious and aware that she's at my house to tell me something important. She says quietly, "Allie…Jessica wasn't feeling well."

"Yeah. I just talked to her. I woke her up, she caught a bug at school." I stand with my arms crossed, fighting the urge to scream, *"Tell me!"*

Audrey brings her hands to her face and shakes her head, then takes a deep breath and holds my arms. Her voice is weak and shaky. She finally looks at me. "Her parents had been out. When they got home my aunt went to check on her. She couldn't wake her up." Tears fill Audrey's eyes. "They called an ambulance, but it was too late." She shakes her head and sobs, "She was already gone."

What did she say? No. This isn't possible. I just talked to her. Audrey's looking at the ground again. She whispers, "I'm so sorry, Allie."

I hear myself scream and turn away from her and run down the hall toward my room, crying and screaming saying something but I don't know what. Finally, I sink to the ground and bury my face in my hands.

I have to call her. I have to tell her this awful story. It's unbelievable. She won't believe it.

Jessica. How can she be gone? This isn't supposed to happen. I remember the conversation we had just a few hours ago. Why didn't I take her to the hospital? Did I tell her I love her? Why didn't I say it?

After a while, Audrey sits beside me in the dark hallway.

Finally I say, "How Audrey?" My head throbs. "How could this have happened?"

"I don't know."

We sit without speaking.

Audrey's phone pings with a new message. It casts a blue light in the darkness and she holds it with both hands to respond.

"I just talked to her a few hours ago," I say.

"Me too."

I don't understand. "What could have happened to her?" I say.

"I don't know. No one knows."

This doesn't seem possible. "How are her parents? And David?"

"Devastated. Everyone's in shock."

Slowly, my senses return and I can stand. I get a box of tissue from the bathroom and blow my nose. We sit on the living room sofa and stare. Audrey says, "I'm sorry to be the one to tell you. I wanted to make sure you found out in person."

"No. Please. I appreciate it." I don't know what I would have done if I would have heard some other way.

"I'm gonna go, Allie," Audrey says as she stands up to leave. "I'll be going over there in the morning. You're welcome to come with me if you want."

When Oscar died, there was a steady stream of people at our house for days. People, most of whom I didn't know, came to offer condolences. It was a somber, miserable time. Is it easier with people around? Does it just give people something to do? I don't know, but I know I want to be there.

"Thank you," I say and I hug her. I can't stop my tears enough to speak. Finally, I choke out the words, "I'll be there in the morning."

It's early Wednesday morning. Ten days before Jessica's wedding.

CHAPTER 43

Cars line both sides of the street at Jessica's parents' house. I'm not completely confident that I should be here. Maybe it's a time for family. If I feel like I'm in the way, I'll leave.

The sun shines and a gentle breeze blows as I walk down the street toward the house and to the front door. People huddle in the front family room. Although the mood is somber, an occasional laugh echoes above the murmur of voices.

The last time I was here was to meet for our trip to Louisiana for our bachelorette getaway weekend.

Jessica's brother, Chris, comes over when he sees me, "Hey, Allison. It's good to see you," he says, hugging me.

"Hi Chris." He and Jessica were close. He always looked out for her.

"Yeah, I didn't expect to see you 'til *next* weekend," he says and coughs a bit.

"I know. Me either." It's heartbreaking to see him like this. "How are you?" I ask him. He looks worn out. Tired and lost.

"Yeah," he says. "I'm good. I'm in shock, of course. I just can't believe something like this could happen. It's unbelievable," he says struggling for words. "Y' know?" he says looking up.

"I know." Chris and Candace's baby is due in a few months. It's hard to move on without someone you love. He's going to miss Jessica for the rest of his life. "You were a good brother, Chris," I say, patting his arm. "She loved you." I choke the words out between fighting back tears. His family will never be the same without her. All these years later I still think about my brother all the time. In my mind, he's still a kid even though I imagine and wonder what he'd be like now. Will Chris wonder about Jessica the same way? I will. I'll think about her on her birthday, how much she loved summer and the beach. Will Petra's ever be the same for me knowing it was the last place I saw her alive? My mind flashes to the moment she walked away from me that day, "It's all going to be okay." Her face bright and happy.

Chris covers his face with his hand, pushing thumb and forefinger into his eyes. And he takes a moment and sighs loudly. "Thanks Allison," he says. "I'm sorry. Come in," he says motioning me further into the room.

"I think my parents are in the kitchen."

"Thanks, Chris."

I don't know what to do or what to say.

Audrey motions me over to the kitchen.

"I brought sweet bread." I hold up two white paper bags filled with Mexican pastry. "I didn't think to bring a platter for it," I say.

"It's okay. I'll get you a plate. Do you want something to drink?" she asks.

"Maybe in a minute," I say. My stomach growls, but how can I eat at a time like this?

"My aunt and uncle are in the back room if you want to go see them," Audrey says.

Mr. and Mrs. Reyes sit forward on the sofa, talking with another couple I don't recognize. *Oh my God. What do I say?* Mrs. Reyes stands when she sees me. "Allison," she says as she reaches out to me.

"I'm so sorry," I say. I try not to cry, but I can't help it. I squeeze my eyes shut and try to tell her with that embrace that Jessica adored her, that she has to be strong, that nothing will be the same without Jessica, but her family needs her. As hard as it will be for her to go on, she has to.

She hugs me and says, "She loved you so much."

I pull away and dab my eyes. "I loved her too. Very much." How can I cry on *her* shoulder?

She says to Mr. Reyes, "Honey, you remember Jessica's friend, Allison?"

I haven't seen Mr. Reyes since Jessica's engagement party. He's been on a diet to lose weight for the wedding and he looks very different from the last time I saw him. "Of course I do," he tells his wife. "Hi Allison," he says, extending his hand.

"Hello Mr. Reyes."

"Thank you for being here. You're a good friend to my daughter." His eyes are swollen and red.

His words touch my heart. I can only hope I was. Is it normal to ask if I could've done more? Called her more? Not been so needy? Do anything different? I don't know.

"Mrs. Reyes, if there's anything you need, you have my number. Please don't hesitate," I say.

"Thank you, Allison."

I go back to the kitchen. Audrey is in the process of putting casseroles, bread, and all the other food they've received on a folding table they've set up in the family room. Mrs. Luna, Audrey's mom, comes into the kitchen and says, "I'm going to make some coffee."

"Hi Mrs. Luna," I say and hug her.

"Hello, Allison. Isn't this just the worst? Poor Jessica. And she would have been the most beautiful bride," she says.

"Mom. Stop saying that," Audrey says. "You're making it worse by saying it over and over."

I've only met Audrey's mom a few times, but I have to think she doesn't mean to sound insensitive. "Can I help you make coffee?" I offer.

"Well, I'm looking for coffee, but I don't see it," Mrs. Luna says, opening cabinet doors.

"Mom, we'll do it," Audrey tells her mom. Mrs. Luna doesn't seem to hear her and continues hunting for the coffee. Finally, Audrey takes her hand and turns her in the direction of the living room. "Mom, people are coming. Please go greet them," she says. "Ask Aunt Diane if she needs anything. Or better yet, take them some water," Audrey says, handing her two bottles of water.

I find the coffee in the cabinet above the coffee pot. Jessica's favorite flavor, Breakfast Blend. I hear her voice, "*Yum,*" and know I won't ever hear her voice again. I wish I could stop these morbid thoughts, but they keep coming. Especially here, in this house, everything reminds me of her. Who she was and what she did. Everything reminds me of what I've lost. Of who I've lost.

Audrey sets bottles of water and paper plates on the counter.

There's a loud, wailing cry in the other room. Audrey says, "I think that's David."

"Oh my God, Audrey," I say.

"I know," she says.

Many people come and go, some I know, some I don't. I stay in the kitchen to help get out the doughnuts, drinks, and breakfast tacos that keep coming. Having something to do helps keep me from collapsing on the ground in a heap.

I want to go to her room and visit with her. I want to see the latest wedding trinkets and hear the latest details. I want to go upstairs to her room, to sit on her bed and keep her company while she finishes getting ready to come downstairs. I want to hear her laugh and see her smile, to hold her one more time.

When we've finished setting out all the food, I ask Audrey, "Can we go to her room? I don't know why, I feel like I want to…I don't know. To be in her space." I can't think of another way to say it.

"Yeah. Let's go."

Audrey leads and I follow her into Jessica's room. She turns on the lamp on the nightstand by the bed. I know there's no reason to whisper or tiptoe, but somehow everything seems fragile, as if I'll break something or disrupt the silence. This is her room, where she grew up. The room she came back to for just a few months before the wedding. She didn't mind coming back. "It's not for long," she'd said. This is her room. It smells like her, like her body spray. Sweet and fresh. Her bed, the comforter tossed, but not tucked, and neat. Dresser with mirror. Closet. Clothes piled on a chair beside the window.

"Audrey," someone calls from downstairs. We both look in the dresser mirror.

"I'll be back," she says.

"Should I go with you?" *Maybe I shouldn't stay.*

"No. Stay. I'll be right back." She closes the door behind her and I'm alone in Jessica's room. I sit on the edge of her chair, on top of the slacks she may have worn to school then tossed here before crawling into bed. I look at her bed across the room. Is that where she was when I talked to her that night? Why didn't she go to the doctor? They would have known it was more than a stomach bug. Why didn't I tell her? Why didn't I help her?

I turn to her dresser. Her makeup bag, dusted with face powder. A necklace, pictures, one of her and David, one of all of us at her bachelorette party. Her brush and comb. Hair dryer. Her water bottle. A package of anti nausea medicine because she thought she had a stomach bug. *Jess.* And then I notice her mini-veil, the one she wore that weekend, on the edge of the mirror.

She was so happy, all smiles, looking beautiful and healthy, ready to be a wife and mom, and always the best friend, always loving and amazing. Always believing in me.

The reality knocks me to the ground in sobs. She's gone. I'll never see her again. *Oh Jess! I'm so sorry. Jessica.* There are no words. I see her under the umbrella on that last misty morning waving at me, "Love you!" My friend is gone.

I want to stay in her room. I want her to walk in, smiling and calling my name, "Allie!" I want her back. I want her back. The tears will not stop. I hear her voice, "It's all going to be okay." But it's not, Jess.

I feel Audrey kneel beside me. She rubs my back.

I squeeze my eyes shut. My face is wet with tears and my head pounds. I lift my head. "Oh, Audrey, this is unbelievable."

"I know." She hands me a tissue.

Audrey and I sit in silence on the floor in Jessica's room. I don't want to talk. Thoughts of Jessica come to my mind, and normally I'd want to say, "Remember the time she …", but I keep them to myself.

Audrey finally starts to stand. "I have to go downstairs."

My legs are stiff and I slowly shift myself to stand.

"No. Stay. Take your time. You're fine," she says.

I want just a few more minutes. "I'll just be another minute."

"Of course. No hurry." Audrey shuts the door behind her.

I stand up and walk over to the nightstand and turn off the lamp. I sit on the edge of the bed and whisper, "Jess," and then I can't speak. I sniff and cry. "I can't believe you're gone. I'm sorry. I..." I want to say something profound, something to let her know how sad I am and how much I'm going to miss her. I want her to know how much I think this sucks. I want her to know how amazing she was and I'm so thankful I had her in my life. I want her to know my life will never be the same without her. Never. I want to tell her I've lost something huge and I feel lost and more alone than I've ever felt before. I whisper, "Thank you for being my friend Jess. I'm going to miss you so much. Don't forget me, Jessica. I won't ever forget you."

I dry my tears with a damp tissue and take a few deep breaths until the tears finally stop.

CHAPTER 44

When I get home, even though I don't want to do anything except sit and think about Jessica, I leash Chewy for a walk.

Her face seems to say, "You okay?"

Chewy's one of those dogs who must be part human. I don't believe in reincarnation or anything like that. I'm still mostly Catholic even though I don't go to mass anymore. But Chewy makes me wonder.

The neighborhood's quiet. Our walk is short.

I get home and sit on the sofa and strum my guitar. I sing Schubert's Ave Maria, the song Jessica asked me to sing at her wedding. I was to be accompanied by a magnificent pipe organ at the cathedral.

As I play, I imagine Jessica in her wedding gown, at the altar with David, smiling at each other through communion. The prelude would have begun and Jessica would have stood up, maneuvering her gown with Audrey's help because I would have been singing, and Jessica would have placed a bouquet of roses at the base of the statue of Mary, then turned and smiled at me.

I play out the scene in my mind again, as I've done hundreds of times while preparing to sing, "Holy Mary, Mother of God, pray for us sinners, now and at the hour of our death." *In hora mortis nostrae.*

At the hour of our death. The words choke me. She was alone. How could someone so loved die alone like she did? Was she afraid? Did she know?

I go to the bathroom and wash my face, "Ugh," I grunt into the towel. "Get it together," I tell myself.

I missed work today and don't know how much time I have and it doesn't matter.

I email my HR rep and let her know I'll be out the rest of the week and give her my cell number and hope it won't be a problem. I'm not going to work right now. That's it. Dock my pay. Whatever.

I think about my mom. She probably hasn't heard the news yet. How would she have heard? She doesn't talk to any one. I should call her. I don't know the best way to say it or how she'll handle the news, but I know she needs to know.

"Mom, I have to tell you something that happened. It's very sad." I don't want to just blurt it out.

"Something sad? What happened?"

I can hear the television in the background and I wish she would turn it off. "Mom, it's Jessica."

"Your friend, Jessica?"

"Yes, my friend Jessica."

"The Jessica getting married?" She sounds distracted, like she's only half-listening.

"Yes, mom. Jessica." I scratch Chewy's ears. "Mom, last night, she wasn't feeling well and she went to bed early and when her parents got home, they couldn't wake her up."

"Couldn't wake her up? What happened to her?"

"They don't know. They called an ambulance, but they couldn't bring her back. She died last night sometime around nine o'clock."

"Oh my God," she says. "Well, how did she die?"

"They don't know for sure. They said it could have been a heart defect or some sort of disorder she didn't even know about. Possibly a reaction to some medicine she took. I don't think they know for sure."

"How could they not know?"

Mom, I didn't press them for the details. "I don't know, Mom. They have to wait for the results of the autopsy."

"How old was she?" she asks.

She knows Jessica and I are the same age. At least she *should* know that.

"Same as me, Mom," I say. "Twenty-eight."

"Well, that's sad. Your brother died when he was only ten. He didn't even have a chance to grow up."

Maybe I half expected my mom to say something callous and uncaring that would make Jessica's death about her, but part of me hoped she would be a normal person, for once, and show some empathy for someone else's tragedy. *Here's your chance, Mom. You can call Mrs. Reyes and offer condolences. It would mean a lot coming from you. Reach out to her and help yourself, Mom.*

But I don't say any of that. Why bother? She doesn't get it. Not even a little bit. "That's true, Mom." I'm disgusted with myself for agreeing with her. "Mom, I gotta go. I have more phone calls to make."

"Okay," she says. "Well, tell her parents I know what it's like to lose a child. Send my condolences."

"Okay, Mom. I'll talk to you later."

Chewy and I step outside to the backyard. It's dark now.

Tell her parents I know what it's like to lose a child. Screw you, Mom. I hope they don't handle it like you have. That they remember they still have a family who needs them. That Mrs. Reyes doesn't blame her husband and drive him away from his family. I hope they'll pay attention to their kids who have to go on living without their sister. I hope they remember their kids, the ones standing right in front of them who still need them.

God, my mom sucks. She couldn't even ask me how I'm doing. Would it have been so hard for her to acknowledge *my* loss? Doesn't she care? How could she not care about me enough to ask how I'm handling it? To ask if I'm okay?

Have I given her too much credit all these years? Do I not know her at all? Is she so freaking selfish that she can't express a little sympathy? Not even to me?

The only person I could talk to without holding back is Jessica. I wouldn't have to explain anything. I could just talk and let it out and rant until I was done.

I sit and cry. *I have no one.* No one. Just me. And Chewy.

My phone rings. It's Joshua. I dry my tears and try to sound normal.

"Hey," he says. "What's goin' on?"

"Hey, Joshua." My voice is nasally, like I have a cold. Not normal at all.

"I was sitting here lining up some auditions this weekend. You came to mind, so I thought I'd call and see how you're doin'."

"It's good to hear your voice." I pull a tissue from my pocket and wipe my nose. "I'm okay. Not great, actually."

"No?"

"No. Something terrible's happened."

"What happened?"

I tell him about Jessica. He remembers her and reminds me that he met her in Waco.

"Oh, my goodness. I am so sorry to hear that, Allison."

"Thank you," I say. "After we got off the phone the other night, Audrey, the other girl you met, that's Jessica's cousin, Audrey was knocking on my door."

I tell him about Jessica and about our long friendship. About her plans for life and babies. How she would have been moving away soon because of David's job. How I already feel lost without her.

"She was the one who pushed me, or I guess she would say, *encouraged* me, to do the talent show at the resort." I laugh even though my tears keep coming. "She encouraged me to go to Waco and audition with you. She was totally down for all of it."

"That's beautiful," he says.

And when he says that, it strikes me how simple and true that is. And I realize what I lost when Jessica died. Her belief that I had something special, her crazy and sometimes annoying persistence for me to not give up, to keep going and find a way to keep singing. Jessica's never-ending faith in me was absolute and perfect beauty. That's as good as it gets. She gave me that and I took it for granted. I pushed her away. I dismissed her encouragement as bias, shrugged off her inspired assistance as nothing special. How ungrateful I was. If only I had a chance to tell her that I get it. I finally get it.

I choke up.

"I'm so sorry, Allison. It sounds like she was a dear friend."

"Yeah, she was. A very dear friend," I say, fighting back tears.

CHAPTER 45

I would have thought that grief makes a person want to sleep more, but it's been just the opposite for me.

Last night, after I got off the phone with Joshua, I stayed up for hours looking through old pictures. Old, old pictures. Printed and in albums and shoe boxes and plastic storage containers. Pictures with names and dates written in my grandmother's handwriting on the back, pictures of my mom and my grandparents, and so many relatives I don't remember or never knew.

I found several of Jess and me from elementary school. At the science fair, the school festival. At her house playing with water balloons, at our eighth-grade dance, at our first day of high school.

Looking at them made me grateful for our past even though we'll have no future.

This morning, I wake up before my six o'clock alarm and lie in bed wishing there was something I could do. At the same time, I can't think of anything I want to do.

I think about work and figure I need to tell Mr. Hernandez I'll be out the rest of the week. He's been good to me. He probably doesn't care to know the specifics, but I want him to know I have a good reason for being out.

I force myself up and email him to let him know I'll be back to work around the middle of next week, then Chewy and I go for a walk. It's a cloudy, dreary day.

When I get home, I wash the dishes in the sink, feed Chewy, and put on a pot of coffee.

Audrey calls. "Hey Allie. How are you?"

"I'm okay. How are you?"

"Fine."

What do you say? It feels like there's not much to say.

"Allie, I have something for you."

For me?

"It's from Jessica."

"Oh."

"Can I bring it by?"

"Yeah. I'm here."

I feel exhausted and wired at the same time. I wonder if there's something I can give Mr. and Mrs. Reyes. Maybe a copy of the pictures I found? They probably have a ton of pictures of her. Maybe just a card, or a letter?

Nothing sounds like enough.

I hear Audrey pull up and open the door for her.

She hugs me and walks in and sits on the sofa.

"Do you want some coffee?" I ask.

"Sounds great. Thanks."

She's looking at her phone when I get back to the living room. She looks worn out.

"Audrey, is there anything I can help you with? Anything you need done that I can do?"

She puts her phone in her purse. "I don't think so. I'm not doing much, just delivering these." She pulls a few pale-yellow envelopes from her purse, looks at the names on them, then hands me one. "Aunt Diane found cards addressed to her bridesmaids. She was probably going to give them to us at the rehearsal dinner."

I take the card with my name on it written in Jessica's handwriting.

"Also, Aunt Diane wanted me to ask you if you would be willing to sing at the funeral mass. Do you think you'd be up to it?"

I would love to sing for Jessica. "Sure. I'd like that."

"Are you sure? It's okay if you say no, Allie. She didn't want to put you on the spot, but she wanted to give you a chance to do it if you want."

I could say no. Maybe I should say no. What if I breakdown in front of everyone?

"Just one song?"

"I think so. She said you can pick the song, but she'd like it as a special, kind of, reflection song. Something like that?" Audrey sits forward on the sofa with her elbows on her knees.

"That's fine. I'd like to do it." I don't think I'd be able to be a cantor and lead the congregation through the whole mass. I haven't done that in years and it would be too much for me to think about, but I can do one song.

"I'll let her know." Audrey grabs her purse and puts it on her lap. "She'll probably be calling you. But even if she doesn't, plan on it, okay?"

"Yeah. How are they?"

Audrey raises her eyebrows. "I don't know. They seem okay, but I don't think they've eaten much. Or slept much. Chris is trying to make sure they eat."

"Hopefully they'll be better once everything settles down a little."

"Yeah. They're making arrangements with the church and the funeral home. I know that's been difficult for them."

"Of course. Audrey, did they say what happened to her?"

She sighs and looks off into the distance.

"I don't know exactly, but they said it was something with her heart. I don't think it was a heart attack exactly, but you know how she felt sick to her stomach that day?"

"Yeah." I nod.

"They said she was probably born with this problem with her heart. But the worst thing, Allie? The worst thing is that if she would have gone to the doctor that night, they probably would have discovered it in time."

It's almost unbelievable. I know it sounds cliche when people say, "She's never been sick a day in her life," when something like this happens, but it was true in Jessica's case. If there were something we could look at and say, *"That was a clue that something was wrong,"* it might be easier to understand, but, aside from her stomach ache that day, there were no signs. Nothing. "Oh my God. Unbelievable. But she had no way of knowing that. I mean, who goes to the hospital for a stomach ache?" I say.

"That's true." Audrey sits on the sofa and stares as if her mind has drifted somewhere else.

"And how are you holding up?" Her eyes are puffy and red. "Are you eating and sleeping?"

She smiles at me. "Not much, to be honest. I'm putting together a video of her."

"Do you need pictures? I found a few from school."

"My aunt had tons. I'm good. It's nearly done." She sighs.

"I'm sure it'll be great." I pat her arm. "But who's making sure you eat and sleep?"

"I know." She wipes tears from her eyes and pulls a tissue from the box on the coffee table. "It's weird. I have no appetite."

I give Audrey a minute. No lectures, but it wouldn't be good for her to get sick. "So you said her parents are making arrangements?"

"Oh sorry." She rolls her eyes. "I forgot to tell you. The rosary will be Monday at St. Teresa's and the funeral mass will be Tuesday. I'm not sure exactly what times."

Hearing the details about Jessica's funeral service brings tears to my eyes and I feel the worst kind of sadness I have ever felt. "Oh my God, Audrey. This is terrible."

"I know."

When Audrey leaves, I go out back with Chewy to read Jessica's card. It's a handmade-paper creation, with the word "Friend" on the front, painted in light pastels, with sticks, flowers, and vines forming the letters. Vintage looking and classic Jessica. Her writing starts at the top left in very small, block letters.

. . .

To my dearest friend, Allie,

I've written and re-written this letter a dozen times and finally decided that I just have to say what's on my heart, so here goes.

First of all, thank you for being the best friend I could have ever hoped for. We've seen each other through the very worst tragedies and the absolute best triumphs. Through grade school and mean girls, and crushes and heartbreak, and family drama, and career struggles. Thank you for never leaving my side, no matter what.

Second, even though I hope to have a houseful of kids soon, I hope you know, I'll still need you to help me show them that friends are to be treasured, that friends help us see the beauty in everyday things, like laughter and kindness.

Third, you're a special person, made for wonderful things. Believe in yourself. However you decide to do it, spread your wings and fly, Allie. You're meant to shine bright. Shine on! And no matter what, I'll be right there with you, kids in tow.

Finally, may I say, you've been an awesome Maid of Honor. Thanks for making my wedding events (all of them) so special. You're the best!

*L*ove you always and forever,
  Jess

I close the card and hold it in my hand. *Friend.* I smile even through tears.

Despite the grief, my heart is full of gratitude. Grateful to Jessica for giving me something to hold on to, something I can hear her voice in, over and over whenever I need to.

Jessica died way before her time, way before she was ready to go. She had her whole life ahead of her and, in that way, her passing is tragic, heartbreaking, and beyond my understanding. But she lived her short life well. She was happy. She helped people. She connected with people. She loved people. She loved life. Is that what makes a good life?

I think about my mom and wonder how long she'll live. Twenty more years? Thirty? It's possible. Has she lived a good life? If she were to die tomorrow, would she be able to say she lived a life worth living?

And then I have to look in the mirror. How can I talk about my mom when I haven't asked myself the same question? Have I lived a life worth living? "Spread your wings and fly," Jessica says.

Oh, Jess. I'm working on it. It's scary, though. You know me. I always think the worst. What if I fall on my face? What if I get hurt? What if, what if, what if…

I look out at my grandmother's backyard and I imagine her walking across the lawn with the garden hose to fill the bird bath and water her roses. What would she say about Jessica? *Que lastima.* How sad. She'd understand that I have to go through my tunnel of grief, but if I stay too long, she'd remind me that I still have a life to be lived. The world keeps turning, no matter what.

CHAPTER 46

*L*ater in the day, I get a text from my dad asking if everything's okay. Weird.

Me: My best friend Jessica passed away. It was sudden and unexpected. It's been rough, but I'm ok.

Him: I'm sorry to hear that. I'm glad to hear you're okay.

Maya probably told him I haven't been to work and maybe he thinks it's because of him. I don't know. Is he really concerned about me? After all these years of nothing?

Mrs. Reyes calls to thank me for agreeing to sing at Jessica's funeral mass.

"I'm honored to do it," I tell her.

The Catholic tradition I've always experienced is an evening rosary and a funeral mass the next morning. The rosary is usually pretty relaxed. After the recitation of the rosary, the service often becomes a kind of "Open Mic" where people can say a few words about the deceased. Sometimes, friends and relatives get up to the podium to share a remembrance about the deceased and start choking back tears, struggling to get through their story. It's understandable, of course. It's painful to lose a loved one, whether they're ten, twenty-eight or eighty-two.

A SONG FOR JESSICA

One of the saddest moments I've experienced at a rosary was at my grandmother's friend, Luz's rosary. Luz celebrated life. She loved to dance and used to go to community dances, by herself if she had to. She'd meet people and make friends. She loved mariachi music. She would stand up and sing with mariachis with passion and fervor. Luz means "light" in Spanish and I always thought she lived up to her name. At her funeral, after people had said what an amazing lady she was in a dozen different ways, her family played a recording of her singing a song with a guitar accompaniment. She sang in Spanish and I didn't know Luz very well, but hearing her voice got to me. I sat beside my grandmother and was moved to tears, amazed how Luz's song touched me.

I can't imagine how Jessica's funeral is going to be. She was young and healthy. She had a large family and knew a lot of people. There's no way to prepare yourself for something like this, but I have to do my best to keep it together while I sing.

I think I should tell my mom about the services and see if she'll come with me. She pissed me off the other day, but I feel like I should give her one last try. Maybe she'll want to go if I pick her up and she can sit with me. She *should* go. Jessica was my best friend for years. There's no excuse for not making an effort here. And it would be great to have someone there with me.

I wait for her to answer and think to myself, *This is it, Mom. Make the right choice.*

After covering our initial niceties, I tell her why I'm calling.

"Mom, Jessica's rosary will be on Monday and funeral mass on Tuesday. Both at St. Teresa's. Do you want to go if I pick you up and you can sit with me? If not to the rosary, at least to the mass?"

"I don't know," she says in a ho-hum voice. "It's probably going to be crowded, right?"

I want to say, *Do you want to go or not? What the hell's the difference if it's going to be crowded?*

"It'll probably be very crowded, I'm sure, but it's okay. I can pick you up and you can sit with me. I'd like it if you'd come with me."

"But you'll probably stay a long time. I don't want to be there all night." She sounds annoyed.

"I won't be there all night, Mom. But if you don't want to go, that's fine."

"She's going to have so many people there. She doesn't need me."

I think about this. How should I feel about my mother not wanting to go to my best friend's funeral? Why can't she see that I need her right now? I shouldn't have to beg her.

"You're right. They don't need you, but I do. Forget it, Mom. It's okay. I thought I'd make it easy for you to do the right thing, but you still… still!…can't think of anybody but yourself." I raise my voice and my hands tremble.

"What do you mean?" She sounds shocked. "You're the one who's always thinking of yourself. No, I don't want to go. Give Mrs. Reyes my condolences."

Give them to her yourself, Mom. For once, get out of your own shit and do something for someone else. Are you afraid you're going to miss your show? Or will you have to get dressed? Can't wear your pajamas? Is that the problem? What the hell is wrong with you?

I hang up without responding. What did I expect? Seriously. Why do I keep setting myself up like this?

That night, I have a dream.

I'm with my grandmother and her friends at a wedding or some sort of party. Mexican music is playing, a polka, and they're dancing and laughing. And my grandmother's asking me to come out and dance and I keep saying no. And there's a young mariachi singer wearing one of those big mariachi hats. He's playing a guitar and his voice is powerful and beautiful. He's singing to me and I feel true love for this guy. He's like a magnet. I'm so drawn to him. All of a sudden he scoops me up, like he's going to carry me over a threshold. He's strong and I feel light and safe in his arms. He puts me down and I start running. I'm running fast and I start breathing hard and tears come to my eyes and I keep running. I'm terrified. I feel as if something's chasing me, like I can't stop or whatever it is will catch me. Finally, I come to a room and it's quiet and peaceful and I feel like I've made it to where I'm supposed to be, to the place where I belong. And there's a woman there, sitting at a table by an open window. She looks familiar, but I'm not sure exactly who she is. She looks at me, smiles and says, "Allie, you're finally here."

I wake up in a panic. *That seemed so real.*

So strange. Why was I running? Who was chasing me? Something that scared the hell out of me. But what about the mariachi singer? He was amazing. And who was that woman by the window?

I don't know what any of it means, but I fall back asleep and feel as if I don't move the rest of the night.

In the morning, Chewy and I go for a walk and the wild neighbors are out. Saturday morning, washing cars in the front yard, kids playing ball in the street.

When I get home, I look around my grandmother's house, my house, and go to the backyard with Chewy. I call Joshua. I hear a hint of concern in his voice.

"How are you doin', Allison?"

"I'm okay. Taking it day by day. I've had my moments."

"Understandable. Sometimes you gotta let it out."

"Yeah. I let it out all right." Squirrels chatter and chase each other in the yard.

I tell him about Jessica's services and that I'll be singing at her funeral mass.

"That'll be a nice tribute to her, especially since she always encouraged your singing."

"True. I hope I don't lose it right in the middle of the song." I've started to doubt whether I can pull it off. I'm not sure I trust myself to do it without breaking down.

"Would you like a guitar accompaniment?" Joshua asks.

"I think they'll have someone playing piano. I thought about playing my guitar, and I probably could. But I'll probably just play it safe and go with the piano."

"What are you singing?"

"*Amazing Grace.*"

"Yeah. That song always makes me cry."

He makes me smile. This isn't a dream. "I know. Something about it."

"So, I'll ask you again. Would you like some accompaniment? I can take my guitar down there and play while you sing. For moral support. If you'd like."

I can't ask him to do that. He'd have to make the trip and he didn't even know Jessica. Only met her once. "Oh, thank you so much for offering, but I can't ask you to do that."

He pauses, as if considering what to say. "You didn't ask, Allison. I'm offering. And it's fine. I'd be happy to be there with you."

His offer overwhelms me and I get a lump in my throat from fighting back tears. If he's with me, I won't have to worry about anything else but singing for Jessica. I'd love for him to be here. Should I take him up on it? "Thank you, Joshua. It's very sweet of you to offer." My mom can't be bothered, but he's offering to travel hundreds of miles to play one song with me. How could I say no? "If you're sure."

"Absolutely."

CHAPTER 47

I pick Joshua up from the bus station Sunday afternoon. I had worried that it would be awkward to have him stay with me, but he's so easy-going it's not a problem at all. We rehearse, walk Chewy, talk a lot, and sing a lot. I tell him about my grandmother and about Jessica.

I ask him if he'd like to come to the rosary with me.

"If it's okay that I go, yes, I'd like to go with you," he says.

Jessica's rosary is way-sadder than I imagined it could be. So many people were there. Most of them were in tears, crying their eyes out for this beautiful, young woman, who had her whole life ahead of her, and who was just days away from walking down the aisle in her wedding gown.

*T*he service is a beautiful tribute to her, but she would have disliked a few things about it. She would have loved a few things, too.

. . .

Things Jessica would have disliked:
    Not saying the full rosary
Seeing her parents, brothers, and David inconsolable
Not enough seats for everyone

Things Jessica would have loved:
    Having her students sing a song she taught them—"I can do my best", complete with hand gestures
    Audrey's photo memorial
    The music selections—"Be Not Afraid", "On Eagles Wings", and "How Great Thou Art"
    The sermon—"Faith, hope, and love…and the greatest of these is love"
    Having her cousins, aunts and uncles all together

Joshua and I get to St. Teresa's an hour before the funeral mass is scheduled to start. Audrey's in the church foyer setting up a photo collage of Jessica and the sign-in book.
Beside the collage, on an easel is Jessica's bridal portrait which perfectly depicts her personality. It was windy the day of her photo shoot at a local art museum. The photographer tried to convince her to move indoors where conditions would be easier to control, but she insisted it would be fine. She was right. Her portrait captures the exact moment the wind caught her veil and sent it floating behind her like a cape. Jessica's face is pure joy.

"Oh, Audrey. She looks so beautiful. I can't get over it."

"Hey Allie. Doesn't she?" She glances at me, and then she sees Joshua. "Hi. Joshua?"

"Joshua, it's Audrey. Jessica's cousin. You met her at the audition in Waco," I say.

"Hi Audrey," he says as he extends his hand. "My condolences to you and your family."

She shakes his hand. "Thank you. I'm so sorry I didn't make it over to see you last night. Every time I headed that way, I got sidetracked."

"It's alright. I'm glad I get to see you now," Joshua says.

Joshua was with me at the rosary last night, but after the service, he opted to stay in place while I walked around to see Jessica's family and old classmates I hadn't seen in years.

Audrey continues, "And thank you so much for coming all this way to play. It's very good of you to do this."

"You're welcome. I'm happy to do it." He opens his walking cane. "Well, if you'll excuse me, I'll give you all a minute. Allison, I'll wait right over here." He walks toward the main area of the church with his guitar in one hand and his walking cane in the other. I've learned in the short time he's been here that he's independent and self-sufficient.

"Thank you," I say.

Audrey clutches my hand and we look at Jessica's portrait. "She was so happy," I say.

"Yeah, she was," Audrey says as she dabs her eyes with a tissue. "I'm going to miss her so much."

"Me too."

After a few minutes, Audrey turns to me and says, "I'm glad Joshua's here with you, Allie. He seems like a great guy."

"He does, doesn't he?" I smile at her. "You think it's okay that he's here? I wasn't sure…" I hope no one thinks it's wrong for him to be here.

"Of course it is. It's fine." She squeezes my hand. "So, do you think you're going to join the band after all?"

I search Jessica's smiling face. "I haven't told him. He hasn't asked either. Part of me feels like I shouldn't go so soon after… I guess I feel guilty leaving when it hasn't been very long …"

"You know if she were standing here she'd say 'Do it.'"

Audrey and I gaze at Jessica's image. *If she were standing here.* It feels like she *is* here. Maybe not in body, but somehow, it feels like she's with us. Her presence. No doubt.

Audrey must be thinking what I'm thinking. We look at each other with tears in our eyes and laugh. And then cry that terrible, all-out sob that makes us laugh and cry even harder.

"Oh my God. Look at us," I say.

We dry our tears and collect ourselves.

"You're going to miss her no matter where you are. That won't change," she says. "Are you excited?"

"Honestly, I'm scared to death. But, yeah. I think I'm ready. If it doesn't work out, at least I tried."

"I have a feeling it's gonna work out." She nods confidently. "It will."

People enter the foyer and stop to look at the portrait. We step to the side.

Audrey says, "Okay. I guess you better go and get situated." She hugs me and whispers, "You're gonna be fine."

"Thank you."

She turns to pack her supplies in a plastic bin, checking to make sure she hasn't forgotten anything.

"Do you need help?"

"No. I think I got everything. Does it look okay?"

"It looks great."

"Thanks. I have to run out to my car. The mass coordinator is somewhere up there if you have any questions. But I'll be right up."

I walk toward the pew where Joshua sits. My heels click loudly on the tile.

"Ready?" I ask him.

"Yes, I am."

We make our way to the front of the church.

"Thanks again for offering to play with me, Joshua. I appreciate it."

"You're welcome. I'm glad I could be here."

We set up next to a podium and a microphone, then sit and wait for mass to begin.

The church fills up fast and soon it's standing room only. Over the past few days, I've reflected over "Amazing Grace" numerous times, "*... I once was lost but now am found, was blind but now I see.*" I think again about the author's story. What sparked his revelation? The inspiration to change his life? Was it a starry night? A whisper in the wind? I don't know. But something touched his heart, something made him see he was on the wrong path. He changed his ways and changed his life. Amazing grace. I think I know how he must have felt.

*L*ater that afternoon, as I'm driving Joshua to the bus station, I know this is it, the perfect opportunity to tell him I changed my mind. I want to work with him. I want to join the band. But what if it's too late? What if he's already got someone else? I don't want it to be awkward. I don't want him to feel obligated.

"What are you thinking?" I tell myself. "No. This is it. You have to do it. Say something." What do I say? My stomach's in knots. I glance over at him. He's wearing his dark glasses and looks relaxed in a t-shirt and jeans. I turn the radio down. "Joshua, thank you so much for coming down for the services."

He shrugs it off. "Of course." Then he says, "I'm sorry about Jessica. I know ya'll were close."

"Thank you. I'm gonna miss her like crazy. I can't even imagine how much, really." I know I'll have to find my way without her. I remember my grandmother's words: You're stronger than you think. The words nudge me forward to speak up, to take a leap of faith. "We haven't talked about it at all but I've been meaning to ask you about the band. Have you found a singer?"

He shakes his head. "Nope. Not yet. Why? Have you changed your mind?"

Okay. There. The door's open. Tell him! "Well, I know I told you I couldn't do it, but I've been thinking about it. A lot."

His eyebrows arch over his dark glasses. "Oh yeah?"

I'm still not positive it's the right thing to do, but it's now or never. "Yeah, I have." I glance at him. "I want to do it after all. If you still think I might be a good fit." He doesn't say anything. "And if not, I totally understand."

"Are you kidding? You're a perfect fit!" He smiles. "Perfect." He slaps his hands on his legs, then stops. "As long as you're sure."

"Absolutely sure."

"Really?" He nods his head. "Alright, Allison. Then you're hired."

"Okay." I feel exhilarated and exhausted. We don't talk about details or logistics or how I feel about it all or why I changed my mind. There's too much to say.

Instead, I drive on and we let the music from the radio fill the space between us.

ACKNOWLEDGMENTS

Thanks to my friends and family who cheered me on while writing this book. I'm grateful for your encouragement. Huge thanks also to my first readers who helped improve the story: Lynda DeLaCruz, Ariana Ramirez, Najentel Chaisson, Nicole Pauley, Dana Gonzales, Carly Hamilton, Emily Whitaker, and Kathryn Mabrito-Palmisano.

And most especially to my husband, Mark, thank you for your love, support, feedback, suggestions, and steadfast belief from start to finish.

BOOK CLUB DISCUSSION QUESTIONS

1. In Chapter 3 Allison says, "Sometimes life buries dreams." Do you agree? Do you think that's what happened to Allison's dream?

2. Friendship is a major theme in the novel. Which character do you think best exemplifies the ideals of friendship?

3. Aside from friendship, are there other important themes and how were they presented in the novel?

4. Which of the characters would you most want to meet? What do you think you would talk about?

5. At the beginning of the novel Allison worries that she and Jessica will drift apart after Jessica's wedding. Do you think she's right to be concerned?

6. Allison struggled making decisions/choices throughout the book. If you had been in Allison's shoes, would you have made the same decisions/choices she did?

7. Allison calls Joshua a "philosopher" and a "Renaissance Man." What do you think of her characterization of Joshua? Is it accurate and what does that say about her?

8. Joshua says his blindness has been more of a blessing than a curse. Does this come across in the novel? How does he show that this is true for him?

BOOK CLUB DISCUSSION QUESTIONS

9. Allison says she feels stuck and she describes her mother as being stuck. Are they stuck in the same way? Do you think Allison sees herself a being as stuck as her mom?

10. Jessica has a large and loving family life. What do you think she gets from her lifelong friendship with Allison?

11. Allison had many influences in her life, some positive, some not. Who do you think had the greatest influence on Allison?

12. Allison expresses strong and sometimes harsh opinions of people. Does this make her a less sympathetic character? Does it influence your opinion of her?

13. Does Allison have what it takes to pursue her dream and see it through?

14. What do the minor characters add to the novel? Did you find them interesting and well-rounded? In what way do they contribute to the plot, theme, characterization, etc.?

15. Allison describes several dreams throughout the novel. Why do you think the author chose to include them? What significance do they have for Allison?

16. How do you think Fernanda Deleon would react if she knew how Allison truly feels about her? How does her unwillingness to discuss things openly affect her daughter?

17. Allison says her mom needs her and that sense of obligation weighs heavily on her decisions. Do you think it should be as big a factor as she makes it?

18. Discuss the dynamics of the mother/daughter relationships in the novel. Do they overlap and affect each other in any way?

19. Music is woven throughout the story in various ways. Does this add to the narrative?

20. Stories sometimes have a lasting effect on the reader. Is there anything about the book (characters, themes, circumstances, etc.) you think may have a lasting effect on you?

ABOUT THE AUTHOR

Ruby Montalvo is a former English teacher and school librarian. She lives in San Antonio, Texas with her husband and their two dogs.

You can sign up for Ruby's newsletter for new releases and blogpost updates at rubymontalvo.com

Lightning Source UK Ltd.
Milton Keynes UK
UKHW040808090120
356646UK00003B/835/P